VICARIOUS VACATIONS

MICHAEL WOJCIECHOWSKI

Black Rose Writing | Texas

ISBN: 978-1-68433-594-7
PUBLISHED BY BLACK ROSE WRITING
www.blackrosewriting.com

Printed in the United States of America
Suggested Retail Price (SRP) $19.95

Vicarious Vacations is printed in Plantagenet Cherokee

*As a planet-friendly publisher, Black Rose Writing does its best to eliminate
unnecessary waste to reduce paper usage and energy costs, while never compromising
the reading experience. As a result, the final word count vs. page count may not meet
common expectations.

VICARIOUS VACATIONS

CHAPTER 1

Megan Lewis visited Mount Rushmore last summer. Her Facebook and Instagram posts averaged 300 likes. Scott Kelson went to Alcatraz and posted a selfie with the iconic prison in the background; the photo received 401 likes. Brock Summerhays spent two weeks in Spain last month. He ran with the bulls—894 likes. Stephanie Riddell vacationed in Bora Bora. Her room photo alone garnered close to a thousand likes, while her swimsuit photos (if you can call what she wore a swimsuit) earned four times as many. Seven months ago, I posted a bathroom selfie. I dressed to the nines to attend the grand opening of a fresh new club. I pouted my lips, sucked in my stomach, and found the angle that best accentuated my figure. The pic received 16 likes. Last week the Starbucks barista misspelled my name: "Page," she wrote. I posted the misspelled cup with a confused emoji face. The cup earned 24 likes. People liked my misspelled name on a coffee cup more than my form-fitting dress? What was I doing wrong?

Everyone's life was better than mine, but no one had a better life than Eric Vandross and Alexis Carter. Their recent wedding and honeymoon photos all earned over 5,000 likes. One photo displayed Alexis, her manicured toes resting on the white Jamaican sand, and the crystal ocean waters in the distance. The photo's caption: "Just another day in paradise #SoBlessed #ToesInTheSand #JamaicanMeCrazy." The post earned 8,000 likes. But the definitive picture showcased Eric and Alexis standing a foot into the ocean. Their bodies faced the horizon, with their heads fixed back towards the camera offering infectious smiles. Eric's right hand extended and met Alexis's left hand. Together their fingers curved and touched, forming a heart. Eric's naked torso glistened in the sun. Shadows outlined the fresh packs of muscle he earned from the hours he spent at the gym. He was designed to make love, and Alexis was made to receive it. Her thong bikini highlighted her taut figure, and her blonde hair complemented her stunning blue eyes with hypnotic perfection. I "liked" their photo and left a comment: "You two are PERFECT together!!! So jelly right now!!! MUAH!!!!" My like brought their total to over 13,000. I hated them and their perfect lives.

I exited Alexis's page and entered my own. For breakfast I ate a bowl of oatmeal with organic mixed berries. I uploaded a photo. Nine people liked it, and no one left comments. Saddened and confused, I checked my followers' list—249. What happened? This morning I had 250.

I clicked into my followers' list, scouring the names, trying to find the deserter and wondering what I had done wrong. I posted nothing political—political posts were a surefire way to lose friends. I kept my opinions neutral, safe. My opinions *were* neutral and safe. Sure, I posted an obligatory message or pic whenever a social event called for one. My thoughts and prayers were always offered after a mass shooting. At the height of the #MeToo movement, I shared a borderline inappropriate experience with an abusive uncle. For a week in 2015, I even changed my profile pic to an equals sign (after I noticed Alexis do the same) to offer my support to the gay community. Like any good social media connoisseur, I made every social issue about me, but I had no strong political leanings because I did not understand what it meant to be liberal or conservative. Beyoncé and Katy Perry supported Hillary in 2016, so I did, too, but I did not vote. Election day is on Tuesday—the same day as Pilates. I would not sacrifice Pilates to stand in line at my old elementary school to vote for a woman with a shrill laugh. And supporting Trump was not an option. He only landed B-minus celebrities on *The Apprentice*, and his campaign celebrities were even worse. Gary Busey? Meatloaf? Kid Rock? Scott Baio? Give me a break.

I found the defector: Craig Stoker. We had been FB friends and Instagram and Twitter followers for seven months. He had sold me my car and even asked for my number during the test drive. I blushed and recited my number while he punched it into his phone. After leaving the dealership in a car several thousand dollars out of my price range—Craig sold me options I did not need yet could not reject—I found Craig Stoker on Facebook and Instagram. I sent him a friend request, and he accepted the request, but he never called or texted.

I searched his name, hoping that he had deleted his entire account—if he abandoned all his friends, it would hurt less than if I were the lone reject. Nope. He was still active. He had even posted a *Game of Thrones* meme earlier that morning. Why had he unfriended me? What had I done?

"Sometimes it seems like life just wants me to give up," I wrote on my Facebook wall. To add emphasis to my cryptic message, I included a distressed emoji. I stared at the like icon for three minutes, waiting for someone to acknowledge what I had written. I retrieved my phone and logged into my "secret" account (Selina Everdean). As Selina, I pulled up my real page. I clicked the like button, and wrote: "Paige, are you okay?" Within seconds the comment appeared on my real account.

I replied: "Yeah, I just don't get people sometimes."

Selina: "I feel you, girlie. I'm here if you need anything. Love ya!"

Me: "Thanks, Selina. Ur an actual friend, not like some cheap car salesman."

With the ball now rolling, three people liked my post, and another liked my oatmeal photo. Screw you, Craig Stoker.

CHAPTER 2

Alexis's popularity was bad for my confidence and worse for my self-esteem. In college I read a psychology study concerning the harmful effects social media can have on a person's psyche. When pictures of "friends" living lives that make your own seem inconsequential bombard your feeds, it can cause depression, anxiety, and FOMO. All those ailments plagued me, and I had the prescriptions to prove it. I am twenty-five and more medicated than my grandparents.

I often considered unfriending Alexis, but I lacked the nerve. Her life became my addiction almost as much as selfies became hers. Alexis was everything I was not: popular, sexy, and adventurous. I already knew, or rather, I already knew *of*, Alexis Carter before I started working at Newage Tech. We attended Grand Heights High School together. She was two years older than me. We never interacted, but I often spotted her across the commons area sitting among her throng of admirers posting updates to her social media accounts. She ran with the most popular girls at the school and served as the group's nucleus. Instagram posts always featured her front and center while her friends jockeyed on the fringes of her popularity for whatever attention she did not hoard. Girls wanted to be her; guys wanted to date her.

The night she graduated high school, while I was home watching old romantic comedies with my mom and sister, I worked up the courage to send Alexis a Facebook friend request. (I was already following her on Instagram.) And, to my surprise, thirteen minutes after my friendship proposition, she accepted! We were official friends! Her friendship brought my total to ninety-six and hers to 2,839. I felt validated. I showed my mom and sister. My mom mumbled, "That's great, sweetie," and my sister, who sat on the floor Snapchatting with her friends, did not even acknowledge the news.

I spent the next eight years liking everything Alexis posted. Sometimes, I even ventured a comment, and occasionally, she liked my comments! When, right before her twenty-third birthday, she announced her engagement to Jason Wilkins, I cried. (Tears of joy or sorrow, I could not tell.) A month later when she posted a picture of herself kissing a man that was *not* Jason Wilkins, I cried harder. The caption under the photo read: "Pretty easy to forget about Jason Wilkins when I have this guy." The photo showed her and the new mysterious man at a party. Alexis flourished a red Solo cup above her head, the mystery man an empty bottle of Jack Daniels. The post smacked of desperation, but I liked it anyway.

Within an hour, she uploaded a series of pictures (most of them shirtless) of her new beau. The new photos highlighted the fun he would provide that Jason Wilkins could not. I navigated to Jason's page. The day before, his profile picture was of him and Alexis. Now it contained a photo of him with a girl who was *not* Alexis. What a scumbag!

A year later, after running through a chain of men, Alexis settled down with Eric Vandross. Eric appeared charming, successful, and, at least from the few photos dotting Alexis's Instagram account, quite handsome. Facebook, Twitter, Instagram, and Tik Tok searches for Eric Vandross yielded no results. I was ignorant to his likes and dislikes, where he grew up, attended school, and what motivational sayings best encapsulated his personality and credos. My knowledge only extended as far as Alexis's online revelations, and for whatever reason, regarding Eric Vandross, she did not reveal much.

She *did* reveal they met at work. Eric was her supervisor. (He, along with two other investors, created Newage Technology, a new software security company that, according to their website, "also explored other fields.") They dated for three years, and then he proposed while vacationing in Niagara Falls. She posted a picture of them kissing, The Falls cascaded in the background, and her slender hand, now weighed down with a three-carat engagement ring, grazed his cheek while they locked lips. The photo left me speechless. I liked it and took an extra dose of my depression medicine before going to bed.

Right around the time Alexis got engaged, I finished my degree from Farmington State University. Farmington State was not my first choice, but my grades and funds were lacking to travel outside the state. So, I applied for student loans and commuted twenty-five minutes to campus each day. Not including my post-high school gap year, I earned my marketing degree in five years. I still live at home, but I am now employed.

About a year after I finished college, Alexis posted on Facebook that Newage Tech needed people with business backgrounds. The following week I found myself in Newage Tech's waiting room. I sat with clammy hands for fifteen minutes before the secretary told me, "They're ready for you now." Through a set of double doors, I entered a sparsely furnished conference room and stopped short when Eric Vandross—and two other executives—stood to greet me. I never suspected Eric Vandross would conduct the interview. He was one of three CEO's, so I assumed someone lower on the totem pole oversaw entry-level hires.

When we shook hands, I regarded his piercing blue eyes and became racked with jealousy. The world has a dating hierarchy. Eric Vandross and Alexis Carter reside right near the top. People like me spend our lives gazing up and wondering what random strategy God employs to determine who is privileged enough to date people like Alexis and Eric.

A layer of fog hangs over most of the interview. My mind kept drifting to Alexis's different posts documenting her and Eric's relationship. Perhaps one day, when I too found someone worth marrying, the four of us could travel together. We could host Super Bowl parties, go for Sunday brunch, and attend other social events that required expensive wine and political discussions. The fantasy seemed so real I almost expected it to materialize on the spot.

To cap the interview, Eric asked if I had any questions. Without thinking, I blurted: "I went to school with Alexis," not recognizing until it was too late that I had offered a statement and not a question.

"Is that right?" he asked, consulting my resume. "Alexis didn't go to Farmington State. She attended—"

"The University of Oppenheimer. I meant high school," I explained.

"Oh, so you're local?"

"Yeah." He expected me to say more, but I had nothing else to offer. I picked at a hangnail.

"Ah…well, I'll tell her you said hello," he said.

"You guys make a great couple."

"Why do you say that?"

"I follow her on Facebook, Instagram, Twitter, and Tik Tok."

"Ah, you're social media friends," he said, leaning back in his chair. "Not actual friends." His tone contained a hint of derision. He stole a glance at the two other executives; they appeared bored with our conversation. Eric took the social cue and got to his feet. "Thank you for coming in. You'll hear from us soon."

Friday afternoon he called and offered me the position. I now work at the same company as Alexis Carter and Eric Vandross! That night, after viewing Alexis's latest YouTube makeup tutorial, I went out for drinks. Although it was a solo adventure, my spirits were high and open to the prospect of meeting new friends. An hour later, I returned home— alone. My mom asked why I was back so soon. I said I didn't feel well. I escaped to my room and pulled up my social media accounts. Earlier at the bar, I posted a picture of my cosmopolitan—cosmos was Alexis's drink of choice—with the caption: "Here's to a new job and a new life! #NewageTech #NewAdventures #WorkingWithFriends." Fourteen people liked my post, including my mom. Work started the following Monday.

CHAPTER 3

With their honeymoon forever catalogued to the annals of social media, Eric and Alexis returned to work. Alexis posted her Monday makeup tutorial video (she had side hustles as a swimwear consultant and a cosmetics ambassador for Pleasantry Cosmetics), along with her outfit of the day (a pencil skirt with sling-back heels) with the hashtag: #BackToLifeBackToReality.

I found her in the breakroom alone Snapchatting. She did not lift her eyes as I entered and ambled to the coffee pot for my morning cup. With my coffee in hand, I retreated to a deserted table opposite hers. From my phone, I entered her Instagram page. I liked her outfit of the day post and on her Facebook wall wrote: "So sad your honeymoon is over. It looked fab! So jealous!!" I sipped my coffee and caught Alexis eyeing me from across the room. I smiled; she sighed and liked my post.

Other co-workers entered, all with their heads in their phones. Like robotic zombies, they found empty tables and continued scrolling through their digital worlds. Five minutes later, Eric and Hal, the regional manager, entered. Eric spotted Alexis and forced a smile that went undetected. Eric brushed past her, while Hal bent his ear about fantasy football strategies and insights. They helped themselves to the coffee and sat at the nearest table—my table. They ignored me; football stats and hypothetical starting lineups merited their full attention.

I studied Eric for a moment, taking in his perfect features, and then returned to Alexis's Instagram page and studied the photos from her honeymoon. I had liked them all and committed their order to memory.

(The champagne flutes they received upon check in, the suite's master tub, Alexis's selfie from her balcony, a side-by-side bikini selfie asking her followers which they preferred—I voted for the pink one because it offered less underboob than the yellow one. The yellow's like total almost doubled the pink's.)

I realized Eric was absent from most of the honeymoon posts. In fact, as I navigated through their documented honeymoon, I only counted three pictures that included Eric. The honeymoon served as Alexis's self-gratification tour. I shook my head while pining for my own narcissistic honeymoon virtual photo album. I came to the last photo, the one that highlighted Eric and Alexis's love ankle-deep in the ocean with their hands joined into a heart.

From my vantage point in the breakroom, I regarded Eric. Something struck me. He appeared quite...pale. Much paler in person than in his honeymoon photo. Had Alexis workshopped his photos to give him a darker complexion? I altered my gaze to Alexis to see if she appeared lighter, too. She did not, but then again, she retained a healthy glow year-round.

Alexis stood and exited the breakroom, never once taking her eyes from her phone, nor acknowledging her husband's presence. Eric caught her right as the door swung shut. He examined the door for a moment, wondering if she would reappear. Then Hal asked him a football question, and Eric forgot about his new bride and began reciting rushing statistics.

A moment later, as I made my exodus, my eyes locked with Eric's. He smiled at me, and I blushed under the weight of his smile. My toe caught the edge of the table leg, and I stumbled for a moment before regaining my balance.

"Are you okay?" Eric hovered on the edge of his chair, ready to spring into action if I needed help. I tried to tell him I was fine, but the words, compounded with my embarrassment, stayed lodged in my throat. I shuffled through the door before making a bigger fool of myself.

CHAPTER 4

Most nights I spent an extra hour at the office. Even on Fridays I never left before 5:00 to gain an early weekend jump. My weekends lacked the usual fanfare. I had no place to go nor people to see—at least not physically. All my interactions occurred through social media, so I had no incentive to rush home. Besides, Newage Tech had faster Wi-Fi than my parents' basement.

As people filed out at the end of the day, I checked social media. I would enter the rabbit hole, and what began as a quick Instagram glance, always evolved into a series of cat videos and nostalgic yearbook photos. Before long I found myself alone in the office liking the latest tattoo designed by my college crush. Often, hours after exiting the office, my car sat abandoned in the parking lot. Such was the case the night Eric Vandross noticed my flat tire.

I exited the office after 6:00 to an empty parking lot save for my car and another two rows back from mine. I could see the outline of someone sitting in the other car, but I paid him no mind. My ignition turned over smoothly, and I shifted into drive when the person behind me honked and pulled alongside my car. It was Eric. He lowered his window and motioned for me to do the same.

"Paige, right?" he asked. I nodded, unable to speak. "You have a flat tire," he said. I heard words escaping his lips, but they refused to create a coherent structure in my head. "Your tire is flat," he said again, pointing to my car's front passenger tire. "I noticed it when I came out to my car."

"What?" I asked. I believed he said something about a flat tire.

"Your tire is flat," he repeated, raising his voice.

What did he expect me to do with that information? "Okay," I said. He stared at me, his eyebrows knitted together.

"Do you need help changing it?" he asked.

"I don't know." I had never changed a tire. I saw my dad do it once, but I had never undergone the task.

"Do you have a spare?" Eric asked.

"I don't know."

"You don't know?"

"No."

"You should look."

"Okay."

"Okay…you'll look?"

"Sure."

"When?"

"I don't know."

He shook his head. "What do you know, Paige?"

His question confused me, so I did not answer it. I grabbed my phone and checked for any messages or notifications. Eric exited his car and approached my window.

"Pop your trunk," he said.

I reached down and tapped the trunk button. I heard the latch release and, from my rearview, saw the trunk lift. Eric walked to the back of my car and opened the trunk. "This may take a minute," he called over the opened trunk. "Shut off your car."

I killed the engine. He retrieved my spare and rolled it toward the flattened tire. "Come keep me company," he said. He unbuttoned his dress shirt and tossed it through the opened window of his car. Underneath he wore a white t-shirt. I took in the outline of his body pressed against the white cotton. An attractive man was getting undressed while changing my tire. It sounded like the plot of an adult film. I blushed at the thought. Eric positioned the jack under the car and stepped back to judge the placement before turning it. "Your parking brake on?" he asked.

"Huh?"

"Is your parking brake on?"

"Oh…I don't know."

He smiled. "Can you check?"

I opened the passenger-side door and pulled up on the brake. My car rose with each new crank of the jack. It thrilled me to watch Eric work. His arm and shoulder muscles pushed and pulled from the effort. It seemed so primitive, so…carnal. I needed to capture the moment with a photo. I spied Eric through my phone's camera and clicked. Eric heard the photo snap and stopped.

"What are you doing?"

"Huh?"

"Did you just take a photo?"

"Yeah."

"Why?"

This was a ridiculous question. *Why?* Because that was what people did. All life events deserved to be documented and shared. "Because," I said, shrugging.

"Delete it."

"Why?"

"Because I asked."

"I want to post it."

"I don't want it posted."

"Why?"

"This isn't something that you need to share," he said, giving the jack two more turns.

"Why?"

He straightened, twisting his torso that had grown tight from sitting all day. "Say something other than why." My natural reaction compelled me to ask 'why,' but I stopped myself before doing so. "You have a flat tire," he said. "I'm helping you change it. The world doesn't care."

I studied the photo. The outline of his shoulder muscles shone through his shirt sleeve. His bicep stretched the fabric. His smooth forearm glistened while his sinewy muscles contracted beneath the skin. It was a great photo, one that could serve as the cover for a romance novel. It deserved to be shared. "This photo is worth at least one hundred likes," I said.

"One hundred people would like that photo? That's pathetic."

"Not for me. I don't have many followers." I lowered my head, embarrassed by my shameful admission.

"That's not what I meant. It's pathetic if one person liked it."

"This is Instagram gold."

"Delete it, okay?"

"How come?"

"Have you ever changed a tire?"

"No."

"That's why," he said. "Delete it or I am done."

"Are you serious?"

"Yes."

"Okay, I'll delete it." I pretended to delete it, but I saved it to my photos and pocketed my phone.

Satisfied, he resumed cranking the jack. The tire lifted off the ground, and it occurred to me that he had forgotten to loosen the lug nuts—this was the one thing I remembered from when my dad changed the tire on our family SUV many years ago. I recalled my mom stepping out from behind our car and asking my father, "Did you remember to loosen the lug nuts?" My dad halted his work and peered at my mom. Having forgotten the imperative step, he sighed with heavy annoyance and began lowering the car, mumbling profanities under his breath.

My tire, no longer bound to the road, would spin once Eric applied the tire wrench to the lug nuts. I debated whether to mention the oversight. He was kind enough to change my tire, so I should not second guess his methods. Perhaps he knew something my dad did not.

"My wife," Eric said, "is always on social media. Every little thing she does, every place she goes, even what she eats, she shares with her, quote unquote, friends. It's embarrassing."

"Your wife is amazing," I said, and Eric laughed.

"She is? What makes you say that?"

"She has over 40,000 Instagram followers," I explained. "She has her own YouTube channel, and she's a makeup ambassador for Pleasantry Cosmetics."

"So?"

"So?!"

Eric pried off the hubcap and fitted the lug wrench over one of the bolts. He cranked the wrench, and the tire spun. "Damn it. I forgot to loosen the bolts."

"Have you ever changed a tire?" I teased.

Eric chuckled and began the disheartening process of lowering the car. "I haven't changed one since driver's ed class. That was fifteen years ago." The car's flaccid tire returned to the pavement, and with brusque force Eric loosened the lug nuts. "So, why is it important to have a lot of followers on Instagram?" he asked.

"Because..." I began, without knowing how to complete my answer. Because...just because.

"Last year I won my fantasy football league," he said.

"What?"

"I won my fantasy football league last year," he repeated. "There were twelve guys in the league. Do you think that's impressive?"

"I don't know." I did not think it was impressive, but I figured it best to keep my opinions unspoken.

"It's not, is it?" he said.

I analyzed his expression, making sure he was not setting a trap. "No, not really," I answered.

"Guess what I got for winning? $500."

"Okay."

"You know the difference between me winning fantasy football and my wife having a lot of friends on social media?"

"What?"

"I have $500 for my accomplishment."

"Did you post it?"

"Post what?"

"That you won?"

"No."

I thought for a moment. "I don't understand."

A hint of frustration invaded Eric's face. "We've both accomplished meaningless things," he explained. "But I got money for mine. She gets nothing."

"She gets noticed."

"By whom?"

"Her friends."

"She doesn't have any friends."

"She has thousands. They like her posts."

"What good does that do?"

"She's popular."

"Hell, Jay Gatsby was popular, and only three people showed up to his funeral."

"Who's Jay Gatsby?"

Eric viewed me, scrutinized my question, and wondered if I meant it as a joke. "He's the literary version of my wife," he said in a serious tone.

"I've never heard of him. What's his Twitter handle?"

Eric laughed, not realizing my question was sincere. "He doesn't have one."

"Why?"

"Well, as I explained, he's dead."

"How did he die?"

Eric removed the flattened tire from the wheel hub. "A mechanic killed him."

"Why?"

"Because he thought Gatsby was sleeping with his wife."

"Was he?"

"No."

"That's a horrible story."

"Yeah? Many people would disagree with you."

Eric maneuvered the spare onto the axle, hand-tightened the bolts, and then dropped the car to finish the task. Once he found his rhythm, he worked with ease and precision. From inside his car, I heard his phone chime with an incoming text message. "Can you check that for me?" he asked.

I walked to his car and found his phone on his seat. I returned, holding his phone out to him. "Can you read it?" he asked.

"You want me to read your text?"

He held up his dirty hands. "Do you mind? Just swipe to unlock it."

"No security code?"

"Nope."

I ran my finger across his screen, and his phone came to life. I touched the message icon, and the screen filled with Alexis's message thread.

"It's from Alexis," I said, reading the message. "She's wondering where you are."

"Tell her I'm at the office, and I'm leaving soon." I typed the message and sent it. I stole a glance at Eric. He appeared preoccupied, so I scrolled through Alexis's message thread. I had not gotten past four messages before I came to a nude bathroom selfie of Alexis. The phone almost slipped through my hands. Her firm, fake breasts stared back at me. She had a towel wrapped around her head, and the bathroom counter covered her lower half. The message read, "Just stepped out from the shower. What are the plans for tonight?" Eric's response came three minutes later: "Dinner with the Murphy's," he wrote and nothing more. He did not tell her she was beautiful, nor did he offer any standard emojis showing he appreciated the selfie. The photo sat unacknowledged. My heart ached for Alexis. How much courage did it take to expose herself only to have Eric dismiss her?

Another chime sounded with an incoming message. "It's Alexis again," I said. "She wants you to bring Chinese food home for dinner."

"Okay."

"That's what I should write?"

"Yeah."

"No emoji?"

Eric shook his head. He finished tightening the final lug nut and pulled the jack out from under the car. "I don't do emojis," he said.

Doesn't do emojis? Who doesn't do emojis? How did he convey emotion?

Eric walked to my trunk and placed the jack and deflated tire inside. "Okay, you're set," he said.

"Should I pay you?" I asked, assuming his chivalry warranted compensation. Eric's face tightened at the suggestion.

"No, you don't need to pay me."

"Thank you."

"Why are you here so late? It's almost dark."

"I…had work I needed to finish," I lied.

"Is that the truth, or are you saying that because I'm the boss?"

"It's the truth," I lied again and bit into my lower lip.

"If I ask you something, will you tell me the truth?"

"Sure."

"Do you enjoy working here?"

"Yeah."

"What do you like about it?"

The question made me reflect. What *did* I like about working at Newage Tech? I enjoyed working with Alexis and Eric, and I appreciated having a job. If my Facebook thread was any indication, countless college graduates struggled finding employment.

"I don't know. It's a good company."

"Come on, Paige, you can give me a better answer than that."

I liked the way my name sounded when he said it. It seemed like no one ever called anyone by their name anymore. Hearing Eric say mine felt personal and, somehow, intimate.

"I like my co-workers," I said. "Everyone is really nice."

"Really nice, huh?"

"Yeah."

"What co-workers?"

"Um…I don't know. Ryann. She's my supervisor. She's nice." Ryann was not nice. "Alexis, too," I added.

"You're friends with Alexis?"

"Yeah," I answered. "I watch her makeup tutorials on YouTube. I subscribe to her channel and follow all her social media accounts."

"That makes you friends?"

"Yes."

"Have you ever spoken with Alexis? In person, I mean."

I considered this. No, I had never *officially* spoken to Alexis, and until that moment I had not realized it. "No," I said, embarrassed.

"Few people have."

"She's out of my league."

"What makes her out of your league?"

"Are you kidding? She's gorgeous."

"And you're not?"

A deep-throated guffaw escaped me. "No," I managed to say.

"Is that what matters?" Eric asked. "A person's appearance?" He sounded like my mom. "Don't ever think she's better than you."

I demurred. "She's so perfect, though."

"You're only seeing the highlights."

"What highlights?"

Eric sighed, ignoring my question. "No one talks with anyone anymore. It's sad."

Before I could ask what he meant, another message notification disarmed our conversation. I handed his phone to him. He took it, careful not to get it dirty, and placed it in his pocket.

"Aren't you going to check it? It's probably from Alexis."

"I will when I leave. We're talking right now."

It occurred to me I had not checked my phone for ten minutes. With that knowledge came the desire to do so; I resisted the sudden urge, however, fearful of disrupting our conversation. I enjoyed talking with Eric. He listened when I spoke. Technology had hijacked that simple courtesy—no one more guilty of that infraction than me. His phone chimed once more, and I expected him to reach for it, but he remained resolute and present. Two messages now sat unchecked. His self-control astounded me.

"Did you have fun on your honeymoon?" I asked, searching for something to say.

"My honeymoon?"

"Yeah. I saw the photos Alexis posted. You must have had an amazing time."

Eric grimaced. "Things aren't always what they seem, Paige."

"What do you mean?"

"I can't say anything. I promised Alexis I wouldn't tell."

"Tell what?"

"Her secret."

"I don't understand."

"I know, and I can't say much more." He checked his watch. "I better get going."

"Thanks again for helping me."

"No problem."

He walked past me and got into his car. I pulled my phone from my pocket and checked it. No messages or notifications. As if on cue, I heard Eric's phone ding again. I viewed him through the driver's side window. I expected to find him hovered over his phone reading whatever messages he had ignored. Instead, he sat motionless, staring ahead as if contemplating something intense. His inscrutable face remained frozen in concerted reflection as I got in my car and exited the parking lot.

CHAPTER 5

Hours were spent examining Eric's photo I saved to my phone. I wanted to post it, to show people he helped me. I imagined the picture appearing on my friends' feeds. Eric's perfect features stunning them silent. They would study the photo and notice that I, Paige Reynolds, had posted it. How did I know such a specimen? Messages would flood my inbox. "Who is the hunk?" they would ask. I yearned for this reality. I appreciated that Eric changed my tire, but I hated that he made me keep it a secret.

"I've been searching for you," a familiar voice said. My eyes lifted from my phone. Eric stood in front of me, one hand in his pocket, the other holding a book. It was my lunch hour, and I spent it alone, in my usual spot, on a bench outside the office.

"Here," Eric said, handing me the book. *The Great Gatsby.* "You mind if I join you?" he asked.

"Sure."

He unbuttoned his suit jacket and sat down next to me. Our legs nearly touched, so I inched away from him to avoid any unintentional contact. His cologne infiltrated the air. It smelled expensive, clean. "That's the book I mentioned the other day," Eric said.

"You mentioned a book?"

"Yeah. That one. You should read it. Tell me what you think."

"You want me to read this book?"

"Well, you don't have to, but I thought—"

"No, I want to," I interrupted. "Thanks." I scrutinized the book. It had been years since I last read a book. "What's it about?"

"It's about a guy who pretends to be something he's not. He throws lavish parties and buys expensive cars, suits, even houses. But it's all pretense, jockeying for the approval of others." He hesitated a moment and then continued: "Anyway, you'll notice some parallels to what we discussed the other day. About Alexis and her social media followers."

"She's very popular. You guys make a great couple."

"Yeah, that seems to be the consensus."

I sensed an air of sadness behind Eric's words. "Are you okay?"

Eric stared at the ground. "Sometimes I think..." but he left his thought unfinished.

His indifference to his wife's social media presence perplexed me. She was an icon. Earlier that morning she posted her outfit of the day— a business skirt with high heels and a button-down blouse with the first three buttons purposely undone. She was stunning. Even Eric had commented: "Wow, honey!!! I'm the luckiest man ALIVE!!! You are GORGEOUS!!!" I wondered what it must feel like to have someone like Eric Vandross make comments with multiple exclamation points and all-capped words. A chain of emojis—several fire symbols and subsequent egg plants—followed his comment. This confused me. Eric had claimed the day before he never used emojis. Even more mystifying was his sudden social media presence. Until this morning when I noticed his public proclamation regarding his wife's beauty, I believed Eric did not have any social media accounts. All my previous online searches yielded nothing. Now, he had an Instagram account, albeit a private one.

"There she goes now," Eric said. I followed his gaze and spotted Alexis walking, coffee and phone in hand, across the square into our building. I wondered if Eric worried she might glance in our direction and see us talking. What would she conclude if she saw me eating lunch with her husband? Eric, however, assessing his wife with tired eyes, appeared indifferent. Had she spotted us, I think Eric would have stared right back at her without reacting.

"She gets coffee at that coffee shop every morning," Eric said, indicating the compact coffee house across the street. "She doesn't even like their coffee. It's too dark, but they make designs with the cream, and she likes taking pictures of the designs."

I unlocked my phone and pulled up Alexis's Instagram page. She had posted a photo nine minutes ago. It was of her coffee; the added cream outlined an owl. I held my phone toward Eric. He assessed the photo and shook his head. To my astonishment, he appeared embarrassed. The photo already had fifty-seven likes. Eric scrolled through her thread, stopping at Alexis's morning post, the one where he had commented with a chain of emojis. His jaw drew rigid and he clenched his free hand into a fist so tight his knuckles turned white.

"What's wrong?" I asked

"I commented on her post this morning."

"Yeah. You guys are cute."

"I don't have an Instagram page."

"Sure, you do. It's private, but you have one." I gritted my teeth, realizing I had just admitted to Instagram stalking him. Thankfully, my admission went unacknowledged.

"No," Eric said. "She created one for me. She posts comments pretending to be me."

"What?"

"Do you think I would post a row of eggplant emojis for the entire world to see?"

"They're not eggplants; they're…penises," I said, blushing.

"I know what they symbolize. I would never do it."

"Well, why would she post comments from you if they're not from you?"

"It's all part of the façade."

"Façade?"

"Yeah."

"I don't understand."

A sharp line formed across Eric's forehead. He checked his watch. "I better get back. I have a meeting."

"Hey, Eric," I called after him. "I'm sorry I showed you. I didn't know she created a fake account for you."

"It's not your fault, Paige. I'm the one who ignored the warning signs."

"Warning signs?"

"Yeah. The addiction to the bullshit."

"What...bullshit?" I stammered at the curse.

"Social media. It's all bullshit."

Eric's comment confounded me. Alexis was popular and beautiful. Her YouTube makeup tutorials averaged thousands of views. Her Tik Tok videos earned more. She mattered; she needed to share her life with her friends and followers. Why did Eric disparage her instead of encouraging her?

"Your wife is amazing," I said. "You're lucky to have her."

Eric held my gaze with a contemplative stare. "Paige, I've never even been to Jamaica."

"What?"

"I've never been to Jamaica."

"Sure, you have. Your honeymoon—"

"My honeymoon is a lie. It never happened."

"A lie?"

"My dad got sick two days before we were supposed to leave. I flew home for a week. I never made it to Jamaica."

"Alexis went without you?"

"She didn't go either. Neither of us did."

"But the photos—"

"They're fake. It was a manufactured vacation." A manufactured vacation? I replayed the words, trying to understand what Eric had revealed. Alexis had posted over fifty photos detailing their honeymoon. How could they be fake? "Vicarious Vacations," Eric said.

"What?"

"Vicarious Vacations," he repeated. "Check it out."

"Okay."

Eric took a step, halted, and turned back to me. "Oh, and if Alexis asks, you didn't hear any of this from me."

CHAPTER 6

Eric and Alexis's popular honeymoon photo stared back at me from the Vicarious Vacations website. The company's homepage contained a slide show of various people exploring a variety of exotic and historic vacation spots. One couple parasailed in Cancun. Another kissed under the Banyan tree in Maui. Another showed a woman, dressed in full belly dancing attire, shaking her hips with the Taj Mahal in the background. And yet another photo showed a man, replete with excited fear, running through the streets of Pamplona with a bull hot on his trail. The last slideshow photo was *the* photo. The one I had studied and scrutinized for the past month. Alexis and Eric's honeymoon photo. Their love displayed for all to see.

Each photo contained the important stats—number of likes, followers, friends—and each photo had at least five thousand likes. No profile had less than a thousand followers and friends, but I was still clueless as to what Vicarious Vacations was.

A pop-up invaded my screen, asking if I needed help booking my next vacation. I closed the pop-up, along with the website, and clicked into Google. I typed "Vicarious Vacations" into the search box. It yielded a plethora of results, but none of them, save for their homepage, had an association with the travel site. I scoured the internet for almost an hour, and I stumbled upon a blog by someone named "Love-me-short-time." Most of his posts were GIFs of kangaroos knocking out celebrities with animated uppercuts. Deep in his archives I found an entry entitled: "The Truth About Vicarious Vacations."

The post said Vicarious Vacations operated as a faux travel organization who manufactured fake vacations for people hoping to improve their social media presence. They operated like Expedia or Orbitz but without the actual traveling. But if Alexis and Eric never went to Jamaica, how did they have photos that proved otherwise? I realized some things on social media were photoshopped or fabricated, but would people lie about going on a trip to gain likes? And pay for it? The idea was absurd, and yet as I scrolled through people's vacation posts and saw the number of likes each photo earned, I became more envious of their popularity. How would it feel to go somewhere—real or otherwise—and have a thousand people like it? How much jealousy would vacation pics elicit from my friends and followers? Numerous times I liked someone's post expecting my generosity would later be reciprocated. Rarely it was, but then I never posted anything extraordinary; my posts were just *extra* ordinary. Would a vacation change that? A real vacation was beyond my budget, but what about a fake one?

I reentered the website and searched for prices. There were no listings, so I clicked on the "contact us" link. I expected an email box to emerge, but instead a smiling emoji filled my screen before disintegrating into several thousand specks of pixelated dust. A thank-you message followed. My phone came to life with an incoming text. It read: "Thank you for contacting Vicarious Vacations. You have an appointment on March 3rd at 4:30. To confirm your appointment, reply 'Y.' To decline your appointment, reply 'N.'"

My finger hovered over the 'N.' I am not impulsive; I seldom try new things. As I weighed what to do, my phone sounded with a new Instagram and Tik Tok update. Alexis had posted a new selfie, modeling her latest sunglasses purchase, and as a bonus, she uploaded a Tik Tok video. In the video, she wore her new sunglasses while lip synching "I'm too Sexy." Seventeen people had liked it in less than a minute. Eric offered the most recent praise. "I love them, babe! You are TOO SEXY!!!" A pang of jealousy struck my chest. I wondered if Eric had made the comment or if Alexis wrote it on his behalf. Even if she had, it still stung having to endure their love, regardless of its authenticity. I wanted a relationship like theirs. I wanted the world to think my life contained an equal amount of adventure and spontaneity. With a steady finger, I confirmed my appointment.

CHAPTER 7

"Paige Reynolds, it's a pleasure to meet you. I'm Shawn Preston," Shawn Preston said, shaking my hand. "Please, have a seat."

I sat in the chair opposite Mr. Preston's desk, and he sat behind his desk in a chair that appeared far more comfortable than mine. His suit looked expensive, and it complemented what I surmised was an expensive haircut. He had a million-dollar smile and never missed an opportunity to flash it. His teeth were white—almost too white—and straight—almost too straight. Next to Eric, he was the most handsome man I had ever seen.

He opened a desk drawer and removed an electronic tablet. He entered a passcode, and it came to life. My Instagram page filled the screen. He tapped a folder icon, and the Vicarious Vacations homepage replaced my page.

"Welcome to Vicarious Vacations," he said. "I understand you're interested in traveling."

"Well, I am, but—"

"You can't afford it?" Shawn said, finishing my thought. "You've come to the right place. We help people, much like yourself, who want the experience and recognition of traveling, but for a variety of reasons, they can't. Some can't afford it, some don't want to endure the stress of it, and some are terrified of it."

"I'm all three," I said. "It's frustrating because I view my friends' vacation photos on Instagram and Facebook, and I get so jealous."

"I understand," Shawn said. "Our services allow you the benefits of traveling without ever stepping outside your home."

"So, I don't actually have to go anywhere?"

"No, *you* won't be traveling, but your friends won't know that, will they?" he winked.

"So how does this work?"

"It's simple," he said, steering through the tablet, showing me past clients and their pristine vacation experiences. "You choose your destination, and we manufacture the vacation. You tell us how many photos you want uploaded to your social media accounts and what type of photos, too. Selfies are obvious, but we can create a variety of moments to document your vacation. We post the photos, and the likes and comments accumulate. You reap the benefits without lifting a finger."

"But it's a...lie," I said.

"So?"

"So...it wouldn't be me. Everything would be fake."

Shawn flashed a furtive smirk. "What social media account isn't?"

"Mine isn't."

"No?" he sneered. I wanted to speak, to defend my online legitimacy, but the symmetry of Shawn's face seized my focus. It was like a scientist had designed him in a lab. "Do you think everything you see on social media is real?" he asked. Before I could answer, he grabbed a remote control from his desk and powered on a TV screen behind me. Kelly Munnz's Instagram page appeared onscreen.

"Hey, that's Kelly," I said.

"It sure is." Operating a wireless mouse on his desk, Shawn clicked on a family photo. "Look at her perfect family." Shawn scrolled through several photos highlighting Kelly's family—she and her husband sipping champagne on a cruise ship, her two kids swimming with dolphins in Cabo, the entire family snow skiing in Aspen. Shawn stopped on a picture showcasing Kelly and her family clustered on a park bench, posing for the camera. I recognized the photo; they had used it for their Christmas card the previous year. "You know what's missing from Kelly Munnz's manufactured life?" Shawn asked. "The husband suffers from insomnia. He spends most of his nights on his computer in his den—

looking at porn." I gasped. Shawn continued, "Don't be so surprised, Paige. His behavior is more common than you might think."

"How do you know this?"

"If it's online, it's never private."

"You track people's online history?" I asked. Shawn gave a slight nod. "That's...wrong," I said. "That's invading their privacy."

"It's all legal."

"How?"

"Congress made it legal. Gotta find the terrorists, right?"

"But Kelly Munnz and her husband aren't terrorists."

"That doesn't matter. The Patriotic Freedom to be Free Act made it legal to retrieve anyone's search history. Even 'cleared' history still leaves a trace. That beautiful act informs us of Mr. Munnz's pornographic proclivities. It's some wild and kinky stuff, too. But of course, you never suspected that based on the 'perfect' life he's presented on social media."

"Wow," I whispered. "Poor Kelly."

"Kelly doesn't mind, and you wanna know why? Because she's having an affair. Found that truth nugget from her own nocturnal online viewing habits. Their teenage daughter, Olivia, aborted a pregnancy last year."

"She's sixteen," I said.

"She was fifteen when she terminated the pregnancy."

"This is...incredible."

"Kelly's first husband—"

"She's been married before?"

"Yeah, it lasted less than a year. The husband left her for...another man."

"No way," I said, trying, and failing, to stifle my gasp.

Shawn sat back and smiled. "Let me ask you something, Paige. Do you enjoy hearing that your friend's life isn't as perfect as you thought?"

I considered Shawn's question. Yes, I *did* experience some level of satisfaction learning that parts of Kelly's life were flawed. It warmed me knowing she suffered and that her perfect life was anything but. What kind of person did that make me, relishing someone else's pain?

"It brings you joy to hear your friend's life isn't as great as she pretends, doesn't it?"

"Yes," I answered. "Why does it make me happy?"

"Because you're human. We like gossip; we like scandals, and social media gives us that. We can view someone like Kelly and realize that every perfect family gathering she shares is for show. From now on you'll see that underneath Kelly's immaculate smile is a woman with an opiate addiction." I opened my mouth to question the authenticity of Shawn's claim. He nodded, anticipating my question. "We're all presenting false narratives, Paige. Even you."

"What? I...that's not true!"

"No?"

"No."

"Who am I talking with right now? Paige Reynolds or Selina Everdean?"

I swallowed. "You know about my secret account?"

Shawn nodded.

"But how—"

"It's not important how I learn these things. What's important is you understand why social media controls your life. Why it controls so many lives." Shawn leaned forward, like a doctor explaining to a patient the intricacies of an upcoming procedure. "Science has proven that when people receive likes on their social media accounts, they get a hit of dopamine."

"What's dopamine?"

"It's a chemical, the 'feel-good' chemical. People who receive a lot of attention on social media get more hits of dopamine than people who don't."

"You keep saying 'hit' like it's a drug."

"In a sense, it is. When you post something on Instagram, Facebook, Tik Tok, whatever, and someone likes it, when you hear your phone ding with a new text message or social media update, your brain has the same response as someone who takes a hit of cocaine or a gambler winning a big hand of poker or someone viewing pornography. Our bodies like to be rewarded. Dopamine is that reward."

"So social media is...addictive?"

"Very."

"But it's just a bunch of people sharing their lives."

"So?"

"So, how is that addictive?"

"Because of your brain's reaction to it. How many times have you wanted to check your phone since we've been talking?" I smiled guiltily. Shawn continued: "You want to check it because you're addicted. Your natural reaction is to always reach for it. The average person checks their phone over four thousand times a day. Check it. In fact, place it on the desk. I don't mind."

I dove into my purse and retrieved my phone. No messages and no updates. I frowned and placed the lifeless device on the desk.

"No messages or updates, huh?" Shawn asked.

"How did you know?"

"You placed it on the desk too fast. How did you feel when you saw that no one had messaged you? How did you feel to learn you had no social media notifications?"

"I felt...like a loser."

Shawn reached across the table and took my hand. "Don't let it discourage you, Paige. You're a beautiful woman, and we will fix this. I will make it so that every time you check your phone, something is waiting for you."

"That sounds amazing."

"Vicarious Vacations can guarantee that if you book a trip through us, each of your vacation photos will yield at least 500 likes."

"500?" I repeated. The number did not seem real.

"Yes."

"How?"

He released my hand and sat back in his chair. "Because we guarantee it."

"But I don't even have 500 friends," I admitted.

"Why do you think that is?"

"Because I'm not popular."

"And why do you think that is?" he asked again.

"I don't know." My frustration shone through my voice. "I upload and share a cat video and ten people like it, but when—"

"But when Alexis Carter does, the same video gets ten times that amount."

"Yes!"

"Why do you think that is?"

"You keep asking me that, and I don't have an answer."

"You don't?"

I sighed. He wanted me to admit what I had spent my entire life denying. Alexis Carter represented what I was not: beautiful, skinny, sexy, successful.

"We will change how the world sees you, Paige," Shawn said. "We will make you relevant."

"How?"

"The better your life, the more popular you'll become. That's where we help." He took his tablet, tapped it a couple times, and rotated it towards me. "These are the different packages we offer. Each vacation comes with a guaranteed number of likes, and often we double or triple those estimates."

The tablet contained a list of popular tourist destinations. Each city contained bullet points outlining common attractions and the projected number of likes for each destination. "A Golden Gate Bridge selfie is guaranteed 500 likes?" I asked.

"Yep."

"The Grand Canyon: 600? Vegas: 800? A Statue of Liberty selfie is worth 1,000 likes?"

"That's right."

"I'm swimming in debt. I have student loans. I couldn't afford—"

"That's okay. We can offer these packages at a fraction of the cost of a real trip."

"How?"

"Because, like I said, you don't leave your house. We manufacture everything, so you get the perks of traveling without leaving your house. No waiting in lines at the airport, no getting lost in unfamiliar cities, no risk of getting robbed or struggling with a language you don't speak."

"That sounds...amazing."

"Where do you want to go?"

"What do you recommend?"

"Well, there's a lot to consider. Would you like to stay stateside or travel international?"

"Ah…"

"Foreign trips cost a bit more." He tapped the tablet twice, and a spreadsheet filled the page. "Here's a list of popular destinations. The first column lists domestic vacations, and the foreign ones are in the third row. Of course, you're not limited to what's listed there. We can custom-make a vacation and send you anywhere."

"Anywhere?"

"If it's on a map, we can send you there."

"But I still don't understand. You said you manufacture all of this. How?"

Shawn opened another page on the tablet and directed me to it. Another data sheet—*my* data sheet—filled the screen.

I scanned the sheet. It contained everything: my shoe size, dress size, bra size, natural hair color, a list of my favorite clothing brands, restaurants, movies, musicians, TV shows, and YouTube channels. It even listed my annual income.

"You know my salary?" I asked.

"That's an estimate. Based on where you work, how long you've worked there, the car you drive, your credit score, your wardrobe, and other variables, we came to that estimation."

"Who gave you this information?"

"You provide most of it, Paige. You offer information through your online activity. Every post, every web search, every online purchase, is a piece of a puzzle. We just put the pieces together."

"Wow."

"How close did we get to your annual salary?" Shawn asked.

"You're within $500," I said.

"By our metrics, you're five-five and one hundred sixty-two pounds. That sound about right?"

I swore off scales since I broke the 150-pound threshold over a year ago. "Ah, I think it's closer to one-fifty."

Shawn smirked and let the lie pass unchallenged. "Okay," he said. He entered my "new" weight and my data points adjusted. "If you lost thirty-eight pounds, re-examined your wardrobe, considered a breast augmentation, we could outfit you for maximum likes. As you are now, you aren't fat or ugly, but we will need some strategic work to present you in a more…fashionable light. Your body structure isn't *as* important if you don't choose an exotic location."

"Why?"

"Sex sells," he said. "Provocative photos garner more traffic and likes. Swimsuit photos, underwear photos, yoga pants, sports bras, sexy Halloween costumes, anything that shows more of who you are, well, people like that. Alexis Carter's most-liked photo, that we didn't manufacture, is from her trip last year at Miami Beach."

I knew the photo. Alexis sunbathed on the beach. Her firm stomach, adorning her latest bellybutton piercing, glistened in the Florida sun. Tiny sweat beads lined her tan body. She lowered her bikini bottom, exposing a preexisting tan line from an old bikini that offered more coverage. I calculated if she lowered her bottoms any further, she may need to consult a gynecologist. Her caption said: "Living Brazilian in Florida! #Smooth. #StupidTanLines. #BikiniBridge." I had to Google "BikiniBridge." I learned it was another feature Alexis had that I did not. The photo received over 6,000 likes.

"I'd never be comfortable posting pictures like that," I said.

"Not even for 6,000 likes?"

"I…" I trailed off. I never considered receiving 6,000 likes. 6,000 was a foreign number. Shawn may as well have promised fifty thousand or a million.

"Paige, you don't have to post anything that makes you uncomfortable," Shawn said. "The beauty of what we do is you get to stay in your comfort zone. We'll post the provocative photos for you, and it doesn't even need to be your body."

"It doesn't?"

"No. Let me show you." He tapped his tablet and another page loaded. It displayed a dozen women, cut off at the head, in their underwear. Their skin tones ranged from "eggshell" to "mocha." Their individual measurements were listed under their photos. "These twelve women have measurements like yours. You need to decide which should represent you."

"I don't get to see their faces?"

"You don't need to," Shawn explained. "We superimpose your face on whichever body you select. If you'd like, one of these women can pose in a provocative swimsuit, a thong perhaps."

"But people will think it's me."

"That's the point."

"But I don't want—"

"Imagine the likes, Paige."

I fell silent and resumed analyzing the different women. It was like selecting produce in the supermarket. "But these women, except for their skin tones, look like me. I want someone more...fit."

"I can appreciate that. We can hold off on any provocative photos until you're more fit. Until then, we'll focus on modest vacation photos. The upside is, often, when customers see their social media status improve, it motivates them to get in shape. If you get in better shape, I can present you with better options. Consider documenting your transformation on social media, and let your friends follow it. People love that."

"I remember my friend Shelly did that. She lost forty pounds."

"I remember Shelly," Shawn said.

"Shelly came here?" I asked.

"Yeah."

"What for?"

"Remember her trip to Key Largo?"

"That was you?"

"Yes. A Vicarious Vacation."

"And her weight loss? You helped with that?"

"Yes. After she saw how popular her Key Largo pics were, she purchased the comprehensive fitness package. We have personal trainers, dieticians, nutritionists, everything you'd need to get in shape."

"Her body is amazing now."

"You can do what Shelly did, Paige. We can help you."

"Did you manufacture that too? Her weight loss, is that fake?"

"Well, in theory, yes, we could fake the weight loss, but you'd have to go into hiding because people could see it isn't true. We offer services and resources to help you reach your ideal weight, but the actual dieting and exercising is your responsibility. Don't be discouraged; as I mentioned, social media is a great motivator. Our analytics prove the most popular social media accounts are those featuring women who aren't afraid to sell their image by exposing a little more skin. With social media, you are the product, so you must sell yourself. A turtleneck won't do the job; a thong will. If you want people to buy you, as a product, you need to show your followers more of what you're selling."

"This sounds so...seedy."

"It's the world we live in, Paige. Humans aren't sentient beings capable of abstract thoughts any longer. They're objects yearning to be objectified. Let the thinkers—the losers—sort out life's big problems. Do you want to cure cancer or be idolized on social media? Do you want to be Kim Kardashian or Katharine Burr Blodgett?"

"I've never heard of Katharine Burr Blodgett."

"That's my point. Let us make you into a minor social media celebrity. People no longer admire intellect; they admire fake breasts and photoshopped butts. Put a taut, smooth backside in front of the Golden Gate Bridge with a clever hashtag, and you'll see your social media feed come to life."

I tried to speak, but words lost their sense of conveyance. I recalled the more provocative social media posts I had seen over the years. Shirtless guys, bikini-clad women. Posts that accrued likes in the thousands. A high school friend became a lingerie model. A year ago, she posted a pic wearing a too small bodice for her too large breasts. The dark areola peaked and teased behind a segment of sheer white fabric. Was it a photographer oversight? Did she intend to post such a revealing pic? The photo garnered over 20,000 likes. The next day she posted another. This time she wore a thong. She bent at the hips exposing sinewy hamstrings and a glistening, oiled buttock. I admired the photo for twenty minutes, and with each page refresh, the likes multiplied. At last check she had 40,000. Bewilderment and jealousy engulfed me.

"We can create any life, any image, you want, Paige," Shawn said, returning me from my reverie. "That's what's so beautiful about what we do. You're jealous of your friends living better lives than you? Well, let's change that. Let's send you somewhere fun. Let's show the world a different side to Paige Reynolds. I will make your friends like you publicly while they resent you privately."

"This sounds…incredible," I said. Tapping the tablet, he restored the destinations' page. "There," I said, pointing to a listing. "That's where I want to go."

Shawn's lips ticked up into an expectant smile. "Niagara Falls, huh? I never would have guessed."

My phone hummed to life with a new friend request. I snatched it from Shawn's desk and gasped. I hit the "accept" button with haste. Shawn Preston, CEO of Vicarious Vacations, was now my friend.

"Thank you," I mouthed, unable to speak.

CHAPTER 8

My instructions were simple—use a week's vacation leave and stay out of sight for the duration. If anyone spotted me, it would expose my sham vacation. Since I was online friends with my mom and nosey teenage sister, I would need to escape their detection, too. I told them some friends and I were going to Niagara Falls. They both eyed me with suspicion but neither questioned my story. Then I drove three miles up the street and checked into a Best Western. Trip Advisor reviews said the continental breakfast left a lot to be desired, the beds were rock-hard, but the Wi-Fi was excellent.

I chose Niagara Falls for the obvious reason—it was where Eric proposed to Alexis. My trip gave us something in common. At our inevitable future gatherings, we could swap Niagara Falls' stories while laughing and reminiscing and becoming nostalgic about the same things. One of us may even suggest we, as a group, revisit The Falls to reconnect with our previous experience. The Falls would unite us and highlight how alike we are. It was the perfect destination for my first vacation.

Vicarious Vacations documented everything: my drive to the airport, me waiting at the gate, my plane seat, my arrival, my hotel overlooking The Falls, The Falls themselves, the people I met, the things I did—all of it uploaded to my social media accounts.

And like a dam finally giving way to the elements, the likes and comments flooded my accounts. My phone had its own pulse. New notifications kept me up at night. Friend requests swamped my inbox; I averaged twenty new Instagram followers every hour. I started receiving random messages on Snapchat and Twitter. One mysterious follower even sent me a shirtless pic on Snapchat and asked that I reciprocate the gesture. I retreated to the bathroom where I took several photos—none of them nude—and hovered my finger over the send button before deleting them and apologizing for my modesty. He called me a tease and stopped messaging me.

My popularity became contagious. I was transforming into the minor social media celebrity Shawn had promised. I loved the attention and wished my vacation did not have to end. When I checked out from the Best Western six days later, fifty-seven pictures documented my trip, and my friends and followers now tallied over 500. All my vacation pictures received at least 150 likes. The picture with the lowest number of likes—a picture of me with my Uber driver in front of a Nathan's Hotdog stand—had 163 likes. One picture of me, the most popular from my trip, The Falls cascading in the background, amassed 1,286 likes—286 more than what Shawn promised. I now had a respectable level of online relevancy. People watched me doing something fun and exciting and they wanted to share my experience. I wondered how many jealous likes I had received. How many people gazed upon my photos and wished their lives contained as much excitement as mine? I relished the attention. I swam in the envious sea that my trip afforded me while dancing on the precipice of the social media elite. I mattered.

CHAPTER 9

Some degenerate stole my thunder. I had settled into my cubicle for a mundane Monday while stealing glances over my shoulder, wondering which co-worker would ask about my trip first. My phone buzzed to life. I grabbed it, confident a new notification awaited me. I was sadly disappointed.

A school shooting occurred less than twenty miles from Newage Tech. A former student, and self-proclaimed INCEL, twenty, entered the school carrying a duffle bag loaded with AR-15's and a variety of handguns, all of which were purchased legally. He waited for the first bell, when 1,800 of his former classmates clamored and jostled to get to their first period classes on time. The shooter took his position on the second floor. His location gave him a bird's-eye view of the common area below. He pulled the first gun from his bag and started firing. Bullets rained down from his elevated position. The school security guard took cover. A handful of students, seated near where the shooter stood, ran in the opposite direction. He fired 1,000 rounds before turning a gun on himself. The latest report listed thirty-six dead and forty-three wounded.

The school, Adams High School, was my alma mater's biggest rival. My freshman through junior year they defeated us in football, all three years kicking record-long field goals in the closing seconds. My senior year we defeated them 42-17, and a group of students, in a wave of excitement, rushed the field and tried pulling down the school's goal post before realizing they lacked the weight to accomplish the task. My upbringing taught me to dislike all things Adams High, but now that they were in the throes of a mass school shooting, my heart ached for the school.

Alexis had already uploaded an obligatory post enumerating her grief: "My thoughts and prayers go out to the victims and families of Adams High School. I remember…" She outlined a litany of memories regarding Adams High School. She even referenced the time she helped a rival Adams High cheerleader who, when struck with an unexpected period, was offered a much-appreciated tampon courtesy of Alexis. She ended her post with the declaration: "It's important for women to stick together. Love knows no bounds! #AdamsHigh #HateNeverWins."

Some guy had just slaughtered thirty-six innocent students, and Alexis waxed poetic about giving a cheerleader a tampon. She made everything about herself. Her post tally: 317 likes in less than ten minutes. Genius.

I countered with my own message offering thoughts and prayers. Unlike Alexis, I had no Good Samaritan act to serve as a sympathy grab. Not counting the immature derision we meted out to the Adams High students after their homecoming defeat, I had zero interactions with the school. Nonetheless, I posted that, "Despite the lopsided victory of my alma mater, the Adams High Grizzlies played with poise and integrity." I studied my post. It was, at least on the surface, heartfelt and sincere. My mom and a handful of high school friends liked it. After five minutes my tally reached six; Alexis's: 408. From my phone, I logged into my second account—Selina Everdeen—and hit the like button, bringing my total to seven. My computer chimed with a pop-up from Vicarious Vacations. Shawn Preston's profile pic filled my screen with a message: "Want at least 100 people to like your latest post? Click 'accept' and we'll guarantee at least 100 likes for only $5.99!"

I stared at the ad. How could he guarantee so many likes?

"Hey, Paige," a strange voice said behind me. I turned and spotted Glenn from payroll standing at my cubicle entrance.

"Hey, Glenn."

"Looks like you had a pretty sweet vacay, huh?"

"Yeah, it was…pretty sweet."

"I've never been to The Falls. They look sick."

"Yeah," I said, smiling. "They were…sick."

"Cool beans, man. Cool beans." He sipped his coffee. We had exhausted all conversational avenues. Our awkward interval lasted another thirty seconds before he tipped his coffee to me and shuffled down the hall.

My computer still displayed Shawn's pop-up, along with my like total that had stalled at nine. Alexis's post had 423 likes. I accepted Shawn's pop-up, and my account came to life. Twenty likes in less than a minute. After five minutes, I neared seventy. Some friends, newly acquired after my Niagara Falls trip, even commented on my post. I reached the 100-like threshold before heading to the breakroom.

Alexis's school shooting post was approaching 1,000 likes as I settled into my usual corner table with my coffee.

"How was your trip?" Eric stood over my shoulder, coffee in hand, smiling down at me.

"What?"

"Alexis told me you went to Niagara Falls. She saw it on your Instagram page, I guess."

"Oh, right." Alexis offered no likes nor comments on any of my photos. Eric sat down across from me. The breakroom was empty, yet Eric still leaned toward me and lowered his voice for dramatic effect and asked, "Was it a real vacation or a vicarious one?" A coy smile breached my lips. "Oh, no," Eric said, sitting up straight. "Not you, too."

"No, I—I went." My lie escaped before I had a second to weigh the consequences of it. The deception was a necessity though. As part of my contract with Vicarious Vacations, I agreed to remain mute concerning the *factual* events surrounding my trip.

"You did?" he asked. He seemed pleased, surprised.

"Yeah," I said, avoiding his stare. "I wouldn't…I mean, why would I lie about that?"

"I don't know, but people do. Hell, I did. Granted, I did not discover I had until I saw my fake honeymoon pictures."

"How many of your trips are fake?" I asked.

Eric thought for a moment and laughed. "Well, that's just it, isn't it? I don't know. Has Alexis posted any other trips since we've returned from Jamaica? Was I in Greece over the weekend?"

"No, Alexis hasn't posted about you lately." I held up my phone with Alexis's Twitter page loaded.

Eric took my phone and read his wife's latest post. His face twisted into a series of embarrassed gestures. "Thoughts and prayers, huh? It's like she's writing for cable news."

"It's a very popular post."

"Popularity is no metric for insightfulness."

"Huh?"

He handed back my phone. "Did the shooter die?"

"Yeah. He killed himself."

"Almost every mass shooter has one common element," he said.

"What?"

"They're all men."

"Is that true?"

"Tell me one that isn't?"

I shuffled through past tweets and Facebook posts about mass shootings. Images of the shooters flickered in my head. They *were* all men. "You're right. They're all men."

"I told you."

"There must be one female."

"Yeah, maybe *one.* I noticed Roberts blamed the shooting on homosexuals again."

"Roberts?"

Eric raised his eyebrows, perplexed with my ignorance. "Senator Roberts."

"Oh, right," I said, feigning knowledge.

"He said mass shootings occur as a way for God to punish society for accepting homosexuality and other alternative lifestyles."

"That's ridiculous."

"He received 78% of the vote last year. He loves Jesus but hates being Christian."

"I didn't vote for him."

"I hope when we die and have our judgment we go into a courtroom. God is the judge and Jesus is the prosecuting attorney, and he is prosecuting us. He has a folder on everyone, and inside is a history chronicling all the times we used him or God as justification for being a prick. And now God and Jesus are charging us for defamation, slander, and libel. Guys like Senator Roberts and every other politician and religious zealot who use God to promote hate under the guise of religion, now they must answer to God and Jesus. If they can't convince God and Jesus to let them into heaven, they don't get in."

I assumed Eric was joking, but his expression suggested otherwise. "Are you being serious?"

Eric sipped his coffee. "Sure. Why not?"

"Would Jesus admit you if that were the case?"

"No. He won't admit me, but not because of that."

"Why?"

"Because I tell mothers their kids are ugly."

I coughed and almost spat my coffee across the table. "You tell mothers their kids are ugly?"

"Yes, if they are ugly, I tell them," he teased. "No one else will tell them."

I wheezed and tried to clear the misplaced coffee from my throat. "Perhaps that's why you will get into heaven. You're the one honest person telling mothers their kids are ugly."

"People want honesty until they get it," he said. I sensed his last comment hinted at something unsaid. "So, what was your favorite part about The Falls?"

"The Falls?"

"Yeah. Niagara Falls."

"Oh, it was…crazy."

"Crazy?"

"No…um…not crazy…amazing. So incredible."

"Did you go on a boat?"

"A boat?"

"Yeah."

"No. I flew."

"I mean, did you go on a boat at The Falls? One of those Hornblower boats?"

"Oh, yeah," I said, recalling the photos from my trip. In one, I stood on the deck of a boat, outfitted in a yellow poncho, while The Falls flowed in the background. I assumed this was what Eric meant.

"Did you Journey Behind The Falls, too?" he asked.

I did not understand what he meant. I bit my lower lip, trying to recall any posts that mentioned a Journey Behind The Falls. The room turned hot, and I prayed I was not flushing under the weight of his questions. The breakroom's door swung open and with it the much-needed distraction from my catalog of lies. I hailed the interruption until I saw Alexis had caused it. She stopped in the doorway, imbued with disappointment.

"What are you two talking about?" she asked, approaching our table.

"Stuff," Eric said.

"What kind of stuff?"

"Personal stuff," Eric said.

"I've been standing at the door for the past five minutes."

"So?"

"So, you were laughing."

"So?" Eric repeated.

"So why were you laughing?"

"Because I'm funny, Alexis," Eric answered and smiled at me for confirmation. I averted my gaze, fearful to endorse an alliance with Eric. "Paige visited Niagara Falls last week," Eric said.

"I know she did," Alexis said. She transferred her gaze from her husband to me. I fumbled with my phone to distract me from her glare.

"I was telling her how much fun we had on our honeymoon," Eric said. Alexis blanched, studying her husband to see if he hid something in his remark.

Alexis forced a smile. "Oh, yeah?"

"Yeah," Eric said, matching her fake smile with his own. "I told her about our snorkeling trip and the SCUBA diving excursion and the food. My god, do you remember how much food we ate?" He burst into a fit of pretend laughter.

Alexis threw her head back and laughed. "Oh my god, yes!" she said, overselling her performance. "I literally couldn't fit into my swimming suit."

Eric halted his fake laughter, staring daggers at his wife; Alexis froze under the weight of Eric's sudden temperament. "You used 'literally' wrong," he said, maintaining his stony expression. It was a struggle to keep from laughing, and I was unsuccessful. The suppressed effort conjured a guttural snort that caused Eric to break character. Eric and I were caught in a fit of uncontrollable hysterics. Alexis was livid. No one ever laughed at Alexis Carter's expense. Her eyes morphed into great fiery orbs of hatred and rage. My laughter ceased, and I discharged a slight whimper. She stared at me for a full minute before forcing her lips upward into a knowing smirk.

"Jamaica was so incredible," she said. "Are you thinking of going?"

"I…ah, I would love to go. Your pictures are incredible."

"It was amazing." Her expression appeared warm, but her eyes remained icy. "A dream come true."

"Yes, Paige," Eric interjected. "All of it was like a dream, wasn't it, sweetie? Almost like it never even happened." He smiled at her, and Alexis frowned.

"Well," Alexis began, attempting to defuse the situation by changing the subject, "I came in here to ask if you want to have dinner this weekend with Gary and Alli. I texted you, but you haven't texted me back."

"My phone is in my office."

"I know. It was on your desk. I wish you wouldn't leave it so much."

"Don't go through my desk," Eric said. "That's where I keep my porn and gummy bears." Eric's delivery was complete deadpan. I choked on my laugh and fell into a coughing fit. Eric smiled, satisfied with his achievement, while I muttered apologies and attempted to stifle my coughing.

"Are you enjoying this?" Alexis asked. I was uncertain if she were asking me or Eric. I shook my head and coughed again; Eric shrugged.

"Please keep your phone with you," Alexis said. Eric nodded, but Alexis knew he had no intention of changing his habits. I sensed they fought often about Eric's phone negligence. His nonchalant attitude about his phone baffled me. He treated it like some insignificant inanimate object, and he did not seem to mind that it upset Alexis.

"So, dinner?" Alexis asked.

"I can't, and you know I can't."

"What should I tell them?"

"Tell them the truth."

"You want me to tell my best friend that we can't do dinner because you're helping your sister plant a tree?"

"Is that the truth?"

"That's how I see it."

"You see what you want to see."

"What does that mean?"

"Think about it, Alexis; I'm sure you can figure it out."

They glared at each other. I was incredulous. Their lives were so...normal, so standard. Bickering over the mundane and routine, arguing in front of strangers, saying things without saying them. Nothing I observed represented what Alexis posted to her social media platforms. They sounded like my parents.

"Fine," Alexis said. She pulled her phone from her back pocket and began writing a text. "I'll tell her, again, that you would rather spend time with someone else than with me."

"That's not true."

"Sure, it is. Your sister needs your help, and you'd rather be with her than your wife."

"I'd love to be with you, but I don't think you're capable of being with me."

"What are you talking about?" Alexis asked, her eyes glued to her phone.

"I will take you anywhere you want this weekend. I'll pick the most romantic place and wine and dine you."

Alexis looked up from her phone, beaming. My pulse quickened. Eric's soft eyes burned with sudden desire. *This* was how I envisioned their marriage. "That sounds great, baby," Alexis said.

"All you have to do is leave your phone at home."

Alexis's smile vanished. The trap had been sprung. "What?"

"Don't bring your phone."

"Why?"

"You want a weekend alone? Let's have a weekend alone. No distractions, no notifications. Just us."

"Eric…"

"Choose between me or your phone." What an unyielding and harsh ultimatum! My mouth dropped, anticipating Alexis's choice.

Alexis shook her head and sighed. "Go with your sister. That's what you want anyway." She then gave me a sharp appraisal and scoffed. She started for the exit and sneered over her shoulder, "I'll leave you alone with your frumpy new friend."

Eric sprang to his feet and blocked the door. Alexis was mystified by his sudden reaction and the speed in which he had moved.

"Apologize to her," Eric demanded.

"What?" Alexis asked. She appeared confused and even a little scared.

"Don't treat people that way. She's a kind person."

"I never said she was unkind. I called her frumpy because she is."

Eric seethed, and Alexis gleamed. She had hoped her comment would sting, and Eric's reaction confirmed it had. "You're an ugly person, Alexis," Eric whispered through gritted teeth.

"No, honey," Alexis sneered. "I'm the sexiest woman you've ever known."

Eric shook his head, resolving that Alexis was not worth the effort required to disprove her boast. He moved to the side, and she walked out the door in mocking defeat. Eric seethed, the pulse in his neck throbbing in rhythm with his breathing.

"You're not frumpy."

I stared at the floor. Frumpy—the word meant nothing to me because I had no metric to weigh its meaning. But Alexis's derision, compounded with Eric's defensiveness, insinuated it was not flattering.

"Are you married?" he asked.

"No."

With his inquiry, I expected him to offer some insight into his marriage, or any marriage, but he had said all he intended to say. I suspect my *not* being married must have muzzled the potential conversation.

Alexis's critique still lingered, still rang in both our ears. Eric fidgeted, and I worried the room's compressed air might compel him to leave. I prayed he would stay; his presence comforted me. I searched for something to say.

"Have you ever had a social media account? I mean, an account that Alexis didn't create for you?"

He nodded. "I had a Facebook account for a few months. I hated it."

"Why?"

"It was an election year."

"So?"

"So, people kept sending me all kinds of propaganda. Memes and graphs and articles that were untrue. Friends kept forwarding me things they'd heard from a friend of a friend of a friend of a brother's sister's wife's stepdad. You know what they call that in real life?"

"What?"

"Gossip. You know what they call that on social media?" I raised my eyebrows in anticipation of his answer. "Sharing."

His observation rang true. "I never looked at it that way."

"Alexis was the worst culprit, too. Always sharing stuff, none of it fact-checked, but still passed along as if it were true."

"Do you enjoy being married?" I asked without thinking. "Sorry, I...I didn't mean...that's none of my business."

Eric waved away my apology, but his expression showed my question had struck a nerve. "The tax breaks are nice," he said, checking his watch. "I should get back to work." He lifted his cup as a parting gesture and walked out the door.

I checked my phone. Shawn promised one hundred likes for my latest post. It now had 134, but weighted against Alexis's comment, my success felt anticlimactic. I switched over to Alexis's profile. She had posted a meme five minutes ago. One of the Hemsworth brothers stood shirtless in the background, with the following scribbled across his body: "Real love is when you are completely committed to someone even when they are being completely unlovable." The quote was from someone named Dave Willis. It was a beautiful quote, so I liked it, hoping my public approval sufficed as an apology for speaking to Eric. Then I Googled the definition for frumpy and removed my like.

Chapter 10

"I want to look like her," I said while Shawn Preston thumbed through Alexis's Jamaica photos. "I want to go to Jamaica. I mean go the way she did—by not going."

"I understand," Shawn said.

"And I want to meet someone like that," I pointed to Eric standing in the surf, his hand touching Alexis's. "You can do that, right?"

"We can create any life you want, Paige."

"I want to go to Jamaica and drink Mai Tai's on the beach, and I want to pose in the ocean with a shirtless guy. Someone that loves me and looks at me like I'm the only person in the world."

"And you deserve that, Paige. You deserve to have the same experience as Alexis. We can make that happen for you."

"I'm tired of being a nobody."

"If you want an Alexis-style life, you'll need to adopt Alexis-style habits."

"What do you mean?"

"You need to transform who you are. It'll be hard, but you'll reap the benefits."

"What do I need to do?"

Shawn came out from behind his desk and positioned himself in front of me. "Will you stand for me, please?" I stood. Shawn stepped back for a better overview. I shifted my feet, uncomfortable with his scrutiny, and crossed my arms across my chest. "Will you put your arms down to your sides, Paige?" My arms dropped. With his thumb and forefinger, he pinched an inch of fat from my arm. He did the same with my stomach. Frowning, he retreated a step and appraised me again, like an art critic evaluating a potential purchase. He strode toward me and gently took hold of my shoulders. His eyes bore straight into mine. "You're a beautiful woman, Paige. Do you believe me when I tell you that?"

My brain dissected Shawn's words, searching for any hint of mockery or deceit. I doubted someone like him could think someone like me was beautiful. I am not beautiful. Some days, if I have enough time to watch and emulate Alexis's makeup tutorials on YouTube, I can pass as pretty; the other days I am simply acceptable. But beautiful? That is a stretch. I am just...there—plain. If forced to describe my physical appearance, the word that comes to mind is...frumpy. The word stung more each time I said it. I hated its accuracy, and I hated the source from which it became part of my lexicon.

I tried telling Shawn he was mistaken, but his hypnotic stare, full of conviction and promise, kept me silent. Was his claim genuine? His visage convinced me that perhaps it was. His steel eyes, which a moment ago shone through my vulnerability, turned soft and engaging. He entranced me, and before I knew it, I had fallen into his chest, crying. He held me, granting me my humiliating reprieve.

Once I regained a moderate level of decorum, Shawn led me to a chair. "I want to help you increase your likes," he said. "Let's get you to Alexis Carter-level numbers." I wiped my tears and nodded. Shawn took my hand. "Paige, I want to ask you something, and I want you to be honest with me, okay?"

"Okay."

"I'm your friend. Remember that. Everything I say is coming from a place of friendship, okay?"

"Okay."

"Tell me why Alexis gets more likes than you."

The answer was obvious. "She has more friends." I said.

"Why does she have more friends?"

"Because she's beautiful."

"Is she more beautiful than you?"

"Yes."

"In what way?"

"In every way."

"Be more specific."

"Her...body."

"Her body. Right. Alexis gets more likes because she has more friends and she has more friends because..."

"...of her body," I said, finishing the thought.

"Exactly," Shawn said, smiling. "I want to help you get the body Alexis has." I did not mean to laugh aloud, but my involuntary outburst escaped without restraint. "I'm serious, Paige," Shawn said. "I mentioned this last time. A better body yields more followers, and we offer a variety of services that can help you improve your body."

"What services?"

Shawn let go of my hand and took his tablet from his desk. He tapped it several times, going into a variety of webpages, navigating the pages like a man on a mission. A minute later, he stopped and handed me the tablet. I viewed a spreadsheet, outfitted with women and a series of before and after pictures. The before photos showed the women, noticeably bigger...*frumpier.* The after shots showed toned bodies, darker skin, happier expressions. Below each picture were their social media stats. As the women got more fit, and revealed more of their bodies, their likes and comments increased.

"I'd like to set you up with a dietician and a personal trainer," Shawn said. I continued scrolling through the thread. The women were stunning, each ranked at or above Alexis's level. And most of them, judging by their before pictures, looked like me. Some were even in worse shape before their metamorphosis. Could I transform how these women had? Did I have a hidden figure concealed under my excess skin waiting to accumulate likes and comments in the thousands? I doubted it, yet the more photos I observed, the more I saw the possibility.

"These women are gorgeous," I said.

"Those women looked like you before they came to us."

"Incredible," I whispered.

"We can market your diet and sell it on your social media platforms. Chronicle your journey to a more desirable weight and body image. Right now, you're common, Paige. That is good. You're relatable; you're ordinary. Let's transfer you into something better, stronger, more beautiful."

"Aren't all body types beautiful," I asked. I had been on the social media grid long enough to witness countless stick-thin models and celebrities hawking a variety of online beauty products, only to navigate to the comment section and read from bitter observers how unrealistic their bodies were. Social Justice Warriors always exclaimed zero-sized models were negatively affecting impressionable young girls, causing them unhealthy body issues. In some arenas, the public even praised obesity, commending and encouraging a lifetime of inactivity. I often "liked" any post that challenged the notion that a small waist heightened by large breasts were a prerequisite for beauty. I had neither a small waist nor large breasts, so I envied those who did. Regarding body image, society had convinced me to side with the majority, and the majority was overweight. So, what caused me to question my indoctrination now? The answer was obvious, even if I was reluctant to voice it.

"Sure, all body types are beautiful, but not all body types get equal treatment," Shawn said. "Publicly, we can pretend thicker is beautiful. That is a smart approach because most people are overweight. It's an excellent marketing strategy to pretend that all bodies, no matter their weight, are beautiful. It's even better if you're doing so while squeezing into skinny jeans and thong bikinis. We love hearing beautiful people, the runway models and goddess-like celebrities, ridicule their own body type to praise the average. It gives them a more human appearance and makes them more approachable. But, Paige, it's bullshit."

"Bullshit?"

He punched his tablet a few times, and the screen filled with side-by-side photos of a woman. In the first photo, she posed at a swim-up bar, a variety of vacationers dotted the background. The woman stood facing the camera, margarita in hand, wearing a smile that said: "I'm on vacation and you're not." She wore a tankini—the perfect swimsuit for her respectable body type. The camera cut her off just below her waist, concealing the parts of her that were less flattering. Next to this photo was another one, nearly identical. The woman posed at the same resort, holding a drink, and smiling. This second photo, however, showcased a woman displaying a body and smile unmistakably more confident. The tankini had been swapped for a string bikini. Chiseled abs stared back at the camera, and her breasts seemed to have grown into two perfect bulbs that struggled against the swimsuit's scant coverage. The photographer did not cut her off at the waist this time but showed her entire body.

"This is Heidi," Shawn said. "She honeymooned in the Dominican Republic. That's the first picture. She came to us and returned to the Dominican Republic two years later. That's the second picture. Now, tell me the truth, Paige, which photo do you prefer? Which body would you rather have?"

Shawn drove his point home. Sure, Heidi looked nice in the first photo, but I could have ripped the second photo from the pages of a beauty magazine. Shawn waited for my answer even though he already guessed which I preferred. I nodded to the second photo.

"Don't worry, Paige. Choosing what's obvious doesn't make you superficial; it makes you normal, human. Judge the results for yourself." He thumbed down the page two inches to the like totals. The tankini photo tallied 229 likes. Most of the comments focused on how much fun it appeared Heidi was having. Her friends envied that she spent the week soaking up the sun while they stayed home trapped in their mundane lives. The second photo boasted 4,136 likes. The accommodating message board focused on her body, not her vacation. Most comments were punctuated with fire and tongue emojis. Jealousy and resentment panged my heart.

"If you want more likes, if you want more attention, if you want to matter, this needs to be your focus," Shawn said. "We can get you a couple hundred likes with this body." He pointed to Heidi's first picture. "Or, with effort and hard work, we can get you to this." He tapped the tablet again and a new picture filled the screen—a back shot of Heidi in a thong bikini. The caption read: "Heading to the beach. Hope I don't burn my cheeks." She included a peach emoji. The post had 8,000 likes.

"That's an 8,000-like butt," Shawn said. "How many is yours worth?"

He was right. Even with the right filter and lighting, I did not have a triple-digit body. I hated the world, so consumed with physical appearance, that 8,000-liked bathroom selfies gauged my self-worth. I recognized how degrading and pathetic my inevitable choice would be, but I lacked the mental and emotional fortitude to stand and walk out on Shawn while he clutched his tablet replete with bikini-clad women. I wanted Heidi's relevance and Alexis's popularity. I wanted to matter.

"Let's do it," I said.

"'Atta girl," Shawn beamed. He held up his hand for a high-five. I smacked his hand with my own. I had never given a high-five before that moment; it would have made an incredible GIF.

CHAPTER 11

Shawn asked if I wanted a male or female personal trainer. I hesitated, and he opened a webpage that featured profiles from each. Every candidate looked like a fitness model. The women's finely tuned muscles and oiled bodies glistened. The men replicated the women but with more rigidity and definition. Their muscles popped and bulged, and veins traversed their bodies like roads and rivers outlining a map. Reflecting about my body, and how much it did not resemble the ones on display, heightened my insecurities. What would these trainers infer when they saw my soft flesh loosely hanging over my hips? How much mockery would I have to endure when my trainer instructed me to run a mile, and I could not complete the task without stopping halfway to catch my breath? Ego and anxieties be damned! This necessary step was a prerequisite to the life I wanted.

Shawn instructed me to choose a trainer I most wanted to date. "If you want to date the person, you'll be less inclined to disappoint him," he explained. I contemplated this as my eyes settled onto Matt Jenkins. He looked like Eric. Same rigid jaw, same hair color, similar complexion. Once inside Matt's profile, a collage of pictures greeted me. Most showed Matt, either at the gym or vacationing, posing—often shirtless—at different popular landmarks. (The St. Louis Arch, the Grand Canyon, Mount Rushmore, Old Faithful, the Lincoln Memorial, the Las Vegas sign.) All his pictures tallied thousands of likes. It did not matter if these vacations were real or manufactured. All that mattered was I had found my trainer.

. . .

I met Matt the next day for my first training session. We met at the gym—the same gym I had been frequenting for the past six years. Once a week I attended an evening Pilates class. I would enter the building, scan my key card, and make a sharp left to the group exercise studio, avoiding eye contact with everyone.

I liked Pilates; the class was safe and unassuming. The people looked like me—on the cusp of life, wondering if their best days lie ahead or behind them. Occasionally, one or two women trickled in wearing yoga pants and sports bras that did little to support their $10,000 breasts. These women always positioned themselves front and center, while the rest of us stayed on the outskirts and judged them for their immodesty and envied them for the same reasons. They rarely returned the following week. The class lacked two elements most fit women craved: ogling men and intensity.

This time when I entered the gym, Matt instructed me to head right instead of left. The right terrified me. Right is where the free weight section, also known as "The Iron Jungle," resided. The Iron Jungle— where everyone who entered was hunting or being hunted. The men, brandishing string tank-tops and archaic tribal tattoos, hunted the women, while the women, adorned in form-fitting exercise apparel, assumed the role of prey. I was the commissioned photographer hiding in the bushes, observing, hoping to get out alive.

I stood on The Iron Jungle's fringes and took in the scene. Hypnotic dance music spewed from the gym's sound system. Mirrors hung from every wall, never allowing members a reprieve from their narcissism. Women congregated around the dumbbells, grabbing different weights and then standing back to watch themselves curl or bend or squat. Some men hovered and the more confident ones approached. They offered instructions and insights, explaining how to improve their movements. Sometimes the women pleaded ignorance, acting as if they had never lifted a weight in their life. This gave the men a spotlight, while engaging in some light physical contact, to demonstrate proper form and technique. The women giggled; the men puffed out their chests and smiled. Everyone played a role while pretending they were not. It was like a dance club with better lighting.

I was out of my element. The loose tank top and looser fitting shorts I adorned were in stark contrast to the other women. My appearance was destined to draw derision and ridicule from the fellow members. I wanted to retreat to the Pilates studio—my safe space—where the lights were low, and one could easily conform. My appointment with Matt was for 5:00. The clock read 4:59. There was not enough time to hide in the Pilates studio, so instead I entered my other safe space: my phone. I entered my Instagram account and navigated through my Niagara Falls photos checking for new likes. I began comparing my numbers when I heard someone call my name. Matt Jenkins stood before me.

I fumbled with my phone while extending my hand for a proper introduction. Matt did not want to shake hands, though; Matt wanted a hug. He pulled me into a warm embrace. I raised my arms and surveyed his back; it felt like a chunk of granite.

"It's so nice to meet you," he said. He released me from his hug and gave me a thorough overview. I shifted my feet while his eyes surveyed my body. He held out his hand to touch my stomach, thought better of it, and asked permission. "Ah...yeah, okay," I said. With a gentle touch, he poked my stomach and frowned. He rotated to my love handles and pinched a healthy inch of fat between his fingers. For the second time in less than a week, an attractive man poked and prodded my fat while frowning. I noticed two women clad in booty shorts and sports bras observing me from the heart of the Iron Jungle. They laughed and resumed exercises that required a lot of bending and squatting. Matt squeezed a hunk of loose skin that hung on the backside of my arm between his fingers. His face contorted, thinking.

"Have you taken before pictures?" he asked.

"Before pictures?"

"Yeah, to chronicle your weight loss."

"No. Was I supposed to?"

"Yeah, we'll want to track your progress. Once you start dropping weight, we'll begin uploading your pictures so people can see your body transformation. It'll create a lot of traffic to your Instagram page. People love when someone takes initiative to lose weight. You'll get a lot of likes."

"My friend Becky started exercising about six weeks ago," I explained. "She's been tracking her progress on Instagram. Her followers have increased."

"Do you 'like' her photos?"

"Yeah. I think she's brave." Becky used *Brave* to describe her journey, so it naturally popped into my head when I thought of her progress. I never thought of dieting and exercising as brave. Most of Becky's friends used the same word in their encouraging comments. *You go, girl! You're so BRAVE!* I decided to adopt the same term when describing my transformation. That was a natural component to social media— adopting other people's trends as your own.

"I can take your photos," Matt said.

"What?"

"Let me take your photos. Sometimes people prefer to take their own, but with selfies, it's hard to get the best angles and include your entire body. I can take them. I'll keep them for you and track your progress."

"Ah…"

"The aerobics studio is not being used." He pointed to the group exercise room tucked into the gym's corner—the Pilates room. "Let's use that."

"Okay," I said, grateful to escape to some place familiar.

"Let's go," Matt said and darted toward the room with a cadence reserved for personal trainers. He scanned his ID badge, and the door clicked open. We stepped inside, signaling the sensor, and the lights flicked on. "Let's go to the far corner," he said. "No one can see us from there." I walked in front of him, concerned that he may have been appraising my backside with the same scrutiny that he did my front a moment ago.

"So, should I just…stand here?" I asked as I neared the farthest corner in the room.

Matt held his phone and checked the lighting. He stepped back and re-checked it. "Yeah, that's good. You'll want to take off your shirt and shorts, though."

"What?" I asked, startled.

"It's for the pictures, Paige."

"You need me in my underwear?" I clutched my arms around my stomach.

"Well, yeah," he said as if I should have already assumed this.

"I…"

"Your underwear is more modest than what half the girls out there are wearing," he said, pointing to the door.

"Yeah, but…"

"What's wrong?"

"I'm not…comfortable with you taking pictures of me in my underwear."

"It's for your fitness journal, so we need to track your progress. Trust me, you'll want to see how far you've come once you have the body you want."

I understood I needed to mark my progress, but I had not considered a stranger snapping pictures of me, especially pictures so…unflattering.

"And you'll store these photos on your phone?"

"Yeah. I'll create a folder for you. I'll upload, photos, workouts, and everything else to the folder."

"I'm not sure I want…"

"It's nothing sexual, Paige. It's what you hired me for, isn't it?"

"I guess."

Matt sensed my discomfort and comprised a plan. "What if I take the pictures with your phone?" he asked. "That way I won't have access to them. Would that make you feel better?"

I thought for a moment. "Yeah," I said. "That would make me more comfortable."

"Okay, but you need to promise you won't delete them. You don't understand now, but you will want these pictures down the road. Can you promise not to delete them?"

"Yeah," I said. "I promise."

"Okay. Hand me your phone."

Matt pocketed his phone as I handed him mine. He spied me through the phone's camera and positioned himself. "Okay, this is the spot."

I shifted my weight knowing that he now expected me to remove my tank and shorts. I pulled at my shirt's hem, willing myself to take it off, but lacking the courage to do so. A lone tear escaped my eye, traveled down my cheek, and became suspended on my chin. My camera clicked. I lifted my eyes; Matt had my phone pointed at me. I opened my mouth to protest, but he lowered the phone before I could voice my displeasure. He retrieved the picture and handed over my phone. My crying visage filled the screen.

"What do you notice when you see yourself?" he asked.

I wiped my eyes to better chart my photo. "I see...me."

"What else?"

"A fat...insecure girl who no one likes."

He blanketed his arm around my shoulders. "I see a beautiful young woman who's this close," he held his thumb and index finger an inch apart, "to becoming the woman she deserves to be." He gave my shoulders a heartfelt squeeze and released me. "You need to see yourself through a different light, Paige. If photos make you uncomfortable, we won't take any, but I need you to do one thing for me," he steadied his eyes, making sure he had my full attention. "I need you to trust that I will get you into the best shape of your life. I will transform you into someone who will beg to have her picture taken."

My doubting disposition, under the sincerity of Matt's promise, became hopeful and optimistic. He smiled. "Let's go workout," he said. He made for the exit, and had not gotten ten feet, before I called his name.

"I want you to take my picture," I said. Matt flashed a knowing smile.

I shed my tank top and shorts and surrendered to the moment. Matt snapped a handful of pics with comforting professionalism. He remained inscrutable throughout and never once ridiculed or mocked my body. A moment later he handed back my phone and gripped my shoulders. "Archive those," he said. "*Now* let's go workout."

CHAPTER 12

My entire body ached. The slightest movements—bending over to slip on my shoes, standing from the toilet, sneezing, breathing—caused every muscle to contract and scream with pain. The past week consisted of doing exercises I had no clue were exercises: burpees, slam balls, mountain climbers, plyo lunges, Supermans.

Matt put me through the ringer. All week I woke in the middle of the night with immense hunger. I would pad my way into the kitchen, throw open my parents' pantry, and grab the first thing I spotted. Graham crackers, potato chips, granola bars, crispy fried onion straws. I returned each foodstuff after reading the nutrition label. Too many calories, too many carbs, too many sugars—too many ingredients that, over a lifetime, had turned me... *frumpy.* I ambled back to my bed clutching my empty stomach.

Matt gave me a crash course, replete with handouts, of nutrition. In summation, my atrocious diet had to change. "You need healthy fats, lean meats, fruits, and veggies," Matt explained while I struggled on the gym's rowing machine. "Avoid simple carbs. Avoid white anything— bread, chips, tortillas, rice. No more fried foods. No more sweets. If you need to snack, eat almonds, carrots, an apple." I stopped rowing. The room spun as Matt continued spouting dietary advice: "People think if the label shows no or low fat it's healthy. That's not always the case. The *right* fats are not bad."

"Right fats?" I gasped. I thought I wanted to avoid fat. Matt laughed at my ignorance. He handed me a towel, and I used it to wipe my face and the puddle of sweat I left glistening on the rowing machine's seat. I spent the next thirty minutes in his office learning the intricacies of fats, carbs, and proteins—macros, he called them. With each new bundle of information, he slid a sheet of paper across his desk with bulleted items outlining, in layman's terms, what he earlier explained in scientific ones. My dietary ignorance was boundless, and I displayed this with each new piece of nutritional information he presented. Matt smirked at my ignorance and replied: "That's what you're paying me for, isn't it?" I forced a smile, recalling that his services were $250 a week. My Niagara Falls vacation, which lasted a week, set me back $300. My travels cost about the same as my trainer. I shook my head at the absurdity of it.

"Vicarious Vacations has supplemental nutrition plans," Matt said. "It's offered from a subsidiary of Vicarious Vacations called Shredded Fitness."

"What do they provide?"

"Well, they provide me," Matt smiled. "But they also provide nutritionally dense meals if you don't want the stress of preparing your own."

"How does it work?"

"It's a weekly meal delivery service. I create meals unique to your fitness needs, and they deliver them to your doorstep. You don't have to prep or cook. Each meal is tailor-made for you."

"Okay…" I nodded, unconvinced.

Matt took the tablet from his desk and entered my fitness spreadsheet. The page listed my age, height, weight, target weight, and pictures from my various social media accounts. He tapped into a folder labeled "food," and the screen filled with different food pictures and recipes I had saved to Pinterest. Another finger tap, and a spreadsheet appeared with a list of different foods.

"It appears you like chicken and turkey," he said, reading from the list. "Almonds and avocados, too. That's good. Both have healthy fats. You're not a fan of Brussels sprouts, huh?" I shook my head to express the disdain I held for Brussels sprouts. "You enjoy several fruits, though," he continued. "That's good. For your snacks you can make smoothies, but we'll use almond milk instead of fruit juice or regular milk, and we'll add a protein supplement. We'll focus on berries—strawberries, blueberries, raspberries, blackberries. Avoid mangos, bananas, and pineapple. They have too many sugars."

"How much will this cost?" I asked.

"Breakfast meals are ten dollars, lunch is fifteen, and dinners are twenty. Snacks are extra."

I did the math: $45 a day, not including snacks. "I can't afford that," I said.

"Can you afford *not* to do it?" he asked. I opened my mouth to explain how budgeting worked, but he waved my impending half-hearted explanation away before I even started it. "All the hard work you're putting in here, will be in vain if your diet doesn't give your body the proper nutrition you need. Think of your body like a car. You can spend hours on the outside. You can wash it, polish it, and make sure it's sparkling. But if you're not putting the best gas and oil in it, and if you're not maintaining what's under the hood, you'll ruin the engine. Over time it will erode, and you'll have to pay to replace it. Our bodies are the same way."

Everything Matt said made sense, and I appreciated him explaining it in a way that was easy to understand, but my budget was far too tight to spend so much on food. I still needed to factor Matt's services into my budget. Student loans accounted for most of my paychecks. If anything remained at the end of the month, I stashed it, hoping soon to have enough for an apartment. I also wanted to take another vacation. The likes I received from Niagara Falls had plateaued, so I needed to budget for another adventure. All these thoughts played through my head, but one thought, or rather one word, kept pushing everything else aside. *Frumpy.* Then, without warning, I heard myself agreeing to the meal delivery service. Matt beamed and told me he would begin developing my meals later that night. It took a week for the meals to process, so I just needed to eat healthy on my own until they arrived. It sounded simple enough; it was not. Food is cheap and easy to access; nutrition is not.

. . .

I woke from hunger pains. I grabbed my phone and began my morning routine of checking my social media platforms. Once completed, I clutched my stomach and rolled out of bed.

I brewed a cup of coffee—black—and made a piece of whole wheat toast—dry. In two hours, I could have forty grams of almonds, and two hours after that, a grapefruit with half a cup of cottage cheese. Two and a half hours later was lunch—half a sweet potato, six ounces of chicken and a small bag of carrots. I licked my lips in anticipation. I was nine days into my diet. Matt told me I should expect my meals to arrive this afternoon.

I still felt sore, but the pain was subsiding. I could now walk without limping, stand without moaning, and the best part—the weight was dropping. I had already lost five pounds. Matt promised the weight would come off, but his primary focus hinged on bringing the different muscles hidden underneath my loose skin to the surface.

Discounting the soreness that still plagued my body, I felt better than I had in years. I was no longer lethargic throughout the day. Sure, I got tired, but the exhaustion resulted from my new exercise regime, not because I filled my body with too many carbs or refined sugars. My mind seemed sharper, my skin appeared clearer, I was happier.

Because I woke an hour before my alarm, I took my coffee to the sofa and sat wrapped in a blanket. With my phone, I tapped into Alexis's Instagram and Twitter pages. She had not posted since last night when she painted her toenails. One foot displayed red polish and the other purple. She asked which people preferred and promised all voters an entry into a raffle for a year's supply of toenail polish, compliments of Pleasantry Cosmetics. I voted for the purple. The last tally read 511-397 for the red.

A new tweet brought my phone to life. "HELP!" Alexis's tweet read. "Eric and I are planning our next vacation and we need suggestions. Respond ASAP!!! #NeedToGetaway #SomeplaceWarm."

They were going on another trip? A legitimate escape or a vicarious one? I wanted to ask but knew better than to expose Alexis's secret (and mine). I could ask Eric if I ever ran into him again. He had been avoiding the breakroom since our encounter with Alexis. I wondered if they fought later that night after work. I pictured Alexis calling me more unflattering, yet accurate, names, and I imagined Eric, once again, defending me. I let that fantasy dance through my head, but understood they likely arrived home and forgot about me.

Meagan Sanchez replied to Alexis's tweet: "Bora Bora, baby!! John and I were there last month. EPIC!!" Brian Denver's recommendation followed: "You should hit up Burning Man. If you do, I'll pitch in for gas. #WeedForSpeed." Heath Klifford weighed in next: "Kilimanjaro. Go before global warming melts the snow and humans kill the wildlife. #PeopleSuck #BePartOfTheSolution."

A plethora of suggestions poured in, all jockeying for Alexis's approval. Alexis's Twitter feed was blowing up at 5:00 in the morning. My stomach groaned, and I sipped my flavorless coffee.

CHAPTER 13

I sat in the breakroom spreading avocado onto a piece of whole wheat toast. My phone rested on the table. Over 300 people offered suggestions for Alexis and Eric's vacation. My recommendation: revisit Niagara Falls. I humble-bragged about my trip and suggested they return to emulate the experience. I even included a picture of me standing at the base of The Falls. This was a classic social media move—reframe someone's post to divert the attention back to yourself.

My recommendation sat on Alexis's thread unacknowledged. The overwhelming consensus favored some place tropical. That logic was ironclad considering people wanted to see, and Alexis wanted to model, her updated swimsuit collection—another Instagram influencer and cosmetics ambassador perk.

I had been nowhere tropical nor anywhere that encouraged swimsuit selfies. I lacked the body and the funds for each. However, with Matt's help (I was two weeks into my new fitness routine), and Vicarious Vacations' services, both were realities hovering in the not-too-distant-future.

I finished spreading the avocado onto my toast and picked up my phone. Earlier that morning I googled the best tropical places to visit in the world. When those results offered locations too extreme or too far, I narrowed my search to the United States. Hawaii ranked at the top of most lists, but several people had already suggested Hawaii. I needed a better suggestion; I needed a *specific* destination, one that demanded Alexis's attention and inspired a like. Alexis had already been to Oahu and Maui (and I remembered the photos from each), so I needed to find a unique place on a different island.

I entered a webpage for the top ten things to do in Kauai when Alexis walked through the breakroom's door. If she noticed me, she did not show it; her phone held her attention even as she poured herself a cup of coffee. She took her coffee and sat at the far table. A place called Queen's Bath ranked number five for the most popular places to visit in Kauai. I clicked on a link that forwarded me to a page that offered directions and photos of the tourist destination. In the photos, people—adorned in swimsuits—lined rocky cliffs overlooking the ocean. It looked exotic and fun and unlike anything anyone else suggested. On Alexis's Twitter feed I wrote: "I think you'd enjoy Queen's Bath. #Kauai." Then I uploaded a couple pics from the website and included them in my post.

From my corner table, I spied Alexis as she sipped her coffee and scrolled through her phone. The distance made it impossible to see what captured her attention, but I assumed she had her notifications activated. As if on cue, her forefinger stopped scrolling. She read her phone and glanced over her shoulder in my direction. Our eyes locked. I opened my mouth to say something, thought better of it, and lowered my head. A second later my phone issued a new notification. She had liked my suggestion!

"Have you been?"

I lifted my eyes, and Alexis stood in front of me. "What?" I asked.

"Have you been?" She held her phone toward me. A picture I attached to my post filled the screen.

"Ah…yeah," I lied.

Alexis leaned closer to me. "Did you *really* go?" she asked, "or did you go in the same way you went to Niagara Falls?"

"I went to Niagara Falls," I said, my voice cracking from the lie.

"You're friends with Shawn Preston," she said. "I noticed him in your friends' list."

"Yeah…"

"I'm friends with Shawn Preston."

"Yeah…"

"So, did you go to Niagara Falls the same way I went to Jamaica?"

"I...don't know what you're talking about."

"You talk to my husband a lot."

"Do I?"

"He told me he told you about our honeymoon."

"What about your honeymoon?"

"Have you told anyone?"

"No."

"You sure?"

"Yes. I swear. I haven't said a word."

"It's in the contract," she said. "If you tell anyone the truth, they'll suspend your Vicarious Vacations account."

"I haven't told anyone. I promise."

Alexis studied me for a moment. My face flushed under her stare. "Good," she said. "Make sure it stays that way." She tilted her head to the side and smiled, changing her disposition. "So, Queen's Bath, huh?"

It took a minute for me to realize what she meant. "Oh...yeah. It's...great there. I think you'd like it."

"Well, I'll do a little research," she said smiling, but her expression offered no real merriment. In fact, Alexis's smile appeared...sad and forlorn. I understood she offered the smile as a passive aggressive gesture towards me, but something deeper fomented beneath her forced expression. The urge to rise and hug her struck me. I wanted to pull her into me and tell her that everything would be okay. If Alexis did not terrify me, I may have followed through with my inclination. But fear kept me immobile.

"Thanks for the suggestion," she said, taking up her phone. I wanted to tell her I had hired a personal trainer and that I had already lost weight and soon I would not be frumpy. Soon we could double date, and occasionally sneak away from work for midday cocktails. From our self-congratulatory perches, we would mock people who wanted to be like us. Those things were left unsaid, though. Instead, I said: "Nothing is going on between Eric and me."

She lowered her phone and assessed me. "What?"

"Nothing is going on between Eric and me," I repeated.

Alexis bellowed a shrill laugh. "Well...duh," she sneered. "Look at you."

"What does that mean?"

"What?"

"What's wrong with how I look?"

"Are you serious?"

"Yes," I stammered. "I follow your YouTube makeup tutorials, and I buy knockoff brands of the clothes you suggest. I follow everything you recommend, so what's wrong with my appearance?"

"Paige, it's not that you're ugly or anything, but, I mean, you're not me. I'm an Instagram influencer, and I'm an ambassador for Pleasantry Cosmetics. Why would Eric be interested in someone like you when he has me?"

My blood boiled. "Because you're cruel," I said. "Because you're shallow."

"You don't get it, do you?" she said.

"Get what?"

"Eric is shallow, too. All men are."

I contemplated Alexis's claim. "Eric isn't shallow," I said. "I had a flat tire, and he helped me change it. What does that tell you about him?"

"He married me, Paige," Alexis retorted. "What does *that* tell you about him?"

I had no rebuttal to this; Alexis's point was irrefutable. She smirked and left the room; I remained seated, hunched over, and beaten.

I logged back into her Twitter page and noted my suggestion. Three other people had liked it, and one even commented saying Queen's Bath was a must. Public affirmation often gave me a sense of approval, but a sudden bout of anger engulfed me. I clenched my fists and stood and kicked while executing a series of ridiculous air punches. I halted my tantrum and pulled out my chair and slumped back down into it, defeated. Eric walked into the breakroom while I was still catching my breath. He smiled and waved as he made his way to the coffee pot. He poured himself a cup and approached my table.

"Morning," he said.

"Hi," I replied.

"I don't suppose you've seen Alexis, have you?"

"You just missed her."

He glanced at my food. "Avocado on toast, huh? That's very…quaint."

"It's healthy," I explained. "Paisley Evans posted about the health benefits on Twitter. I'm following a similar diet."

"Paisley Evans, huh?"

"Yeah."

"Diets don't always work."

"Mine does. I've already lost six pounds."

"It won't work unless the things you do to get fit become habit. You can eat avocado on toast to get to your ideal weight, but unless you make it a permanent part of your lifestyle, you'll put the weight back on."

"I won't go back to how I used to eat. I'll monitor my macros." Eric raised his eyebrows, impressed. "Do you know what macros are?" I asked, hoping to showcase my newfound knowledge.

"Yeah, I know what macros are. You're not doing high fat, low carb, are you?"

"No. Moderate fat, moderate carb."

"Sugars?"

"Only natural ones."

"Protein?"

"Sixty-five grams a day," I said. "Who taught you about dieting?"

"Paisley Evans," Eric jeered. "It's not complicated. If you want to lose weight, eat right and exercise. If you want to stay fit, eat right and exercise. It's simple, yet difficult for most to maintain."

"This diet will work," I said. "I have a trainer and everything."

"Oh, yeah? What does 'and everything' entail?"

"I'm on personalized meal plans, too. He creates my meals, and they're sent to my house."

"He sends them?"

"No. He creates the meals. A meal delivery company sends them."

"Sounds expensive."

"Yeah. It's draining my savings."

"I hope you're not thinking of asking for a raise," Eric teased, and I smiled. "Well, good luck to you. It's admirable you're taking care of yourself. You already are a beautiful woman, though." His comment cracked and struck a chord in me.

"You don't think I'm frumpy?" I asked.

"Frumpy?"

"Yeah. Remember when your wife called me frumpy?"

Eric massaged the back of his neck and wondered how to address the elephant I had just let enter the room. "Have you ever heard the expression, 'Hurt people hurt people'?"

"No."

"Well, now you have. Don't let her comment get to you."

"Beautiful people never worry about hurting ugly people."

Eric furrowed his brow. "Who said that?"

"I did just now. Your wife is so beautiful."

"On the outside, sure. But inside, where it counts, she's...well, she struggles."

"So, you married her for her looks?"

"Excuse me?"

"I'm sorry," I fumbled. "I shouldn't have said that."

Eric stared at me for an uncomfortable beat. Thoughts played through his head as he tried to decide which, if any, to share. His jaw flexed under the weight of the words he would not say. "Never apologize for speaking your truth," he said. "I married Alexis because..." but he did not finish his thought.

"You okay?" I asked.

He settled into the chair next to me. "I will not lie," he began. "Her appearance played a role. But something else mattered more."

"What?"

"Getting married made financial sense."

"I get that. If I were married, I could afford to move out of my parents' house."

"No, that's not what I mean. Newage Tech was on the verge of bankruptcy, and Alexis's father gave us enough capital to stay afloat. I met Alexis's father before Alexis. He is who introduced me to her. I co-founded this company with two other people. Charles Carter, Alexis's father, cut us a hefty investment check. It came with some strings attached."

"Her father leveraged the investment?"

"It was more...intricate than that. He may have still invested, but it helped that I was dating his daughter, and it helped more when I proposed."

"Wow."

"Pathetic, isn't it?"

"Why do you say that?"

"I'm a sellout."

"No."

"On some level I am. I love this company. I have a vision for it, and I'm doing what I can to make it a reality."

"It's an impressive company," I said. "And I'm sorry for prying into your marriage. I had no right."

"Alexis and I had...*have*...very little in common," Eric said, willing to disclose more marital secrets. "But I figured why not? The love would come later, right? I'd pay that price if it allowed me to fulfill greater ambitions." Eric halted to reorganize his thoughts. I wanted to offer something in response, but I lacked any insight worth sharing. "Now," he continued, "we can't even be in the same room together. She's always on her phone, and I'm always wishing we had something to talk about."

"Are you considering..." I began but stopped myself before I asked what I wanted answered.

"Divorce?" he said, finishing my thought.

I nodded.

"No," he said, but disappointment drenched his answer. "I'm trying to make us work. We're going to counseling, and we've made some progress. We're even planning a trip."

"I know. She sent a tweet asking for vacation ideas."

Eric ran a frustrated hand through his hair. "I should have guessed."

"Kauai was my suggestion."

"I've never been to Kauai, and I don't think Alexis has either."

"She hasn't."

Eric flickered a defeated smile. "You may know more about my wife than I do. I can't tell you how much I hate social media, and I hate it more that it's an essential component to the company. Heather is creating a whole social media marketing team."

"Who's Heather?"

"The head of marketing. Co-CEO."

"That's a great idea."

"That's what Heather says."

"It's a brilliant way for people to connect."

"You sound like everyone in our board meetings. If it's so great at connecting people, why does everyone on it feel so alone?"

Eric's question deserved an answer, but I could not provide one.

Eric glanced at his watch and stood. "I better get going," he said, fixing a critical eye to me. "You better get going, too. What am I paying you for?" he smiled. "Nice talking to you, Paige," he said, heading for the door.

"Hey, Eric," I called after him. "Why do you talk to me? Why do you confide in me about Alexis?"

Eric shrugged and said: "You listen." He stepped through the door but reemerged before it could close. "Hey, have you read my book yet?" he asked.

"Your book?"

"*The Great Gatsby*," he said.

On a mental cloud, I drifted to my house, ran down the stairs, and into my bedroom where the book sat untouched on my desk. The first night Eric lent it to me, I read the first page but did not get further.

"I started it," I said.

Eric squinted at me, and I suspected he deduced the truth. Any cheerfulness he may have clung to drained from his face. He exited the room without calling my bluff.

CHAPTER 14

Alexis tweeted an official announcement—Kauai! My suggestion! My heart swelled with pride. I liked her tweet and posted a comment. "You will LOVE it there!! So gorgeous! #Jealous #BeachLiving." Her followers weighed in, offering suggestions of what to see and where to eat. Alexis gave a rough outline of their itinerary. Most days were beach days, but sandwiched in between, on day three, she and Eric planned to visit Queen's Bath. My other suggestion! I was beside myself. I giggled and posted another comment underscoring how beautiful Queen's Bath was. Three minutes later Alexis liked my comment! I forgave the hurtful things she had said in the breakroom. We were friends again.

Then the loneliness seeped in. I had no one to share in my joy, and no one to brag to about my accomplishment. My depression and anxiety medications sat on my nightstand. I took two pills from each bottle, clutched my phone to my chest, and rolled over in my bed. How I wished it were me going on vacation with Eric. My FOMO was cranked to eleven. Hot tears welled up at the corner of my eyes. I took a deep breath and another. Alexis and Eric's vacation would crush me. Jealousy would lace each new photo; every like would sting my heart and quicken my pulse. I must combat the impending envy. I needed to take a vacation, too.

. . .

I stood in the middle of Shawn's office like a waxwork on display in a museum. Shawn rubbed his chin, evaluating what he saw. He muttered "incredible" under his breath but loud enough for me to hear. He lingered behind me. I wore a shirt that extended below my backside. "May I?" he asked, and I nodded. He lifted my shirt tail and scrutinized my butt, nodded approval, and dropped my shirt.

"Your body is transforming, Paige," Shawn said. "How many weeks have you been working with Matt?"

"Six."

"Wow. And how much weight have you lost?"

"Fifteen pounds."

"You're tracking your progress, right?"

"Yes. Matt takes a photo every Monday."

"Have you compared them yet? You have not posted anything."

"I'm too embarrassed to look at them."

"May I?" Shawn asked, holding out his hand for my phone.

I blanched. "Um…"

"I will give you an honest critique."

I took my phone, opened my "dieting" folder, and handed my phone to Shawn. There were six sets of pictures, one for each week, of me outfitted in my sports bra and underwear. Each week contained a front and back shot.

"You need to post these," Shawn said. "Look at the improvements." He came beside me and held my phone so we could observe the photos together. My week one photo filled the screen. "See," Shawn said, and then he thumbed forward to the most recent photo, the one Matt had taken a few hours ago. "The changes are subtle if you go from week to week, but if you skip from week one to week six, you can notice massive improvements. When you started, your stomach and arms didn't have much definition and about four inches' worth of your inner thighs were touching. Now, skip ahead to week six." He shuffled to this morning's picture. "See the difference?"

And I did. My stomach, although still…frumpy, had undergone subtle changes. It appeared more toned, as did my arms and legs. "See there," Shawn said, pointing to my inner thighs. "Look how much your thighs have shrunk in the past six weeks. Now only two…three inches are touching. In another six to eight weeks, you may have a thigh gap, Paige." A thigh gap! It was a struggle containing my mirth.

Shawn handed back my phone. "You need to post," he said. "Start today. Create a post telling everyone that you've started a weight-loss journey. Explain the struggles you've endured your entire life concerning your weight and your diet. People love that because everyone struggles with their weight and diet. Your story is very relatable, so people will respond. They'll encourage you to keep up the outstanding work, and it will inspire you to do so. Let your followers see your progress. Let them take this journey with you."

"I don't...I can't," I stuttered. "I'm almost naked in these pics."

"You're wearing a sports bra and underwear in those photos. Some women workout in more revealing clothes."

"I'm not comfortable putting my body on display like that."

"You have to, Paige," Shawn said. "Your likes and comments will skyrocket. There's nothing sexual or provocative about those pics. They're...honest. You're an incredible, beautiful woman. Let people see that. You'll inspire them to undergo their own journey. Share your beauty with the world, Paige."

I brought my thumb to my lips and chewed my fingernail. Shawn sensed my trepidation.

"Trust me about this," he said. He took my wrist, and with a supportive smile, guided it back to my side. "Will you trust me?" he asked.

I hesitated, then nodded.

"Good," he said. "And there's one other thing."

"What?"

"You need to buy better underwear," he said.

"Better underwear?"

"Yes. Sexier. Start wearing underwear that reflects the body you're working towards, not the body you have, Get bras with lace and distinct colors. Make sure they lift your breasts to emphasize your shrinking waistline. Stop posing in your sports bras. Get push-up ones, and your panties—"

"Panties?" I repeated. I had never used the word 'panties' before to describe my underwear. Panties sounded so...sexy, so...scandalous.

"Yeah," Shawn said. "Panties. Right now, you're wearing underwear. I get it. They're practical and comfortable, but they're what girls wear.

You're a woman. Be one. Wear sexy clothes. Women want to feel sexy and men want to view sexy things. Get thongs, cheeky panties, French cut panties. For now, post photos of your front; backsides take more time to tone. We'll hold off on backside pictures for now. Also, let your followers see you become more womanlike. Dress like a confident, sexy woman. Give your female followers someone to envy and give the men a taste of your seductive side."

"I don't have a seductive side."

"Get one," Shawn said. He retrieved his tablet and opened his Instagram page. He typed, "#HumpDay" into the search box. Hundreds of pictures filled the screen. "Notice these women," Shawn instructed. "Each one is in a thong. Each one posing at the perfect angle, with optimal lighting. This needs to be your inspiration, Paige." He tapped on a photo of a woman in a white thong, bent at the waist, peeking into the refrigerator. "Count her likes," Shawn said. "87,499." He tapped on another photo—a woman in a black thong straddling an ottoman. Over 60,000 likes. "People want to see this. This is what you need to post, Paige. This is how you become an influencer. Study these women, and evaluate which photos receive the most attention." I nodded, absorbing Shawn's wisdom. "And your meals?" he asked. "How are they?"

"They're great," I said. "Everything is made specific to my tastes and needs."

"Great," Shawn said. "Have a seat, and we'll get to the real reason you are here." I eased into the chair opposite his desk. "So, you are ready for another vacation?"

"Yes."

"Are you experiencing FOMO?" Shawn asked, smiling. I reddened, embarrassed by my transparency. "Don't be embarrassed. The fear of missing out is one reason Vicarious Vacations exists."

"Alexis and Eric are going on a trip, and it's driving me crazy."

"Yeah. They leave for Kauai in two weeks."

"Is it a vicarious vacation?"

"No, it's a real one."

"How do you know?"

"We track anyone with a V.V. account. Alexis has posted several times about her trip, and her credit card has airline transactions and a hotel in Kauai for seven nights."

"I'm the one that suggested Kauai."

"Yeah, we noticed that on her Twitter feed. Our database flags and authenticates any potential vacations."

"I'm happy for them, but ever since Alexis announced they were going, my jealousy has skyrocketed."

"That's understandable. You can anticipate what she'll post. Alexis is a master at eliciting jealousy. You're having a very human reaction to her trip."

"I figured a trip would help."

"I agree. Where would you like to go?"

"Kauai?"

Shawn shook his head. "I must advise against that."

"Why?"

"Kauai looks like you're stalking her. You suggested Kauai on Twitter. Her followers saw that. Had you suggested it as an invitation because you were already going, that'd be different. But since you offered a cold recommendation without first saying you were going there too, well, now you'd look like an obsessed fan. Also, it would appear disingenuous if you were there, and you didn't get together for dinner or snorkeling or something else, especially since you recommended Kauai."

"Yeah. That makes sense."

"Now we could create photos of you hanging out with her and Eric in Kauai, but I don't think she'd go for that."

"She wouldn't."

"Also, Kauai is tropical," Shawn continued. "Kauai means bikinis. Your body is coming along, but are you ready for bikini selfies?"

"No."

"And you wouldn't want to go to Kauai alone. It's a romantic getaway, so going alone reeks of desperation. You want to choose somewhere more pragmatic."

"Like where?"

Shawn considered this and asked, "You ever been to New York?"

"No."

"Let's send you to New York. You can run through Central Park, see the Statue of Liberty, hit a few Broadway shows."

My pulse quickened with excitement. "I've always wanted to see *Wicked*."

"Perfect."

"Won't it seem desperate if I go to New York alone?"

"No." Shawn said. "Tropical vacations are for couples. Big city ones are for anyone, and we could send you with someone."

"What do you mean?"

"We can create a boyfriend for you." Shawn grabbed his tablet, tapped it a few times, and handed it to me. Thumbnails of guys outfitted the screen. "Pick a guy," Shawn advised.

"Who are they?"

"They're accounts we've created for people like you. People who want to meet someone without meeting someone."

"I can have any of these guys?"

"Just point."

"These guys are out of my league."

"Quit being so hard on yourself. We're working to bring out the full potential of your sexuality. You can have any of those guys. Pick one."

"Wouldn't people be suspicious? I mean, I haven't ever mentioned a boyfriend before and then I'm in New York with a random guy?"

"There are a few ways to approach this," Shawn said, anticipating my concern. "We can create a narrative that you met someone in Niagara Falls. One of those guys," he pointed to the tablet. "You didn't post about him because you didn't want to be presumptuous. As it turns out, the mysterious man you met in Niagara Falls lives in New York City. You've kept in touch. You've sent messages, you've snap-chatted, you've sexted, and now he wants you to spend the week with him. He surprised you with *Wicked* tickets."

My lips, absorbing the believable narrative, crept into a smile. "I like that." I clicked on the profile of a man with dark skin and darker hair. "What about him?" I asked.

"Great choice. He complements you well. What should we call him?"

My first impulse was to name him Eric, but that exuded falseness. "How about Sean?"

Shawn's eyebrows jumped halfway up his forehead. "Like me?"

"No," I said. "S-e-a-n. Not, S-h-a-w-n."

"Whatever you want." Shawn took the tablet and archived 'Sean' into my profile. "He will no longer be in our database. Once someone selects a partner, we remove them from the selection poll, so you need not worry about *Sean* appearing on someone else's platform. He is all yours. I'll have a team compile a back story. Nothing too difficult to remember, just bullet points, and we'll begin constructing and chronicling your relationship on your different social media platforms. We'll introduce him to your followers later today and upload some Niagara Falls pictures of the two of you. You'll say you didn't post them earlier because you and Sean were just friends. The photos will serve as a coming out party, a celebration of your new boyfriend. This is good for you, Paige. You'll receive a lot of traffic. A trip to New York with a new love interest will do wonders for your profile."

I smiled and clapped my hands. "When do I leave?"

"Do you have a week's worth of vacation time saved at work?"

"I think so."

"How about the day after Eric and Alexis leave?" Shawn said. "That way you can vacation while they do, and it won't bring you down when she posts pics from her trip. You'll be on your own adventure to combat any insecurities her vacation may cause you."

"I like that."

"There is one problem, though."

"What?"

"You need to disappear for your vacation, remember? People can't see you working out."

I had not thought about my training sessions. "I would not advise taking a week off from training when you're making so much progress."

Taking a hiatus from training was unimaginable. Yes, the first week was torture, but once the soreness subsided and my meals arrived, working out had become intoxicating. Even mentally, I was sharper and more focused. Some days the exertion high was so profound I even skipped my depression and anxiety medications.

"What can I do?" I asked.

"Let's call Matt," Shawn said, taking his phone and placing the call. Matt answered after the third ring.

"Matt, Shawn Preston here," Shawn said. "I'm here with Paige Reynolds."

"Hey, guys," Matt said.

"Paige is planning a trip in a couple weeks to New York."

"Great."

"The problem is she doesn't want to take a week off from her training."

The call fell silent for a moment while Matt examined a solution. "Paige, where are you staying during your trip?"

I leaned toward the phone and said, "Ah...my parents' house. I mean...er...my house."

"You live with your parents?" Shawn asked with surprise.

"Yeah," I said, my face hot with embarrassment. "I'm saving for a place, but I have student loans, and—"

"Who else lives with you?" Shawn asked.

"My sister."

"Are you friends with your sister or parents on any of your social media platforms?" Shawn asked.

"Yeah. My mom and my sister, but my dad doesn't do social media." This sudden interrogation confounded me. "What's the problem?" I asked.

"If you're living with them," Matt explained, "they'll know you're not in New York City."

Understanding dawned on me. Shawn must have assumed I lived alone, so he never inquired about my living situation. It was a marvel that of all the personal elements Shawn had deduced about me, this fact eclipsed his algorithms. Maybe because I never posted anything regarding my mom and sister, so I never left a trail linking them to me. Matt knew I still lived at home, which was why he asked where I was staying. With my first trip, I stayed in a hotel. I had become so enamored with my latest trip, that it had not occurred to me, at least not yet, that I needed to follow the same protocol.

"With Niagara Falls," I explained, "I stayed in a hotel to hide from my family. I never left the room, and my parents and sister suspected nothing."

"Good," Shawn said, relieved. "Is that your plan again?"

"I'll figure something out."

"You can block them," Matt offered. "But it may look suspicious."

"No," Shawn said. "Blocking them won't work. It's social media. She'll have friends of friends of friends of friends. It will get back to her family."

"My dad isn't on social media," I repeated.

An idea struck Shawn. He opened his desk drawer and grabbed a pen and a notepad. He wrote something, but from my angle, it was impossible to decipher what it said. "You need to stay out of sight for the duration of your trip," he said, scribbling on the notepad.

"I'll get a hotel room again."

"Hey, Shawn," Matt interjected, "if we could negotiate discounted hotel rates for people like Paige—"

"Way ahead of you, Matt," Shawn said. "I just made a note to meet with our marketing team." Shawn took his pen again and scribbled something else on the notepad. "Anyway," he said, "let's get back to why I called. Is it possible to train Paige after hours?"

"Yeah," Matt answered. "I have another client I'm working with from eleven till midnight. I could work with Paige from midnight to one. Would that work for you, Paige?"

"Yeah, but won't the gym be closed?"

"That's the point. No one will see you."

"Will this cost extra?"

"Double."

I winced, and Shawn detected my apprehension. "I can give you 10% off your vacation, and we'll cover your hotel the first night," he said.

I ran the numbers through my head. Even applying the discounted rate, this trip was too expensive. How would I ever get an apartment and pay off my student loans if I kept traveling and training with Matt? But how could I *stop* using Matt? How could I *stop* traveling? Both were unthinkable. Twenty-six more pounds stood between me and my ideal body weight. Alexis and Eric were heading to Kauai in two weeks, so now was not the time to falter. I needed to work out, and I needed to travel. Ten minutes later I left Shawn's office with a one-week trip to New York City booked.

CHAPTER 15

I closed my eyes, exhaled, and tapped the upload button. *One-two-three...* My phone chimed when I hit seventeen; I continued counting, *eighteen-nineteen-twenty...* It chimed again at twenty-three, twenty-six, thirty, thirty-nine, forty-one, forty-two, forty-eight, fifty, fifty-six, and sixty. I opened my eyes. Eleven likes in one minute. Another minute passed—eleven more. At the five-minute mark, I already had 100 likes. The comments arrived as quickly as the likes. My friends and followers called me brave, beautiful, courageous, hot, and sexy. Several others told me I was inspiring them to start their own weight-loss journey. They admired my progress, commended my dedication, praised my developing body. Then the unthinkable occurred: My like total rose from 118 to 119 with a comment: "You go girl!!! You look AMAZING!!!" Several fire emojis followed the all-capped compliment. It was from Alexis Carter.

I covered my mouth and wept.

The response, fueled by Alexis's public affirmation, compelled me to retrieve my running shoes and head outside for a post-workout run. I took my phone, and each new like and comment gave me more incentive to run faster and farther. By the time I stumbled into my bedroom for the second time that night, I had clocked an additional six miles. I completed them in under an hour—a personal best.

A week later, my mom and sister drove me to the airport. I told them about Sean, my new boyfriend, and how he had bought *Wicked* tickets and asked me to come to New York. My mom seemed skeptical, and my sister feigned indifference. I told my mom I wanted to take an Uber to the airport, but she insisted on driving me. I asked why she did not insist when I went to Niagara Falls and she said, "This is different. You weren't meeting a boyfriend." Her point eluded me, but I did not expend the energy arguing it.

I watched my mom and sister pull away from the curb as I entered the airport. It buzzed with life. People walked with purpose, fearful of missing their flight while trying to outwit their fellow travelers through the TSA lines. It had been ten years since I had last flown, and I did not recall the airport being so chaotic. My youth must have made me oblivious to my surroundings. I was a teen trying to navigate my way through adolescence, and my immaturity still required that my parents assume responsibility for my livelihood and well-being. Children go where their parents tell them. To a teenager's existence, the world is just background noise. Now that I had more independence, I did not envy people who fought airport crowds and the stress of traveling.

Confident that my mom and sister were gone by now, I stepped back outside and called an Uber. Less than an hour later, I checked back into the Best Western three miles from my parents' house.

Alexis and Eric arrived in Kauai the previous night. As expected, Alexis was documenting their entire trip: the trek to the airport, their airplane seat assignments, their arrival, their experience at the rental car counter (it took FOREVER!), their hotel view, and which bikini Alexis planned to wear to the beach the next day. All her updates received triple-digit likes, but her bikini laid out on her hotel bed with the caption: "What you can expect for tomorrow" tallied close to 5,000 likes.

I entered my social media accounts and watched my trip materialize. Vicarious Vacations already posted a selfie of me at the airport. It had 214 likes. The most recent comment came from Sean, my faux boyfriend. It read: "SOOOOOOOO excited to see you! I'll be the guy waiting with flowers making the other ladies jealous and their boyfriends mad." His comment was five minutes old, and it already had fifty-seven likes.

Vicarious Vacations spent the previous two weeks rolling out mine and Sean's relationship. Two days ago, Sean posted a picture of two *Wicked* tickets alongside a boarding pass with my name printed on it.

My friends were astonished! 567 likes! My fabricated relationship was generating unreal traffic. My new relationship, along with my newfound popularity (because of my weight-loss journey) made me into a minor social media star. This past week, Matt started taking videos of me working out so I could showcase the hard work I logged at the gym. He also tasked me with creating new pictures, "pensive" pictures he called them. This entailed snapping pictures where I looked solemn and reflective. The trick was to look anywhere but the camera, as if I were posing for a boy band album cover. The objective was to appear contemplative and thoughtful. At first these photos seemed ridiculous, but when the likes accumulated, I got on board snapping photos where I pretended not to know my picture was being taken. Even something as innocuous as a protein shake post earned a response. Included with the picture would be an ingredients list, and without fail, my followers asked follow-up questions. (How often did I have a shake? Were they meal replacement shakes, or did I use them to supplement my meals? How did they taste? How many calories?)

Being relevant meant everything. People cared about what I did and enjoyed watching my life. They admired me; they envied me. My life had purpose and direction. I was important.

. . .

Shawn was wise to suggest I take my vacation while Alexis and Eric took theirs. Every morning when I woke—not that I slept much—I found Alexis's platforms filled with new thousand-liked photos. My depression, coupled with an insatiable envy, would crystalize. Then I navigated to my Instagram page and observed my vacation and love life in full swing. Sean and I ran every morning in Central Park. One day we visited the Statue of Liberty, the next day The Met, on the third day we saw *Wicked.* All my photos received over 600 likes and several even reached into the thousands. I spent each day hiding in my cramped motel room, eating my diet-specific microwaved meals, and watched mine and Alexis's vacations unfold. When I was not on my laptop smitten with my fabricated life, I was at the gym after hours with Matt. It was the happiest week of my life.

Until it wasn't.

A strange thing happened on day five of my vacation. Alexis had not posted anything new for nearly twelve hours. Her most recent post was a selfie at the Queen's Bath trailhead. She and Eric had planned on visiting Queen's Bath on day three of their trip, but a heavy rainstorm set in, delaying them a couple days.

I anticipated waking to a plethora of pictures showing Alexis at the iconic tourist stop, but after a fretful night of sleeping, I checked my phone and she had posted nothing new. I checked her Twitter and Facebook pages. Nothing. I concluded she must have lost service, and once she was back in range, pictures would flood her accounts.

I clicked into my own Instagram account and found Sean and me standing in Rockefeller Center eating New York-style pizza. My mouth watered, and I padded across the hotel room to my suitcase and retrieved my sack of almonds. I spent the day watching my vacation unfold while also keeping tabs on Alexis's Instagram page. By the time I left to meet Matt, she still had not made any recent posts. I guessed she must have damaged or lost her phone. Maybe it slipped out of her pocket and fell into the ocean. Maybe she dropped it on the rocks, and it no longer worked. My heart ached imagining the torture of losing one's phone on vacation.

Two hours later, after returning from the gym, I learned why Alexis's social media platforms were dormant. One of my Twitter followers shared a news article. The headline read: "Tourist Dies Taking a Selfie at Kauai's Queen's Bath." The article had over 500 likes.

CHAPTER 16

When I suggested Alexis and Eric go to Queen's Bath, I did not realize it had a history of killing tourists. Nowhere on the travel websites did it say that people die each year trying to navigate the technical terrain outfitting the lava-shelf tide pools. Most victims die once they reach the cliffs. The scenery is awesome, the tides ferocious, and selfie-seeking tourists are vulnerable.

My guilt assailed me for two reasons: I recommended Queen's Bath, and like the school shooter had done after my Niagara Falls vacation, once again someone else's tragedy overshadowed my joy. I still received hundreds, and in several cases, thousands of likes from my various posts, but no one at work wanted to discuss my vacation nor my newfound love interest. Alexis's death dominated all conversation. Even in death her popularity eclipsed mine.

My life was lost without Alexis. Who would teach me how to do my makeup without her YouTube tutorials? My wardrobe needed her insights and recommendations. She gave so much to the world. She gave so much to me. I struggled to cope, and I seldom ate and rarely slept. I increased my medications and worked out twice a day.

The lone silver lining to Alexis's death was my expedited weight loss. I was no longer racked with bouts of hunger. I cut my daily caloric intake by half and doubled my physical activity. Fifteen pounds stood between me and my target weight. My weight-loss photos were earning more attention every week. I spent hours each day admiring women who dared to pose in their bras and thongs on Instagram. My body now adopted features like the women I ogled. Armed with a new credit card and an insatiable superficial ambition, I treated myself to a Victoria's Secret shopping spree buying sexy bras and panties that were more complementary to my new physique.

For my latest weight-loss post, I selected a pink lace bra and matching panty. I tried, and failed, to capture a flattering photo. The angle and lighting were never right, and my picture filters made me look cartoonish and bewildered. Frustrated, I packed my delicate new sundries in my gym bag so Matt could take pictures for me.

An hour later, when Matt and I escaped to the darkened aerobics room, I told him to scout the ideal lighting while I changed. I crouched behind one of the room's oversized audio speakers and emerged in my new bra and panties. When Matt saw me, he did a double take. I blushed and struck a pose.

"What do you think?" I asked.

Matt started to speak but hesitated. He gathered himself and asked: "Are you sure you want to go down this road, Paige?"

"What road?"

"This road. Getting your picture taken in that?" He gestured to me, brandishing a disgusted air.

"What's wrong with these? These are sexy."

"Yeah, they are."

"So, what's the problem? You didn't have an issue when I wore my other bras and underwear."

"Those were different. You're...you're changing, Paige."

"I know I'm changing. I'm losing weight and getting toned. People love my posts."

"What people? A bunch of strangers?"

"No. My followers."

"You're right," Matt hissed. "Your followers. I'm sorry."

"What's going on with you?" I asked. Matt no longer brought enthusiasm and excitement to our photoshoots. He always seemed upset and distant.

"It's nothing," he said. "Hand me your phone."

He took my phone and opened my camera. I sucked in my stomach and pushed out my chest and asked how I looked. Matt eyed me through my camera and moved me two feet to the left where the lighting better stressed my best features and hid my worst. He snapped a handful of pics and handed my phone back without even looking at the photos. I critiqued them alone, disbelieving what I saw. The self-consciousness and body-image issues that used to stifle my inhibitions had all but vanished. I looked sexy; I looked beautiful. My metamorphosis was in full swing. Alexis's death somehow made me impervious to my own insecurities. I now lived because she no longer did. It became my responsibility to live for both of us.

.   .   .

The funeral was brutal. Alexis's parents spoke and then Eric. Her mom blubbered through her address, pausing every ten seconds to blow her nose into a wadded tissue. Her father appeared stoic and inconvenienced. Eric had always exuded confidence and self-assurance, but when he mounted the church's pulpit and began eulogizing his dead wife, he seemed lost and confused. Was he harboring guilt? Was he in denial? I wanted to rush the podium and take him into my arms and hold him until he broke whatever spell held him. My heart ached for him.

Once Eric concluded his talk, we made our way to the cemetery. A priest consecrated the grave, and then Eric stood, removed his boutonniere, and with a trembling hand, placed it on Alexis's casket. A pair of dark sunglasses hid his eyes, but they did little to conceal the tears lining his cheeks. He leaned toward the casket and mouthed something no one heard. The scene was gut-wrenching. He sank into his chair and cradled his head in his hands. No one moved for three minutes, and then slowly, reverently, people dispersed.

Then something peculiar happened. A gaggle of women, who I recognized from Alexis's girls-night-out pictures, approached the casket. They all displayed abstract countenances of solemnity and grief. They surrounded the casket and Marci (Alexis's yoga friend) pulled a selfie-stick from her purse and placed her phone on the end. The entourage leaned in and eyed the phone. Marci snapped a pic and examined the photo. Displeased, she instructed the cronies to face more north to capture the mountainous backdrop. The pride rearranged for a better photo as Eric raised his head.

"What the hell are you doing?" he said through gritted teeth. Some women squinted in his direction, while some kept their eyes fixed on Marci's phone. Eric rushed over to Marci's outstretched phone. He yanked the phone from the stick and threw it twenty yards where it crashed against a tree. Bits of phone scattered, and Marci yelped as if Eric had shot her through the heart.

"This is a funeral," Eric said, seething. "Show some fucking respect."

Marci ran past Eric to where her phone lay shattered on the cemetery grass. She began reassembling the pieces, praying that she could fix whatever Eric had broken. The other women peered at Eric with confused expressions, each thankful it was Marci's phone that Eric tossed and not their own. Eric told the women to go home. Go home, they marveled with puzzled expressions. They had not yet taken a photo.

Eric returned to work the day after the funeral. I did not see him, but I overheard Ryann, my supervisor, tell a co-worker she saw him enter his office around noon. I asked how he looked. She shrugged. "Like someone whose wife just died."

I took longer and more frequent breaks that day, hoping to catch Eric if he came into the breakroom. He never did. Every time the door opened, I sat up hoping to see him stride through, only to find someone else enter. When I was not waiting in the breakroom, I trekked to the bathroom, taking a detour that crossed his office. I hoped to bump into him as I passed, or at the very least, catch him open his blinds as he gazed at the maze of cubicles occupying the floor. No such luck, though. Eric stayed concealed.

The month following Alexis's death, Eric became a ghost, arriving early and working late, all the while staying hidden in his office. My co-workers and I could only speculate how he was coping. I checked different social media platforms stupidly hoping that Alexis's death had inspired him to create an account to document his grief. The searches returned a slew of Eric Vandrosses, but none of them were *the* Eric Vandross. Even the fake account Alexis had created for Eric no longer existed. What's more, two weeks after Alexis's funeral, her social media accounts vanished. Even though she had passed, I still checked them daily, foolishly expecting to find recent posts. Now her accounts were gone. A lifetime of makeup tutorials and outfits of the day erased from the cloud as if she never existed. To be removed from the annals of social media—that was a fate worse than dying.

CHAPTER 17

I began receiving private messages from a variety of men. It seemed each time I logged into my accounts, half a dozen sexual offers awaited me. With each inquiry, I scoured the sender's online profiles. Several were married or in committed relationships. (And as far as they knew, so was I. As of late, my accounts were a collage displaying mine and Sean's New York love story.) The few senders whose social media accounts indicated they were single, appeared to be crusaders of narcissism, materialism, and hedonism. The extra attention flattered me, but their propositions always went unanswered.

Sometimes, discounting my silence, a guy would send another message asking for a nude picture. I dismissed these too, and that often ended the propositions. But on more than one occasion, men met my silence with yet another message. These typically included a naked picture of the guy, his head cut off, with his erect penis in his hand. Some variation of, "Can you handle this?" always accompanied the photo. I would blush and delete the inappropriate inquiries, but the last couple, I am embarrassed to concede, I archived. However, because of my inexperience, sex scared me.

I lost my virginity my junior year in high school. My boyfriend and I had sex at his house while his parents were at a movie. It was painful for me and quick for him. Afterwards, he retreated to the bathroom and returned with a towel. He tossed me the towel so I could clean myself. "I'm hungry," he said. He eyed me for a moment, waiting for me to recognize his pronounced hunger. He stuck his finger in his bellybutton, removed a piece of lint, and flicked it onto the ground. "I'm gonna make a Hotpocket." He left the room and returned five minutes later with two Hotpockets. I assumed one was for me, but when he wiped his greasy mouth on his comforter and reached for the second, I realized both were for him. We slept together one other time, then he dumped me with a text message.

There were other guys—three to be exact—each a short-lived college romance. We would go out twice, and on the third date sleep together. I would sleep with each one two more times and never hear from them again. Unlike my high school boyfriend, my college lovers never even extended me the courtesy of ending things with a text message. They ghosted me and later unfriended me, cutting off all prospects for any relationship. That was my sexual history. The last three years had been met with involuntary celibacy.

Now that I posted weekly progress pics, and those pics got more provocative as my body became more desirable, sexual proposals became a common occurrence. Yet I was unprepared to frolic with random guys considering their lone agenda. It felt incredible that strangers were perusing my social media posts and enjoyed what they saw. My hard work did not go unnoticed, but letting followers ogle me from a distance is different than sharing a bed with them. I wanted to date and get to know someone before sleeping together. So, I resisted the seedy proposals that inundated my social media inboxes. Until I received a message from Clint.

Clint Glasgow's message read: "Hey, I'm friends with Matt. He told me to check out your fitness progress. You're killing it! Keep it up. Your legs are toned AF!"

With my interest piqued, I clicked into Clint's Instagram page and spent the next hour engaged in some astute online stalking. Like Matt, he too was a personal trainer when he was not working at his uncle's body shop. He was fit, handsome, and loved enormous trucks, fast cars, and tattoos. He was a year older, had never been married, and did not have kids. I messaged him back, and we exchanged twelve more messages, each more flirtatious than the one before it. I expected he would ask for a date, and then…nothing. The messages stopped without explanation. I was disheartened until, a week later, I asked Matt about Clint, and he eyed me with suspicion.

"What?" I asked.

"Don't date Clint Glasgow," Matt said.

"Why?"

"He's…typical."

"Typical how?"

"He's just…kind of a prick. No, that's not accurate. He *is* a prick."

"How so?"

"He dates a lot of women."

"Well, he doesn't want to date me. He won't ask me out."

"You can blame me for that," Matt said.

"What?"

"I told him you have a boyfriend. A serious one."

"Why would you tell him I have a boyfriend?" I asked.

"Because as far as he and the rest of your followers believe, you do. Have you forgotten about Sean? The dreamboat guy you traveled to New York for. Remember?"

I finished my set of lateral raises and racked the dumbbells. "He thinks I'm dating that guy?" I asked.

"Yeah," Matt explained as we made our way towards the squat rack. Matt began sliding weights onto the barbell. "Clint thinks you're in love. If it weren't for New York Sean, he would have asked you out a week ago."

I stared at Matt with my mouth opened trying to decide which emotion overwhelmed me more: frustration towards Matt for not saying anything, or admiration for Clint because he respected what he thought was a legitimate relationship between me and my manufactured boyfriend. "Why didn't you say anything?" I asked. "I'd forgotten about Sean."

"Contractually, I couldn't. Vicarious Vacations created Sean for you. I can't tell a third party he's not real."

"You could have told him we were having problems or something."

"I don't meddle, Paige. If you wanted to maintain the facade that you and Sean were dating, it wasn't my place to say anything."

"You could have said something to me," I said, taking my position under the squat bar.

"I cannot discuss anything pertaining to Vicarious Vacations unless you bring it up first. And since you brought it up, I'll say this: You're better than Clint. He'll use you, and you shouldn't waste your time with him."

"That's just it, Matt. I'm not wasting my time with anyone. My last date was…it's been a long time."

Matt shook his head. "Well, it's your life. If you want to date Clint, tell him you and Sean broke up."

So that was what I did. I finished my workout, mounted the stair-stepper, and sent Clint a message explaining that Sean and I were now dating other people. A minute later Clint responded with a smiling emoji and asked if I wanted to get dinner Friday night. My giddiness enraptured me, causing me to stumble and hit my shin on the stair-stepper.

CHAPTER 18

I cursed Eric for deleting Alexis's YouTube channel. I had a date in less than an hour, and I needed Alexis's makeup tutorial on smoky eyes. My YouTube searches yielded charlatans explaining makeup techniques that were laughable compared to Alexis's aesthetic acumen. Did Eric understand the gravity of his decision to erase her online presence? Alexis was a makeup ambassador. Over 50,000 people subscribed to her YouTube channel. We depended on her, and I needed an exotic yet innocent look for tonight. One that frightened but also welcomed. I needed Clint to want me, and I needed smoky eyes for that to happen.

At five past the hour, Clint sent a text message telling me he was pulling into my parents' driveway. I stole one last glance at myself—frustrated that I did not have Alexis's wisdom to assist my appearance—and rushed up the stairs. My parents and sister stood at the living window peeking through the curtains to the lifted truck parked in the driveway. The truck's idling engine invaded our living room, shaking pictures and other loose objects.

"That thing is bigger than our RV," my dad observed. "Who is that?"

"That's Paige's date," my sister answered. "She posted about him an hour ago."

"What about Sean?" my mother asked. She retreated from the window and saw me standing in the middle of the living room.

"They broke up," my sister answered on my behalf.

"We broke up," I confirmed. My sister and father turned at the sound of my voice.

"Who's Sean?" my dad asked.

"Sean is Paige's ex-boyfriend," my sister answered. "He flew her to New York."

"When was this?" my dad asked.

"Like a month ago," my sister answered, again assuming it was her place to speak for me.

My dad's lips pursed into a disapproving frown. "You met a guy in New York?"

"Yeah, well…" I trailed off.

"What happened between you and Sean, honey?" my mom asked.

"It didn't work out."

"Did he get jealous because of your bra and panty pics?" my sister sneered.

"Bra and panty pics?" my dad asked, his eyebrows raised. My phone buzzed with another text from Clint asking if I was coming.

"Paige, are you posting pictures of yourself in your underwear?" my dad asked.

"It's not like that, dad," I said, walking toward the door.

"Yes, it is," my sister said. "Here." She thrust her phone in my dad's face. His eyes widened as he examined my latest photo—an artistic matching bra and panty pic.

"Oh, my goodness," he muttered under his breath.

"She posts one every week," my sister said.

"Shut up, Kelsey!" I snapped.

My dad remained fixated on my sister's phone. My mom observed from a distance. "Did you know about this?" my dad asked.

"I knew about Sean," my mom answered.

"What about the underwear pics?"

"Not those," my mom said, pointing an accusatory finger at the phone. "The photos I saw, her underwear wasn't so…stringy."

Stringy?

"It's not like you can see anything," I said.

"I can see quite a lot," my dad retorted, raising his voice.

"Read the comments, dad," Kelsey instructed, grabbing her phone and scrolling to the comments. She handed the phone back and pointed to the screen. "Guys keep asking her when she will post a picture of her butt."

"Shut up, Kelsey!" I yelled. I made a mental note to unfriend my sister later. My mom, too.

My dad, squinting, read the various comments. "What's with the peaches?" he asked.

"Those are asses," Kelsey said.

"Kelsey!" my mom interjected.

"What are these purple things?" my dad asked.

"Those are boners," Kelsey revealed.

"Kelsey, watch your mouth," my mom screeched.

"That's what they are, mom," Kelsey explained. She pointed to a comment. "See, they're asking Paige to post ass-er-butt pics, and Paige said she still needs another month before she's ready."

I crossed the living room and snatched the phone from my dad's hand. Startled, my entire family cast forlorn stares at me. I was not sure when, but under the weight of this sudden intervention, I had started crying. Tears traversed my cheeks, creating crevices down my meticulously made-up face. I wiped my tears, and in the momentary lull, Kelsey reclaimed her phone from my hand. A full minute passed before anyone spoke.

"What's going on, Paige?" my father asked.

"Nothing," I answered.

"Why are you posting underwear pictures? Why are you promising to post pictures of your butt in a month?"

"It's part of my weight-loss journey."

"Weight-loss journey?" my mom said. "Honey, you don't need to lose weight. You're beautiful the way you are."

"No, mom," I snapped. "I'm not. I'm…I *was* gross and overweight and ugly, but I'm improving. Can't you see how I'm improving? I've lost thirty pounds."

"You seem thinner," my mom said, "but I just assumed you were depressed again."

"I am depressed, mom," I said, wiping my eyes. "But I'm getting better. I feel better, and I want to share that with my friends." My phone buzzed. Clint asked if he should leave. "I gotta go."

"Where are you going?" my dad asked.

"On a date," I answered.

"A date?" My dad gave me a discerning overview. "You're dressed like a…woman of the night!"

"This was an expensive outfit, dad."

"It was? You're hardly wearing anything."

"That's a nice thing to say to your daughter," I said.

"Is that your date?" my dad asked, pointing to the widow. His face was incredulous. "You're dating a man who won't even come to the door? You deserve better than that, Paige."

I shook my head. "You guys don't get it," I said. I opened the front door and walked into the night.

. . .

Clint did not notice my tear-stained face when I first climbed into his massive truck. From his phone he watched a YouTube video of a Ford Mustang tethered to a Dodge Charger, each trying to pull the other in the opposite direction. The cars' tires burned, emitting a plume of smoke that engulfed the two muscle cars while each struggled to gain traction on the other. After a minute, the cars stopped, and the smoke cleared. Shards of rubber littered the area. A heavyset, bearded man entered the picture carrying a measuring tape. He evaluated the scene, blazing a path through the discarded rubber. He placed the tape on the ground with a discerning eye. I had not the slightest idea what he measured. After a suspenseful delay, he stood up straight, and declared the Charger the winner. The Charger's driver let out an astounding *Whoop!* while the Mustang's driver bowed his head in gracious defeat. Clint chuckled and pumped his fist. He scrolled through the recommended video thread, bookmarking the ones he wanted to watch later, before lowering his phone and acknowledging me.

"Hey," he said.

"Hi," I said.

"Where do you want to eat?"

"I don't care," I answered, but this was a lie. I wanted something in line with my strict diet. Something under 550 calories.

"Have you been crying?"

"Yeah. I've been crying."

"Why?"

My mind raced. He did not need to know about my family's impromptu social media confrontation. I stuttered and then lightning struck. "I've been thinking about my friend Alexis. She died a little over a month ago. It's been hard for me."

I expected my answer to elicit a sympathetic response, but I was not sure Clint even heard me. His phone chimed, and he checked the message halfway through my explanation. He typed a quick response. "Sorry, what did you say?"

"My friend died."

"When?"

"Over a month ago."

"How?"

"Taking a selfie."

Clint laughed, yes, he actually laughed. "Man, that sucks." Another message interrupted our conversation. He read the text, released a slight chuckle, and began composing a response. I checked my phone. No messages, no updates. Clint sent his text and put his truck in reverse. "How about we hit up Applebee's," he said, but it was not a question.

Was I foolish to expect to go somewhere nicer than Applebee's? I spent a quarter of my paycheck on my new outfit (a form-fitting skirt and stylish crop top) and worn cheetah-print heels for dinner at Applebee's? Several heads swiveled in our direction as the hostess led us to our table. Onlookers must have wondered why I had gotten so gussied up for a family establishment. Clint, however, fit in perfectly. He wore a t-shirt, frayed cargo shorts, and tennis shoes. To top it off, after he carefully parked his truck, he grabbed a baseball cap from his dashboard and put it on—backwards.

I did my best to hide my irritation, not that Clint would have noticed anyway; he spent most the night on his phone. He ordered a hamburger, and I got a salad. When our food arrived, he devoured his hamburger and wiped his hands with his napkin before grabbing his phone. When the check came, Clint glanced at it, but made no movement toward it. His phone held his attention. Did he expect me to pay? Frustrated, I excused myself and headed for the bathroom.

I sat in the bathroom stall and urged myself not to cry. The desire to abandon the date and head to the gym for a late-night workout struck me. Then my phone buzzed. In my absence, Clint had posted a picture of me sitting across from him in the Applebee's booth (how did he snap it without me knowing?) with the caption: "On a date with this hottie!" He tagged my name, so everyone could see he was with me. The likes ticked in, and I became giddy. Clint had ignored me for most the night, so his pronouncement boasting my "hotness" came as a surprise. The post already had twelve likes by the time I finished in the bathroom. I hit the like button and wrote: "Hopefully, the date has just begun!" A second later, Clint liked my comment. There was a bounce in my step as I exited the bathroom.

I returned to the table and noticed Clint had paid the bill. He lowered his phone as I approach and offered a boyish smile. "So, what should we do now?" he asked.

"I'm up for anything."

"Cool."

We drove to a park. Clint killed the ignition and explained we could not go to his house because his parents were home.

"You still live at home?"

"For now, but I'm saving for an apartment. Student loans are killing me."

"Where did you go to school?"

"Northern State."

"What's your degree?"

"I didn't finish, but I'm only two classes away from graduating. Maybe I'll enroll next fall. Who knows?"

"So, what do you do?"

"I personal-train and work for my uncle. He owns a body shop."

I feigned interest, but I had already learned all of this from my online sleuth skills. I realized Clint retained the same genetic code as most other guys my age. A mid-twenties kid trying to pass as an adult while suffocating under the weight of stifling student debt. He still lived at home and believed he would save enough to move out without yet crunching the numbers to realize he could not. Clint worked for a family member, so common sense dictated his potential earnings were topped out. Student loans accounted for most of his income, and his truck's maintenance milked the rest. Clint was the poster boy for my generation.

And I was the poster girl.

His story was my story—mid-twenties and living at home trying to earn enough to move out, while my savings diminished from personal trainers, faux vacations, strict meal plans, and a new wardrobe. This explained why Clint and I were spending our evening in a parking lot instead of some place less dispiriting.

I pondered the elements arresting people like Clint and myself when, without warning, he began rubbing my thigh. My skin came to life, awakened by his touch.

"I can't get over how hot you are," he said. His words came out heavy, like he had just run up a flight of stairs. He began sliding his hand up my leg. I shuddered, and he leaned forward and kissed me, circulating his tongue into my mouth. By the time I understood his intentions, his hand was up my skirt, prying for a seam into my underwear. I recoiled and grabbed his hand.

"Stop," I hissed.

"What's wrong?" he asked.

"I need...a minute."

He winced and removed his hand from out my skirt. "I'm so hard right now. Feel." He stole my hand and placed it over his shorts. I felt a significant bulge. His forwardness repulsed me, yet...the obvious effect I had on him flattered me. I was torn, so I kept my hand where he placed it, not sure what to do next, not sure what I *wanted* to do next. Clint sensed my hesitation and said, "We don't have to have sex if you're not ready."

His understanding moved me. I was not ready, and I said as much.

Clint discerned me, disappointed and dejected. I sensed he expected a different answer. He peered through his windshield and into the night. "Maybe you could just give me a blowjob?" he offered as a consolation prize.

I tried to speak, but his modest proposal sucked the words from my lungs. I had given one other blowjob in my life, and it was not a resounding success. The guy, my college boyfriend, was so unimpressed he stopped it—complained my teeth kept getting in the way. The next day I googled how to give a proper one, but before I could pilot my newly researched technique, I was single again.

During the midst of my past recollections, it occurred to me that my hand still rested fretfully where Clint had placed it. I searched for an escape, silently reciting words harsh enough to deny his request, yet laced with enough politeness that he would want to see me again. If I flat-out told him I wanted to take things slow, would he respect my morals or scoff at my prudishness? My uneasiness eclipsed Clint because before my mind cleared enough to weigh my options, he had moved my hand and unzipped his pants. He worked his face into a beguiling smile and gestured to his lap. I assessed it, skeptical and frightened. I did not want to do what Clint wanted—and I did it anyway.

. . .

Three nights later, Clint and I had our second date. It replicated our first except for a change of restaurant. This time he took me to Texas Roadhouse. We said less than fifty words to each other, both of us lost in our phones. When we left, he took a selfie with me and posted it to his Instagram page. I did the same. By the time we pulled into the desolate parking lot, his post had thirty-seven likes and mine had eighty-three. My social media superiority served as my focus while I performed what Clint expected of me.

For our third "date," he invited me to his parents' house—they were gone for the night—and he told me to "wear something sexy." The request made me giddy, even if I recognized the objectification it entailed. I purchased a new dress from Macy's and a lace thong from Victoria's Secret. I enjoyed wearing new form-fitting clothes and sexy underwear. When I arrived at his parents' house, Clint opened the door and gave me a satisfactory appraisal. "Damn" he said under his breath.

We entered his kitchen, and he asked if I was hungry. Without waiting for an answer, he opened the fridge and retrieved a bowl of leftover pasta. I wish he had something healthier, something with fewer carbs, but I figured it best not to complain or suggest he make something else. He reheated the leftovers and dished them onto paper plates. (He did not want to dirty dishes, he said.) After we ate, and discarded the dishes, we retreated to his bedroom. Car posters coated his walls, dirty clothes lined his floor, X-box controllers lay on his unmade bed. He tossed the controllers onto the floor and reached for me. Disregarding all foreplay, his hands were on me, with his sour tongue plunged down my throat.

He pulled my dress over my head and snaked my underwear down to the floor. I did not resist his advances, nor did I encourage them. I became an inanimate object, struggling to comprehend the expediency of the moment. He lowered his pants, took my hand, and ushered me onto his bed. I was motionless throughout. It lasted less than two minutes. After one last repulsive thrust, he rolled off the top of me and reached for his phone. He tapped into the YouTube app and began watching car videos. I lay naked and ashamed and waited for him to acknowledge what we had shared. I expected him to reach for and comfort me, hold me, and together savor the moment which, I assumed, now certified us as a couple. Instead, his phone demanded his attention. I covered myself with a sheet and placed my head on his chest.

"What are you thinking?" I asked.

"I don't know," he mumbled. "Nothing."

"Hey, Clint, do you like me?"

A five second pause. "Yeah, I like you." Tires screeched from the video he watched.

"Do you love me?"

"Love?" he repeated the word as if it stung his throat.

"Yeah."

A ten second pause. "I don't know."

"Have you ever loved anyone?"

"I don't know."

"Are you even listening to me?"

A heavy sigh. "Yeah, I'm listening."

"What are you thinking about?"

"You already asked me that."

"You didn't answer."

A heavier sigh. "I'm thinking about how many more questions you're gonna ask before you'll let me finish this video."

I sat up and stared at him, but he paid me no attention. I reached for his phone, and he pulled away.

"What are you doing?" he asked.

"You are so rude," I said.

"Why?"

"We just made love."

Clint laughed.

"What's so funny?" I asked.

"We didn't make love, okay? We had sex. There's a difference."

"Is that all I am to you? Just a chic to bang?"

Clint shrugged. "What do you think this is, Paige?"

I was incredulous, with Clint and myself. I cursed my stupidity, got to my feet, and began gathering my clothes.

"Oh, come on," Clint said. "Don't be a bitch about this."

"Matt was so right about you."

"Matt?"

"Yeah. He warned me about you."

"What did he say?" Clint asked, sitting up and giving me, for the first time, his full attention. "What did that faggot say about me?"

My mouth dropped, and I shook my head in disbelief. "Just the truth," I said and left the bedroom, pulling on my dress as I fled.

When I got home, I laced my gym shoes and escaped for an evening run. I needed to clear my head and burn the pasta calories I had consumed earlier. Later that night, after showering and ruminating on the evening's events, I tried sending Clint a message. It did not go through. He had unfriended me and blocked my accounts. Somehow, getting blocked hurt more than anything else I endured in his bedroom.

CHAPTER 19

The feeling that I caused Alexis's death plagued me. Had I never mentioned Kauai, had I not pretended to have visited Queen's Bath, had an overwhelming desire to gain Alexis's approval not suffocated me, she may very well still be alive. I needed to clear my conscience, not with a shrink or religious authority or someone else who grants absolution, I needed forgiveness from the person who mattered most: Eric.

Three months had passed since Alexis's death, and although Eric worked every day, I never saw him. He avoided the breakroom, the cafeteria, and somehow the bathroom, too. The two other company executives—Weston Goodman and Heather Keller—sometimes entered his office, but they never stayed long, and they never shared with anyone what they discussed nor how Eric was doing. It drove me mad.

. . .

Friday arrived, and people were dispersing early. As usual, I did not have plans. It had been weeks since I last saw Clint. He still blocked my accounts and, my texts remained ignored. It was best he ignored me. I had nothing to say, and I had no desire to cultivate a friendship beyond social media. All I wanted was a more amicable parting. I felt used, and I convinced myself that if Clint accepted my online friendship, then maybe our brief relationship was more than just another notch on his bedpost.

Yesterday while lifting, Matt asked how things were with Clint. I dropped the fifteen-pound dumbbells and burst into an ugly crying fit. Matt ushered me from the gym, and we walked to a nearby coffee shop where I explained everything that happened. After purging myself of the retelling, Matt responded: "Well, now you know who *not* to date."

Thanks to Vicarious Vacations, I now had over 6,000 friends and followers, but while sitting in that coffee shop, I realized Matt was my best friend, and we were not even social media friends—at least not anymore. He had disabled his accounts months earlier. When I asked why, he said he had a nasty breakup and private things had become public. I wondered what he meant, but he would not elaborate, and I did not press him.

Now with the weekend rearing its ugly head, I wanted something more than a night in my parents' basement. By the time I shut down my computer, it was approaching six. Eric had the blinds pulled in his office, but with the dying day, I determined the lights were on inside. I wondered if he slept in his office. The temptation to knock on his door and ask for a minute of his time teased me. I wanted to apologize for recommending Kauai, and I needed him to hear my confession if I ever hoped for forgiveness. I made a beeline for his office, arrived at the door, lifted my hand to knock, and...froze. For over a minute I stood outside his office and willed myself to tap on the door, but something kept me still. Abandoning the inner struggle, I dropped my hand and left.

As I drove out from the Newage Tech parking lot, I spotted Eric exiting the building. I pulled to the curb and watched him enter his car. He exited the parking lot and sped past me without glancing in my direction. I pulled away from the curb and followed him. I did not have a plan, nor did I have any idea how long, or how far, I would follow him. After trailing him for ten minutes, he slowed and made a left down a tree-lined street. He was driving to the cemetery.

Without giving my actions much thought, I proceeded down the same road. I braked as I approached the cemetery's clearing. Eric had already parked and, holding a flower bouquet, was walking toward Alexis's grave. I slowed to a stop and parked behind a line of trees. It was easy to make out Eric, but the trees concealed me from him. He stood still, staring at his deceased wife's grave. The headstone was not yet set;

in its place stood a temporary plastic marker with Alexis's name printed on it. Eric kneeled and placed the flowers next to the plastic marker. I got out of my car.

With a measured step, I walked toward him. He did not appear to sense my approach. When I got to within ten feet of him, he stood, and I stopped. His eyes remained fixed on Alexis's grave. "Did you follow me from the office?" he asked.

"Yeah," I answered.

"What do you want?" He turned; his eyes were bloodshot and cold. His hair disheveled, and his sunken cheeks sported an unkempt beard. I had not seen him since the funeral. He seemed older, tired. "What do you want?" he asked again. His voice was rough, stern.

"She died because of me," I said. "I...I'm the one who told her about Queen's Bath."

"Yeah. She told me."

"I need you to know I'm sorry. I shouldn't have recommended it."

"She told me you'd been there before. Is that true?"

"Ah...yeah," I lied.

Eric leveled me with his eyes. "You haven't, have you?"

"No."

I watched as every muscle in Eric's jaw contracted and fought against his sallow cheeks. "You made her jealous."

"Who?"

"Alexis."

"I made Alexis jealous?" I snickered at the absurdness.

"She thought I liked you."

"That's ridiculous. Why would she think you liked me?"

"Because I changed your tire. Because we talked a couple times in the breakroom."

"You were just being nice."

"That's not how she saw it."

"Eric, I'm so sorry. I never meant to cause problems. I loved Alexis. Hell, I wanted to *be* Alexis. My entire life that's what I wanted."

Eric kicked at a twig on the grass, lost in his own thoughts. "Did you go to Niagara Falls?" he asked. I pursed my lips, determined to maintain my lie, but understood he already perceived the truth. "Well, Paige, you're more like Alexis than you think. You take fake vacations and tie your self-worth to your social media popularity."

I had no rebuttal to his claim, so I remained silent.

"I found all of Alexis's usernames and passwords. I logged into her Instagram account. Her Snapchat, Twitter, Facebook, Tumblr, all of them. I intended to cancel everything, then I did a little searching. I searched for you. You liked everything she posted. You watched all her makeup tutorials on YouTube. Any little innocuous thing she did, you liked. And I started noticing *your* posts. You took a fake vacation to where I proposed. And now you're posting pictures in your underwear, so the world can see how much better you are because you're a little skinnier. I also noticed you were in New York at the same time Alexis and I were in Kauai. Did you go to New York, Paige? Or was that another fake vacation to help you cope with your insecurities?"

Words failed me. All my faculties were numb.

He continued: "As I scrolled through your 'weight-loss journey,' and I can see that may be the *one* area of your life that isn't a lie, I noticed something: You are just like Alexis. Posting pictures so people can objectify you is the exact thing Alexis would do. It's what she did. And where did her popularity get her?" He pointed a trembling finger at her grave. "Right there. Died trying to get the perfect selfie. Is there a more pathetic way to go?"

His question was rhetorical, but his expression indicated he wanted an answer. My chest heaved; my breathing was labored. I was on the cusp of a panic attack. "What do you care?" I said, my voice breaking. "You never even loved her. You married her for her dad's money. She deserved better than you."

He analyzed my words, while I pondered the audacity with which I spewed them. "She and I got exactly what we deserved," he said, his own voice breaking. "She died doing what she loved, and I have to live with the consequences of knowing I could have stopped it."

"How could you have stopped it?"

Eric hesitated, conflicted and distressed. Was a confession on the horizon? His torment lingered on the fringes, pulsating and begging to be revealed. He wanted to purge, to rid himself of his guilt.

"She was cheating," he said. "Some guy started messaging her on Facebook two years ago. I found out and threatened to leave. She ended things with him and begged me to stay. I stayed, and another guy came into the picture. Same thing—began sending her messages on social media. The second time, I didn't care. I didn't threaten to leave or kick her out or go stay in a hotel. I just told her to get the divorce papers."

"What happened?" I asked.

"She blamed you."

"What?"

"She used you as justification for cheating. It was a bullshit excuse, but she claimed I drove her away because of you."

I was floored. "Me?"

"She hated that I enjoyed talking to you. It made her feel insecure. It baffled her that I could be drawn to someone so...unlike her."

"Someone frumpy, you mean?" I asked.

"No," Eric said. "Someone who listened when I talked. That's all I ever asked. Listen—be present. Her insecurities made her jealous. She wanted to work things out, give us one more chance. We started seeing a counselor, and she suggested we take a trip. I agreed under the condition Alexis leave her phone home. That was too harsh; she said it was unimaginable. The counselor told me I needed to accept her for who she was. Uploading pictures was part of her identity, and I needed to come to terms with that." Eric halted to clear the sobs stuck in his throat. "The entire trip Alexis kept saying, 'We must go to Queen's Bath. We have to go to Queen's Bath.' It was closed every day because of the rain. On the second to last day, Alexis said we needed to go regardless of the weather. I fought her on it. I told her it was closed, and it was dangerous. One of her Facebook friends told her to jump the fence. Said people did it all the time. I asked why it was so damn important to see Queen's Bath. And guess what she said?" Eric peered at me. "She said: 'So I can show your work wife proof that we actually went. Unlike her.' That's why it was so important. She wanted to prove something to you. When she told me that, I lost it. We got in a fight. I left the room, and she took the rental car to Queen's Bath without me. She skipped the fence at the trailhead, hiked to the cliffs, and lost her footing while trying to take a selfie. A group of teenagers saw her stumble and then a rogue wave carried her into the ocean. One jumped in after her, but…"

My mouth hung open in stunned silence. I had followed Eric hoping to apologize for a simple vacation recommendation. It was absurd that a few innocent workplace conversations drove Alexis mad with jealousy. How was it that someone so perfect struggled with so much insecurity? It made no sense. She had everything, including *my* envy.

"Did Alexis have a reason to be jealous of me?" I asked.

"What?"

"Was she just insecure, or did you give her a reason to be jealous?"

"Are you asking if I liked you?"

"Yeah," I mumbled. "I guess so."

Eric ruminated on how best to answer. "I thought…"

"What?"

"I thought you were different, and I liked that maybe you were, but I was wrong."

"How do you know you're wrong?"

Eric's face contorted in a series of expressions—all of them sad. "You never read the book."

"What book?" I asked, but even as I said it, I understood what he meant. At home, in my nightstand, it sat ignored like a forgotten dream. *The Great Gatsby.* "I started it, but…"

"You don't need to explain anything, Paige. I get it. I see who you are. Alexis was jealous of a version of herself."

As if expecting my meager rebuttal, Eric waved me away, uninterested in hearing any half-hearted explanations I might offer. He brushed past me and walked to his car with a broken step. I remained at the cemetery musing how, once again, I found myself jealous of Alexis Carter.

CHAPTER 20

I stood on the bathroom scale and stared, disbelieving what I saw. I rubbed my eyes, and the number did not change. The red digital digits glowed, confirming my success. One hundred and twenty pounds—my target weight. I had done it. I let out a joyful whimper and rushed to my bedroom for my phone. With a measured step, I returned to the scale, cautious that if I stepped too quickly, the number might increase. It did not. One hundred and twenty pounds! I snapped a picture of the number and posted it to my social media accounts. "120! I made it! #LiftToGetFit #Goals #IDidIt."

Within seconds the likes and comments flooded my page. Most were congratulatory, yet some did not acknowledge my achievement but rather used my success as a springboard to talk about their own weight-loss struggles and accomplishments. The standard sexist messages from men asking when to expect the promised backside picture followed. Soon, I promised, soon. To some I was an inspiration, to others I was an object; both made me swell with pride.

A new notification invaded my phone. A private message from Shawn Preston. It read: "Congrats, Paige! You look AMAZING!! Can you come by the office tomorrow at noon? I have a business proposition for you."

. . .

Shawn greeted me with outstretched arms when I entered his office. I fell into him, welcoming the comfort of human touch. After our embrace, he held me by the shoulders and gave me a kind appraisal. "You are stunning, Paige," he said. "Matt has transformed you."

"I've never felt this good," I said.

"I bet. You are glowing. Please, have a seat." Shawn and I settled into our familiar chairs. "It thrilled me to see you kept your promise."

"Promise?"

Shawn smiled and, taking the remote from his desk, powered on the television behind me. My morning bathroom selfie greeted me. Earlier, after my morning workout, I weighed myself again and dropped to 118 pounds. I updated my progress and could no longer deny the requests. After my shower, I stepped into a purple lace thong, positioned myself, found the best lighting, and snapped a handful of pictures. I dissected each, scavenging for the best one. My thumb hovered over the "upload" button for over a minute. Could I do this? Was I ready to reveal this much of me? I steadied my breathing, counted to ten, and tapped the upload button. The response was immediate; my like total hit 1,000 within thirty minutes.

"This photo will reach 10,000 likes by the end of the day" Shawn said. "You now have over 15,000 followers, and we expect with more photos like this, you will reach 50,000 by the end of the year."

"50,000?" The number seemed unreal.

"You are on track to become a social media influencer," Shawn said, and my mouth dropped. "We'd like to market your story."

"How?" I asked.

"We want you to be the weight-loss ambassador for Vicarious Vacations."

"An ambassador?" Alexis was an ambassador.

"We want to use your story," Shawn continued. "Your photos, your diet plan, your exercise regime, everything you've done in the last year to get where you are today. We want to use it for marketing purposes. Every woman who comes to us hoping to lose weight, wondering if they have the fortitude and will power to do so, we want to show them your story."

"That sounds incredible!" I said.

"Include your diet. Sell people on the personalized meal plans. Give workout tips, diet advice, anything you can share that's related to fitness."

"Am I qualified to do that? I don't have an exercise science degree."

"It's social media; everyone is an expert, and no one is qualified. We've created a contract, and corporate will email it to you soon. You'll just need to accept the terms and conditions."

"What are the terms and conditions?" I had not finished asking the question before the notification arrived. Shawn smirked, foreseeing what awaited me—my ambassador contract!

"It's boilerplate stuff," Shawn said. "You agree to let us use your images, your story, anything you upload to social media. We'll show potential clients your profile, pictures, your journey. Everything you've been documenting you agree to let us use for promotional purposes."

"Will I get paid?"

"Of course."

"How much?"

"You'll receive a commission based on referrals and fitness packages purchased. Post more pictures like the one this morning. In addition, we'll start sending you workout clothes and other things we want you to model and sell to your followers. The more traffic you create, the more traffic we'll receive, resulting in more money and swag for you. You are now the product, Paige, so you need to sell yourself. You'll have a referral code for people to enter if they want to register for any of our services. We'll text it to you later today. Always include the code in your posts. The company you'll work with is a subsidiary of Vicarious Vacations called Shredded Fitness. That's who you work for—Shredded Fitness, not Vicarious Vacations. You sell people on the fitness packages, and then we contact them about vacations. With each post, forward people to the

Shredded Fitness website where they can enter your promotional code. Each time someone enters your code, you'll receive a percentage."

"So, I need to keep doing what I've been doing?" I asked. "Post pictures, gain followers, and get paid for doing so?"

"That's it."

"I love it!" I opened the email from Vicarious Vacations. The attached contract was thirty-six pages. "Thirty-six pages?" I asked.

"Just legal jargon. Read it if you want, but it says what I just explained." I began skimming the contract, and Shawn shifted in his seat. "If you sign up in the next thirty minutes, there's a bonus."

I looked up from my phone. "Bonus?"

"A free vicarious vacation anywhere in the world."

"Anywhere? Even Jamaica?"

Shawn smiled and grabbed his tablet from his desk. He worked quickly, and after a moment pointed to the TV screen where myself and Sean (my forgotten New York boyfriend) were standing in the ocean's crystal blue waters. Our bodies faced the horizon, but we swung our heads back towards the camera. I wore a green thong string bikini. My bronzed skin glistened, my muscles appeared toned and smooth. Sean stood next to me. His body the perfect complement to my own. My right hand touched his, our fingers curved, creating the shape of a heart—it was the perfect facsimile of Alexis and Eric's honeymoon photo. My heart stopped, and I gasped, stricken by the beauty of the recreation.

"Wow," I said. "Whose body is that?"

"That's yours. I pulled your body from the photo you uploaded this morning. I just added the bikini."

"That's me?"

"Yes, that is you. You could leave this weekend, and this picture could be on your feed in forty-eight hours."

"But Sean and I broke up, and I started dating Clint."

"I noticed that, but you're not dating Clint anymore, right? Neither of you have posted anything together in weeks."

"No, we're not dating."

"So, get back together with Sean."

"Just like that?"

"People break up and get back together every day. Imagine how jealous a Jamaican vacation with your New York boyfriend would make Clint."

"He wouldn't know. He blocked me."

Shawn laughed. "I'd wager he does plenty of online stalking. Each of your New York posts averaged over 3,000 likes, but a photo like this," Shawn pointed to the screen, "I can guarantee 20,000 likes."

"20,000 likes?" I asked. "That's more than Alexis and Eric's photo."

"With your body, the right bikini, and the right destination, we can get you 20,000."

I pondered Shawn's promise. The appeal teased me to where I began laughing aloud. Then I remembered Eric and how hurt he was at the cemetery. I replayed the words he had said. They danced in my head, forcing me to respect the memory of Alexis. I sped to the bottom of the contract and hit "accept."

"I want to be an ambassador, but I don't want to recreate Alexis and Eric's photo," I said. "That's their memory. I want to create my own."

"That's not a problem."

"Send me somewhere exotic, and send me with Sean."

"How about…Costa Rica?"

CHAPTER 21

I spent the next week "preparing" for my trip. As an homage to Alexis, I bought three new bikinis—each one skimpier than the one before it—and displayed them on my bed. I asked my followers which one I should wear first. To no one's surprise, the third bikini earned the most votes. I began posting more provocative bathroom selfies. Each recent picture received over 5,000 likes, and the thong photos always earned over 10,000.

Vicarious Vacations began posting photos and updates informing my followers about my upcoming four-day Costa Rica trip. (I wanted to go longer, but I had used all my vacation days and squandered all but two hours of sick leave.) I again arranged to workout with Matt after hours, and Shawn covered the cost of my hotel—another perk to my newfound ambassador status. My life was on the rise. I now had a body to die for, thousands of followers on each of my social media platforms, and a second income whose sole requirement asked that I post photos of myself while offering fitness advice.

Friday morning arrived, and I woke early to pack for my trip. Shawn had arranged an Uber to take me to my hotel. So, with my suitcase in hand, I opened my bedroom door and found my dad standing outside waiting. He gave me a quick glance then held his cell phone at eye level for me to see it. The selfie I had taken twenty minutes earlier filled his screen. I wore a tank top, a seductive expression, and nothing else. The tank fit me perfectly, and I had positioned it so it exposed a healthy amount of side boob. It extended just enough to cover the top half of my backside. My smooth white cheeks emerged from beneath the tank, and the lighting and artful filter I used kept the most important part of me concealed in the shadows. In less than twenty minutes it already had 3,800 likes.

"Did Kelsey show you?" I asked. I had blocked my sister and mom over a month ago, but they could still find my accounts online. None of my accounts were private.

"No," my dad said. "A co-worker showed me. He said, 'Boy, Tom, your little girl has grown up, hasn't she?' I had no idea what he meant, so he showed me what you've been doing online. He said, 'All you have to do is type your daughter's name into Google, and you'll find her.' And there you are," he added, showing me his phone again.

"It's for my new job."

"You got a new job?"

"Yeah."

"Are you a stripper?"

"No."

"Are you...selling your body for sex?"

"Of course not."

"What is your new job?"

"I'm an ambassador for an online fitness company. I inspire people to lose weight by sharing my weight-loss story. For each person who signs up, I get a percentage."

My dad shook his head and thrusted the phone toward me again, brandishing it under my nose like I were a misbehaving dog. I noted the photo now had over 4,000 likes. "You're not wearing any pants, Paige," my dad said, trying, and failing, to stay composed.

I reached out and lowered his outstretched arm. "It's for work, dad. I needed to get a second job so I can move out of here."

"How are you going to afford to move out if you keep spending your money on these vacations?"

"My job is paying for my next vacation."

"You mean the one you're going on today? The one to Costa Rica where you're meeting a guy named Sean? Some guy I've never met?"

"It's not like that, dad."

"Oh, it's not?" he said, his voice rising. "Tell me you're not meeting a guy in Costa Rica for four days, Paige. Promise me you won't share photos of yourself in skimpy swimsuits."

"I have to, dad," I said, my voice rising to meet his. "It's for my—"

"It's for your job. You've said that. How about this, Paige? How about *I* make you a deal? Don't go on this trip, okay? Don't go to Costa Rica and stop posting naked pictures and I'll—"

"They're not naked pictures—"

"And I'll pay you whatever this extra job pays. How's that? I will pay you not to go to Costa Rica so you can sleep with a random guy and post naked pictures. What do you say, Paige? Do we have a deal? I will pay you to keep your dignity."

Tears invaded my eyes. "It's not like that," I whispered.

"What?"

"I said it's not like that."

"That's how it looks. You start this crazy diet, you exercise three hours every night, and now you're whoring yourself out online!"

My tears came fast and hot and all that mattered at that moment was stopping my father from saying anything else. "They're fake," I said.

"What?"

"The vacation. The guy—Sean—none of it is real."

My dad stared at me, trying to make sense of my revelation. My phone rang, and I pulled it from my pocket. It was Vicarious Vacations. I forwarded it to voicemail.

"W-what...what do you mean it's not real? It's right there." He tapped his phone's screen.

Vicarious Vacations called again, and I again sent the call to voicemail. "Sean isn't an actual person," I explained. "He's made up."

My dad failed to process my words. "What are you talking about, Paige? There are pictures of you two together. There are pictures of you two kissing in New York!" he yelled.

"They're fake, Dad!" I screamed. "It's photoshopped!"

He was incredulous. He began thumbing through more photos, squinting at each one. "These are fake?"

"Yes," I whispered. My phone rang again.

"You're...you're lying to me."

"Vicarious Vacations."

"What?"

"Go to Vicarious Vacations.com. It's a company that manufactures vacations."

My dad pondered my revelation. "Why would people create fake vacations?"

"For likes, dad."

"Likes?"

"Instagram and Twitter likes. Facebook comments and Tik Tok views. It feels good when people like me. The people who like my photos, they don't know it's fake." I wiped my eyes. "I'm not going to Costa Rica, and I'm not seeing Sean. Sean isn't real; he never was. I'm going down the road to the Best Western. I'll be there for four days."

My dad stood dumbfounded and bewildered. He kept reviewing my photos and glancing back at me. He sensed a cruel trick was being played, and he expected me to make clear what my explanation muddied. He learned my secret, and no matter how nonsensical it seemed, it was the truth.

I stepped past him, careful not to bump him with my suitcase. "The underwear pics," he said. "Are those fake?"

I sighed and shook my head. "No, Dad. Those are real." This admission seemed to sting the most. "I've never looked this good, and I want to share who I am with my friends."

"What kind of friends want you to post naked photos?"

"I'm not naked, Dad," I retorted, frustrated with his defiance. "The photos show the progress I've made, and the benefits of exercise. I'm no longer depressed, Dad, and I'm not anxious like I used to be. Doesn't that count for anything?"

He readied himself to say more but decided against it. His eyes, soaked in disappointment, said it all. He pocketed his phone and walked away as I ascended the stairs and began my vacation.

The clock read 1:29 in the morning when someone knocked on the door. I feared it was my dad. Ever since our morning encounter, I expected he would come to the hotel to confirm what I had told him. My exhaustion overwhelmed me. Matt put me through the ringer at the gym, and I wanted nothing more than to climb into bed, check Instagram, and go to sleep. I lacked the energy for another argument. He knocked again, and I padded to the door and opened it. Shawn Preston stood outside.

"Shawn," I said. "What are you doing here?"

"We need to talk, Paige. Can I come in?"

"Yeah, sure," I said, moving aside to let him enter. "Is everything okay?"

He entered, and I closed the door behind him. He pursed his lips and examined my room with a critical eye. I wondered if he had ever stayed somewhere so modest.

"Once you're home from Costa Rica, we're suspending your social media accounts for ten days," he said.

My heart stopped. "Why?"

"Breach of contract."

"What?"

"You told your father about Sean and about Vicarious Vacations."

"How do you know that?"

"We heard you."

"You heard me? How?"

"Through your phone. We can hear every conversation you have."

"What? How?"

"You gave us permission when you accepted your new contract," Shawn explained. "If you reveal to anyone what we do, the services we offer, we can suspend your accounts. Ten days for your first offense. The next will be a month. If you violate your contract a third time, it's a permanent suspension."

"I didn't know I agreed to that, and I didn't know you could hear my private conversations. That's not fair. That's not...right."

"It was in the contract."

"You didn't give me time to read the contract. It was thirty-six pages!"

"Ten days, Paige," Shawn said, refusing to argue the semantics of the contract. "If you tell people what we do, you violate your contract. If everyone learns about Vicarious Vacations, everyone will think the vacations are fake. People won't take fake vacations if everyone is privy to the lie."

"It was my dad. He doesn't even have a social media account."

"It doesn't matter. People talk."

"Isn't that what you want? How are you going to build your business if you keep it a secret?"

"*We* contact people, not you. Your job is to post fitness pictures and keep your mouth shut about Vicarious Vacations. We don't need you to sell our product. We sell our own product."

"How?"

"Think about it," Shawn began. "You go back to work and Steve Philips in accounting asks about your Costa Rica trip. He says he saw your photos on Instagram. He read your tweets, and they piqued his interest. We know this because we hear your conversations. So, we track Steve's internet history, see him searching for vacations. We learn what he likes and dislikes and determine his budget. Next thing he knows, Steve is receiving emails and special offers from us for trips to Costa Rica. We arrange a meeting, and I sell him on a Vicarious Vacation—like I did with you. Before he leaves, he signs a contract allowing us to listen to his conversations and promising not to discuss what we do. If he breaks that contract, he gets banned."

"No one will agree to that type of contract," I said.

"You did."

"I didn't read it," I argued.

"Exactly."

"It's wrong! You can't force people into letting you spy on them."

"We don't force anyone to do anything. Anyone can refuse our terms of service. We are not the problem, Paige, you are. If people like you kept their mouths shut, we wouldn't need to listen. The original Vicarious Vacations contracts stipulated customers could not discuss our business operations, but we didn't have any way to enforce it. We couldn't access users' phones, so we needed to amend our agreements to protect our business."

"You tricked me," I said. "You're tricking everyone. People never read online contracts."

"Is that our fault?"

"It's wrong."

"It's capitalism. We've started updating contracts with the new non-disclosure clause this week. Clients were never supposed to discuss Vicarious Vacations, but now we can suspend them if they do. We listed the unfamiliar terms into software updates, and like you, people will agree without reading them."

"You're like a car salesman."

"And you are someone who loves to drive. We need to protect our business brand. We can't have people talking about what we do."

"If you ban me, I won't travel with your company anymore. You'll lose a customer."

Shawn kicked his head back and laughed. "You can't afford to travel otherwise, Paige. You are broke and addicted. We own you."

"Please, Shawn, don't do this."

"Vicarious Vacations is not responsible for your ignorance. You could have read your contract, but the prospect of social media popularity blinded you. Don't blame me for your vanity."

"This is so wrong," I repeated like a broken mantra.

"And yet when you take a vacation and you get likes and comments, it feels so right, doesn't it? We want the entire world taking Vicarious Vacations, and we don't want anyone talking about it. No one will ever discover what's real or what's fake. Everyone will pretend. Everyone is already pretending, so why not profit from it?" I paced the room and sat on the edge of the bed. I felt violated, cheated. Shawn sat down next to me. "Even if you read the contract, Paige, you still would have agreed to it. Should I tell you why?"

"Why?"

"Because you're an addict," he said. "You post a picture, and that picture gets ten likes. That means you get ten hits of dopamine. Your brain wants more, so you post another photo, a better one. That photo gets one hundred likes, and that's ten times more dopamine than before. So, you post another photo, a better photo—a thong photo. Now you're getting thousands of likes, and that's a thousand hits of dopamine. You can't stop. You need your daily dose of dopamine, so the photos become more frequent, more provocative. The addiction consumes you; you cannot function without it.

"None of this is news to you, Paige. If you recall, I explained it the first day we met. Your brain, all brains, respond to social media likes the same way someone's brain responds to gambling, pornography, and hard drugs. You are a drug addict; your drug is just different. It's not stigmatized because social media is cheaper than gambling, less embarrassing than porn, and more acceptable than cocaine. Social media is the drug everyone is taking, and no one is getting off, and the intervention isn't coming, Paige. Do you know why?"

"Why?"

"Because the enablers are also addicts. Drug dealers don't hold interventions for their customers. Use your head. You got your first smartphone when you were twelve. Who gave it to you?"

"My parents," I said. "I got it for my birthday."

"That's my point. Your parents gave you a phone because *they* have phones, so they excuse their behavior by giving you what they already have. Your parents may have been better off giving you a heroin needle."

"That's absurd."

"Is it?"

"Yeah."

"Are you not listening? Chemically, biologically, hard drugs give you the same feelings that social media can; the brain activity is identical."

"But drugs kill," I countered. "People get addicted, and they die. People don't die from social media."

"Alexis did," Shawn said, and I fell silent. "The brain stops developing at twenty-five. Most kids get their first smartphone by age twelve. At twelve, parents give their children devices that link them to a variety of sordid networks determining their self-worth through likes and comments. You post a pic, you don't get enough likes, you get depressed, you kill yourself. Your friends go to fun places without inviting you, they post the pics, you get jealous, depressed, you kill yourself. Your personal relationships suffer because you don't dare escape social media. If you try and escape it, your FOMO kicks in. What are your friends doing? You don't know, so you get anxious, you kill yourself. Every year, since the inception of social media, suicide rates have increased for teens and young adults. I'm not talking about slight upticks in the stats. I'm talking about a pandemic. Social media depresses kids and those kids are anxious and they're suicidal. People attach their self-esteem to their social media profiles. Someone takes cocaine or heroin and they feel great…until they don't. They become addicted and often suicidal. It's the same with social media. Social media is the drug accepted by society.

"I just cashed in on it by exploiting poor parenting. If your parents didn't buy you that smartphone for your twelfth birthday, had they gotten you a bike or a book instead, I would not need to explain what you are too ignorant to admit. They gave you the needle, you stuck it in, and you've been addicted ever since. And now your dad has the audacity to confront you and ask why you're posting naked pictures? He shit the parenting bed, that's why. You are what he raised you to be. He provided the means to create an unhealthy addiction because he didn't do any research. He did not care enough to learn how harmful a smartphone is for a twelve-year-old. Parents don't parent, Paige. They allow devices to do it for them, and the real tragedy is if you ever have kids, you'll do the same."

"I won't," I cried.

"Yes, you will. You're not unique, and you're not exceptional. You are average and on a quest of conformity with the rest of us. Are you going to be the *one* parent who takes a stand? The mother of the lone child who doesn't have a smartphone? Imagine the embarrassment your daughter will have to endure if she can't connect with friends through social media. You'd let your child be the outcast? Allow her to get bullied for your noble cause? Bullshit, Paige. You won't parent because you have your own addiction to feed. You will neglect your child just as your parents neglected you. Parenting is hard; technology makes it easy which in turn makes me rich. This problem is not going away, and it will get worse."

"I'll stop," I said with no real conviction. "I'll kick the habit."

"You can't break this addiction because social media is your identity. Take it away, and you are nothing."

"I can try."

"You will fail."

"I won't."

"Do it right now."

"What?"

"Disable your accounts right now. There's your laptop," he pointed to my laptop sitting on the far desk. "Cancel your accounts right now. Log off for good."

"I...I'm on vacation," I justified.

"No, you're not. You're at a Best Western three miles from your house." I offered no rebuttal. Shawn understood I lacked the mental fortitude to suspend my accounts. "Tuesday at midnight we are suspending your social media accounts for ten days. You will not have access to them, but people can still find you, observe your profiles, even like and comment. They won't know you're offline and unable to see your own pictures and posts."

"Will you make posts to my accounts?"

"Perhaps."

"Why?"

"To keep you hooked. The not knowing will drive you mad. You'll wonder what, if anything, we've posted. What comments are you missing? How many likes are you receiving? Which pictures did we create? What story did we invent about you and Sean?"

"You're treating my life like it's a game."

"A game you signed up to play."

"I used to think you were kind."

"I don't enjoy doing this, Paige, but it's necessary for my business." He paused, giving me an opening to speak. I stared at the floor. "Your ten-day suspension will be the hardest ten days of your life. And just so you are aware, most people, when they breach their contract, have their accounts suspended immediately. I'm letting you finish your trip, so you're welcome. I hope there isn't a next time, but if there is, you won't have a grace period." He stood and walked to the door. "See, I'm not as cruel as you think. Enjoy the rest of your vacation," he said and exited the room.

CHAPTER 22

I could not function nor concentrate. I doubled and tripled my depression and anxiety meds and worked out longer. Nothing helped. What were my friends doing, where were they going, what were they wearing? I checked my phone a thousand times a day hoping Shawn, in a moment of compassion, lifted the ban. With each failed attempt to log into my accounts, my anxiety increased and my depression soared. I was nothing without my online profile. Even my fake account—Selena Everdeen—did not work. I had never felt so alone.

Sickness overcame me. My head spun, and I became nauseous and disoriented. I stumbled to my supervisor's office, hoping she would grant me a few additional sick days. She sat at her computer drafting an email. Upon my intrusion, she stopped typing, annoyed by my interruption.

"Hey, Ryann," I began, trying my best to sound sick, "I'm not feeling well."

"So, go home."

"I can't. I've used all my sick leave."

"Use your vacation leave."

"I've used all that, too."

Ryann sighed, demonstrating the inconvenience of her subordinates. "You can request additional days through a CEO."

"You mean Eric Vandross?"

"Him or Heather Keller or Weston Goodman."

I knew of Heather Keller and Weston Goodman, but I had never said more than five words to either. "Who's the nicest?" I asked.

Ryann rolled her eyes and continued composing her email. "Well, no one sees much of Eric since his wife died. Heather will want to see your sales stats before even considering giving you fifteen minutes of additional leave. Once she sees those, she'll want to fire you. So, I guess I'd go to Weston." Ryann lifted her eyes and gave me a critical overview. "Yeah, I'd go to Weston. You look like the type of girl Weston wouldn't say no to."

"What does that mean?" I was wearing a button-up top and a pencil skirt with heels. It was a professional but sexy outfit—it helped that I kept an extra button conspicuously undone. I modeled the outfit on Instagram when I first purchased it two weeks ago. A pair of dark-rimmed glasses completed the ensemble. Several fans said I looked like a sexy librarian.

"It means what it sounded like, Paige" Ryann said.

"You don't like me, do you?"

Ryann stopped typing and looked at me. "I don't know you, Paige. It's hard to get to know a person when she only pays attention to her phone." She paused, giving me the opportunity to offer a defense; I had none.

The three CEO offices lined the far side of the building. Weston Goodman's sat stationed between Heather Keller's and Eric's. Heather and Eric's doors were closed, and Weston's was not. I peeked inside and found him at his computer, his back to the door. I glanced at Eric's office and debated if I should take my chances with him. We had not spoken since the cemetery. I replayed our conversation several times in my head, and it was impossible to determine if he felt anger, sadness, indifference or all three towards me. I needed to rectify things between us, but the timing was not right. Not in my current state. My unimaginable social media withdrawals required me to get home and into bed. Eric would not sympathize; I prayed Weston Goodman would. I tapped on his door, and he turned.

"Can I help you?" he asked.

I stepped into his office, and he gave me a sharp glimpse as I came into full view. I knew nothing about Weston Goodman, but he exuded privilege. He struck me as someone who spent his entire life expending minor effort and received maximum rewards.

"Hi," I said. "My name is Paige Reynolds. I work in marketing."

Weston stood and offered his hand. I stepped forward and shook it. "I'm Weston Goodman. What can I do for you?"

"Can I talk to you about requesting a few additional sick days?"

"Sick days?"

"Yeah."

"Did you talk to your supervisor?"

"Yes. She told me I needed to speak with you."

"You said you're in marketing?"

"Yes."

"That makes sense. Ryann defers most decisions to me. Please, have a seat." Weston motioned to the empty chair in front of his desk. "What's your name again?"

"Paige Reynolds."

"How long have you been working here?"

"A little over two years."

"And you've used all your sick days?"

I nodded. "I got influenza the first year I worked here, and a month later, I got strep throat. I burned all my sick days and even took a couple days off without pay."

"Ouch. And what's wrong with you now?"

"Nothing is wrong with me."

"Why do you need the sick days?"

"I'm nauseous and dizzy."

"You're not pregnant, are you?" Weston asked, trying, and failing, at making a joke. I forced a smile—anything to get additional sick days. "I'm assuming you're married?" Weston asked, backtracking.

"No, I'm not married. And I'm sure I'm not pregnant."

"Got a boyfriend?"

I thought about Sean. "Ah...it's complicated," I answered, wondering why my relationship status needed this level of scrutiny.

"Relationships always are. Why don't you use vacation days?"

"I've used those, too."

"Wow, you must really dislike your job, huh?" Weston laughed at his joke, and I forced another smile; my cheeks burned with irritation. "Take however much time you need, but you must make it up once you're feeling better. Work late, maybe put in a couple weekend hours."

"I can do that."

"Great," Weston said. I stood to leave, but the sudden movement sent my head whirling. I clutched the arms of the chair to keep from toppling over.

Weston sprang to his feet. "Are you okay?"

I took a moment and waited for my equilibrium to find its footing. I offered an embarrassed smile. "Yeah. Just a little dizzy."

"Can I call you an Uber?"

"No, I'll be fine. Thank you, Mr. Goodman."

"Please, call me Weston."

I nodded, and with a deliberate step, got to my feet. Weston asked that I close the door as I left. I did and collided into Eric who was exiting his office at the same time. He stammered an apology before realizing who he had bumped into.

"Sorry about that," he said. "I didn't see you."

"It's fine," I said.

He gave me a curious stare. "Were you meeting with Weston?"

"Yeah."

"How come? Never mind. I don't need to know."

"I needed to ask for some additional sick days." I glanced past Eric and noticed someone sitting in his office, his back to me.

"Your supervisor can grant those."

"Mine wouldn't."

"Is Ryann your supervisor?"

"Yes."

My head spun. I closed my eyes to regain some clarity, but the darkness seemed to exacerbate my dizziness. I opened my eyes and squinted back at the man in Eric's office. He rose and walked to the far wall and studied a picture mounted there. A shock of recognition seized me; the man resembled Kenny Waters. I shook my head, trying to clear the hallucination, but the movie star doppelganger remained vivid and clear.

"Are you okay?" Eric asked.

"I'm dizzy and I'm going through withdrawals and I'm seeing things."

"What kinds of things?"

"Kenny Waters," I said. "I see Kenny Waters in your office."

Eric pulled his door shut. "That is Kenny Waters."

"Kenny Waters is in your office?"

"Yeah."

"Kenny Waters the actor?"

"Yeah."

"Why is Kenny Waters in your office?"

"We're friends. We grew up together."

"Are you serious?"

"Yeah. He couldn't make the funeral so..." he trailed off.

"Wow," I said, examining the closed door that concealed one of the biggest movie stars in the world. "Can I ask him for a picture?"

Eric's expression hardened. "For your Instagram page?"

"Yeah."

Eric shook his head in disbelief. "Nice seeing you again, Paige," he said and stepped past me. I watched him round the corner, saddened he did not consider looking back at me, and enter the bathroom. I approached Eric's door and tried the handle. Locked. I lifted my hand to knock, calculating that I had enough time to get a selfie before he returned. But I froze from the supposed anger my request would invoke from Eric. My hand hung suspended for half a minute before I dropped it to my side.

Then I noticed, through a slat in Weston's office blinds, the glow from his computer screen. I squinted and recognized my Instagram page. Weston clicked on a photo—the one featuring me in a tank top and nothing else. He leaned forward, examining the photo. I tried discerning the like total, but the text was too small. He exited from the photo and scrolled further, clicking into different pictures. I wanted to enter his office and join his perusing. Had Vicarious Vacations posted anything since my ban? Had I lost or gained any followers? My elevated anxiety put my world into disarray. I needed deep, drug-induced sleep.

I floundered home to an empty house. My mom had tucked the Ambien behind an expired Pepto Bismal bottle. I stole two pills, put the bottle back, returned to the cabinet, and stole eight more. With a glass of tepid tap water, I swallowed two of the pills, rolled into my bedroom, and collapsed onto my bed. I spent the next four days passed out, waking only to use the bathroom, check if Shawn had lifted my suspension (he had not), and take more Ambien.

CHAPTER 23

I sat on my bedroom floor clutching my phone. I rocked back and forth staring at the clock. 11:59 It had been 11:59 for ten minutes. My suspension ended at midnight. *Come on, come on, come on.*

The clock changed.

I unlocked my phone and tapped the Instagram icon. Success!

I froze, my eyes glued to a picture uploaded to my page. Sean, my fabricated boyfriend, had found another woman—Trinity. The photo showed Sean and Trinity kissing in front of the Eiffel Tower. Below the picture, *I* had written: "Just learned that my boyfriend, or who I *thought* was my boyfriend, is screwing some floozy. Aren't they cute?" The picture had been posted at 11:59.

Why have Sean dump me? I felt nothing for him because he was never real, so what purpose did it serve to invent his infidelity? Then I understood: Shawn did it because he can. He was demonstrating his authority, proving that if I refused to fall in line, he had the power to control and change my life.

I exited Instagram and entered Facebook. Shawn made the same post on my Facebook and Twitter accounts too. I clicked into my friend requests; I had forty-seven. Forty-six were strangers, but I still accepted their friendship. The request who was not unknown: Weston Goodman, one of three CEOs at Newage Technology.

I spent the next few hours perusing my social media platforms, trying to catch up with everything I missed during my ten-day absence. It was almost three a.m. when I powered off my phone and got into bed.

I woke three hours later to a message from Shawn. "Sorry to hear about your breakup. Welcome back online. Remember to post a picture today and include the discount code. Make it sexy."

The reminder was unnecessary. I had already planned to post a fitness picture after my morning workout. Earlier in the week, Shredded Fitness sent me a low-cut sports bra and matching booty shorts. I packed the sports bra and shorts in my gym bag and showed them to Matt later that morning.

"Those *are* sexy," he conceded, holding up the shorts to appreciate the design.

"I need you to take some photos," I said.

We were, as usual, in the group exercise room alone. I withdrew to my corner and began changing while Matt kept watch on the door. "Okay," I said. Matt spun around. I struck my-now-customary pose and punctuated it with a fluid flourish.

"You look...incredible," he said, almost choking on the praise. The compliment, although heartfelt, contained a tinge of sadness. Mine and Matt's recent photoshoots had taken on a strange dichotomy. He always proffered unabashed praise about my body, but each approbation seemed regretful and contrite.

I removed a spray bottle from my gym bag and handed it to Matt. "Spray my chest, stomach, and butt. I want it to seem like I just finished working out."

"You came prepared, huh?" he asked, his voice maintaining its regretful air.

"I've seen other Instagram influencers do this. Besides, I get a percentage of every client that registers for a fitness program using my code. I'm an ambassador," I added to further highlight my importance.

"Yeah," Matt said. "I used to be an ambassador, too."

"You were?"

"Well, yeah, Paige." Matt appeared insulted with my surprise. "That's why Shawn recommended me as your trainer."

"Are you still an ambassador?"

"No."

"Why not?"

"I quit a few weeks ago."

"How come?"

Matt drifted to a distant memory, and once arrived, he became even more distant and forlorn. I sensed he wanted to share whatever kept him despondent, but he recoiled and decided against it. "It's a long story," he said. "Let's get started."

Matt pointed the water bottle at me and began spraying. The water droplets stabbed my skin and chilled me. "Turkey's done," Matt quipped. I spied my breasts and found two erected nipples poking through the soft fabric.

"It's cold," I explained.

"I'm sure your followers won't mind." Matt swapped the spray bottle for my phone. I faced the camera, sucked in my stomach, lifted my chest and stuck out my butt. I gazed into the distance looking pensive and innocent.

"Pop your heel," Matt instructed.

I did as instructed. "How's the lighting?" I asked.

"It's good. Did you want backside shots too?"

"Yes." I spun and assumed my familiar backside pose. I smiled, scowled, flirted, demurred, and Matt captured them all.

Once I had enough options, I selected the best pictures from each angle. I posted them, along with some generic motivational quotes, and sat down and watched the likes invade my post. I held my phone to my chest and drifted away as the dopamine flooded my brain.

. . .

19,998 likes! Unbelievable! Two shy of 20,000! 20,000 was unprecedented territory. Nothing Alexis posted ever reached 20,000. *Two more...two more...come on, two more...*

"That's quite the photo." Startled, I turned and found Weston Goodman standing over me, his eyes craned on my computer monitor. I exited the page.

"Sorry," I mumbled. "I had to check...I wasn't on it for very long."

"Hey, don't exit for my benefit," Weston said, flashing his million-dollar smile. "I liked what I saw."

"I rarely check my account from work."

"Relax. Eric is the social media stickler around here. I don't care if you check your accounts. Besides, I've been following your fitness journey. It's incredible. You should be proud." I felt my skin flush. "So, do you do the training?"

"Excuse me?"

"Your post this morning," Weston said. "You mentioned that if people want to get in shape, they can sign up for your fitness program. You included a discount code."

"Yeah. Fifteen percent off."

"So, do you train the people that sign up?"

"Oh, no. I am an ambassador. My discount code is a link that will forward you to the company website."

"Yeah, I did that. The company is called Shredded Fitness. I did a little research, and it's a subsidiary of a company called Vicarious Vacations. What's that?"

I glanced at my phone. Was Shawn listening? "Ah..."

"I Googled them, and I can't tell what they do." Weston said. "I think they're a travel agency of sorts. Like Expedia or Orbitz."

I bit my tongue, fearful of another contract violation. I hid my phone in my desk. "I've never heard of Vicarious Vacations."

"Oh, I thought maybe you used them to book your recent vacations."

"What?" I asked, feeling hot.

"You travel a lot. Do you use them when you travel?"

My back started sweating. "No, I don't use that company. I've never even heard of them."

Weston peeked over his shoulders, surveying the surroundings, and leaned closer to me. "Wanna hear something crazy? On their homepage, they have a photo of Alexis and Eric from their honeymoon."

"They do?" I asked, playing dumb. "Eric Vandross? The CEO?"

Weston straightened. "Assistant CEO," he said. "I'm the main CEO."

"You are? I thought—"

"It doesn't matter. Anyway, I wonder if Eric knows there's a picture of him and his dead wife on a vacation website. It would drive him batty. He hates that stuff."

"Yeah...maybe. I don't know Eric that well."

"It's a great picture though. They're standing in the water and making a heart with their hands. Alexis is wearing this tiny thong. It's hot."

"That's...interesting."

"I've received half a dozen emails from them."

"From whom?"

"Vicarious Vacations. I clicked into their website, and a pop-up asked me to confirm an appointment. I declined, and since then, I keep getting emails asking when I want to meet for a free vacation consultation. One day you're shopping for running shoes online, next thing you know you're inundated with ads for running shoes. Everything is connected. Nothing is secret anymore."

"Tell me about it," I said and blanched, fearful that my slight may constitute another suspension.

"That's how business is done today. I want to streamline our products that way. Eric keeps dragging his feet, though."

"Why?"

"He's old school. Believes in privacy and all that jazz. Truth is, he may be on his way out."

"What are you talking about?"

Weston again checked for any interlopers within earshot and whispered, "His father-in-law, well, ex-father-in-law is a major investor. He's considering pulling his funding. Now that his daughter is dead, he doesn't see the point in investing in his son-in-law's company. Without that funding, Eric becomes obsolete."

"Well, if Eric becomes obsolete, what happens to Newage Tech?"

"Heather and I will buy his stake."

"Is that what will happen?"

"Either that or we find another investor or...we fold."

"Wow," I whispered. My concern was for Eric, but Weston surmised my fretful expression was for my own employment uncertainty.

"Don't worry about it," Weston said. "I'm sure you'll be fine. You seem to have quite the skillset." I was not sure what his comment insinuated, and my expression said as much. "I mean with your fitness stuff," Weston explained, sensing my confusion. "It seems like you have a few irons in a few different fires."

"Should I worry about my job here?"

Weston laughed. "Oh, no. I didn't mean to imply...I'm sure everything will be fine. We have made no decisions. We haven't even seen this quarters numbers yet." I nodded, unsure how to interpret this new information. "I wanted your input on a few items, though."

"My input?" I asked. No one wanted my input on anything.

"Yeah. You're young, you're beautiful, you seem to have a pulse on what people like. Newage Tech needs to adapt, and we need to find a fresh marketing angle. That's your wheelhouse, right?"

"What?"

"Marketing."

"Oh, yeah. Marketing, right."

"I was wondering if you could stay late a couple days this week. I'd like to pick your brain about new marketing strategies. See if we can't find an unconventional approach to sell our products, help spread our name, you know?"

"Okay."

"You need to put in a few extra hours anyway because of the sick leave I granted, remember?"

"Yeah, I remember."

"So, let's hash out a few ideas. Come by my office tomorrow after we close shop."

"Sure," I said, masking the disappointment in my voice. I wanted to spend my night exercising, not feigning interest talking marketing strategies. But I owed Weston. He had granted me additional sick leave in my moment of crisis. "I'll plan on tomorrow."

"Great. Oh, and sorry about what happened between you and Sean."

"Who?"

"Sean."

"How do you know about Shawn?"

"He's all over your social media accounts. He cheated on you with that Trinity chic."

"Oh, *that* Sean. I was thinking of a different...never mind."

"You've dated more than one Sean?"

"No."

"Well, sorry about your breakup. He seems like a real prick."

"That's okay. We weren't that close anyway."

"He flew you to New York, and you spent four days in Costa Rica together."

"Yeah, but...yeah."

Weston waited for me to elaborate, but I figured it best to keep my mouth shut. "Right," he said, not giving voice to his confusion. "Well, you're single now, so the world is your oyster, right?"

"Right."

"I'll see you tomorrow."

"Okay." Weston turned and started toward his office. I watched him recede out of sight before restoring my Instagram page. 20,002 likes!

CHAPTER 24

I watched, stricken with pangs of jealousy, as my co-workers made their way to the exits. A few passed my cubicle offering perfunctory smiles and half-hearted head nods, but most crossed my threshold staring into their phones, eager to leave work, oblivious of my presence.

At twenty past the hour, I made my way to Weston's office. He had emailed earlier and asked that I bring my third quarter reports. I feared when he saw them, he would not be impressed. I produced average work on most days and below average on the rest; my sales figures reflected that. My lone 'attribute' was my consistency. In the three years I worked at Newage Technology, my stat sheet always hovered right in the meaty part of the curve; I existed contentedly in the middle.

I arrived at Weston's door and knocked, and a moment later he opened it. He smiled and invited me inside. I entered and noted the surroundings. Yesterday Weston mentioned that he was the main CEO, and if office size were the determining metric, his claim appeared to be accurate. His entire back wall was tinted windows overlooking a park. An oversized mahogany desk rested in front. The far wall featured a Banksy knockoff, the opposite wall, an Andy Warhol, and in the center of the room stood an antique table with four out-of-place chairs circling it. I did not recall any of these ostentatious furnishings when I asked for additional sick days two weeks prior. He must have redecorated, or I must have been too self-absorbed and dizzy to notice the gaudy Feng Shui.

He directed me to the table. Atop the table rested a folder with my name scribbled on the tab. The folder appeared slim, sparse, and I had no clue what it contained. On the far wall, under the Banksy print, rested a cart. It housed a variety of liquor bottles, their varying colors shone under the office lights. Weston walked to it and took two glasses from a shelf underneath.

"Can I get you a drink?" he asked.

Drinking was not my vice. I knew too little about alcohol to know what I liked. In high school, I never attended parties where friends raided their parents' liquor cabinet and told everyone to help themselves. On the few social occasions that encouraged drinking, I ordered wine to appear sophisticated. When the waiter inquired what kind, my usual reply was, "Whatever you recommend." Often, the server brought a red wine that tasted like bitter Kool-Aid. These thoughts circulated my head, and the most obvious question struck me: What did drinking have to do with my third quarter stats and innovative marketing strategies? Maybe drinking had everything to do with it. Outside of Newage Tech, my business experience did not extend beyond the fast food industry. Perhaps having a drink at 5:30 on a Wednesday night in your boss's office was the most natural thing in the business world.

"Um…what are you having?" I asked.

"Scotch," Weston said in a tone meant to impress. "I always drink scotch."

"Okay. I'll try it."

Weston gave me an incredulous sneer. "You drink scotch?"

"On occasion," I lied.

"What's your brand?" My face flushed, exposing my ignorance. "That's what I thought," Weston laughed and poured the drinks. I took the offered drink, and he sat down next to me. He lifted his glass, and I did the same. He clinked his to mine and took a drink. I brought mine to my nose and sniffed. It smelled like the rubbing alcohol I used in elementary school to kill spiders.

"Are you gonna smell it or drink it?" Weston chided. I took a sip; it tasted like liquid fire. I coughed, and Weston laughed. He reached for my drink, and I surrendered it without protest. He asked if I minded and then downed it without effect. The performance was meant to impress, but it did little for me. He returned to the drink cart and poured himself another scotch and then uncorked a different bottle and poured something into my glass. "It's vodka with a splash of coke," he said, handing me the new concoction. "It won't burn as much going down."

I took a sip to be nice, but I had no intention of consuming the calories. I feigned approval and placed the glass on the table.

Weston took the folder from the table and opened it. It contained a single sheet of paper. He pulled his chair closer to mine—his scotch-soaked breath invading my nostrils—and read the sheet of paper. It was a spreadsheet, my spreadsheet, chronicling last quarter's sales. I had the same sheet with me. (He had asked me to print and bring my own, so why did he print one, too?) The difference between our two data reports was mine had two pages instead of one—I had enlarged my font to necessitate an additional sheet.

"These are your sales figures," Weston said. "They are...lacking."

"It's been a rough quarter."

"I can see that." Weston dropped my sales sheet on the table. "Newage Tech needs to reinvent itself. I want to see us go public within the next five years. That requires more innovation, and we need to offer what our competition can't." With a fluid motion, he lifted his scotch and downed it in a single gulp. He returned to the alcohol cart, poured himself another drink, and settled back into his chair. He had, without detection, inched his chair closer to mine. "I need ideas," he said, sipping his drink. "Your specialty is marketing. How can we market a better product?"

I pondered his question, but I did not have an answer. I took my drink and pretended to take a sip, using the action to buy time. "Marketing is simple," I said, returning my glass to the table.

"How so?"

My answer served only to interrupt the silence, so I had nothing else to add. From my purse, I heard my phone buzz with a new notification. Had I received a new like? An additional friend request? I wanted to reach inside and check it. I wanted to do anything other than discuss company sales stats and earnings.

"Well, consider your products, our products," I began without any idea of where I was going, "and consider what sells."

"And what's that?"

The buzzing resumed. I *needed* to check my phone. My like total must be climbing. Weston somehow, undetected, had moved even closer to me. I could *feel* his breath. My thoughts scrambled. I thought of Vicarious Vacations, Alexis, her death, Eric, and how much I missed his friendship. Our conversation in the cemetery still seared in my head. I thought about Shawn and how I was now a fitness ambassador for Shredded Fitness. I thought of my recent photo and how sexy...

"Sex," I said.

"What?"

"Sex sells. It's the old adage in advertising, right?"

Weston gave me a thoughtful nod. "How does that apply to us?"

"What was the marketing budget last quarter?" I asked because this sounded like a reasonable question.

"I'd have to check."

"Do you know how much of it was geared towards sex?"

"None."

"Well, there's the problem." I sounded like my technical sales professor from college. He too spoke around questions when he did not know the answers to them.

Weston considered this, pretending like what I said made sense, and offered a wry smile. "So, sex, huh?"

"Yeah."

"You seem preoccupied with sex."

"It's not that. It's...that's advertising, right? Sex is used to sell everything from hamburgers to washing machines."

Weston nodded and leaned closer to me. Our legs touched. I recoiled, and he moved even closer. "You may be onto something," he said. "Sex is a powerful tool. For instance, sometimes sex can sell a boss on why he shouldn't fire a lackluster employee." Weston smirked at his own threat and touched my leg with his hand. At first, I thought the contact was incidental, but when he made no effort to remove his hand, I understood his intentions. Weston did not care to talk about marketing strategies; he expected me to save my job. My poor sales were leverage to get me into bed.

"Mr. Goodman, I—"

"Call me Weston," he said. He leaned closer and stopped his face inches from mine. He expected me, driven mad with desire, to bridge the remaining distance to feel his lips on mine. I remained motionless, however. He interpreted my lack of defiance as permission. He covered the last inches separating us and kissed me on the mouth. I did not resist the kiss, nor did I receive it. I remained immovable, frozen in time. "You're good at using sex to get what you want, aren't you?" he whispered, drifting away from my mouth and onto my neck.

My skin crawled. I shuddered from fear and he misconstrued my displeasure for passion. "I don't know what you mean," I whispered.

"Yes, you do. I've seen your Instagram posts."

"I'm a fitness ambassador. Those pics are for a job."

Weston laughed. "Speaking of jobs…" He began, unbuckling his belt. Without warning, I was thrust back to the abandoned parking lot where Clint had expected me to fulfill his sexual whims. Now Weston expected I do for him what I had done for Clint. Weston leaned into me, peppering my neck with kisses, each one stinging more than the one before it.

"No," I managed to say

"What?" he asked, kissing the base of my neck.

"No."

"You don't mean that."

"I don't want this."

He grinned. "Sure, you do."

His hand again found my thigh. I grabbed it. "I don't want this," I said. My voice sounded distant and unlike my own. Weston stopped; his ravenous eyes were sharp and wanting.

"Trust me, Paige," his fiery breath pricked my skin, "you want this."

"I don't…I can't…" I whispered.

"You can't or you won't?"

"What's the difference?"

Weston shook his head, frustrated with my ignorance. "This could cost you your job, you know?"

His threat silenced me, and he took my silence as my acquiescence. His hand crept further up my leg, while the threat of losing my job still permeated the air. I needed my job because it was my lone connection to Eric. Without it, I may never set things right with him. I needed the money, too. I needed the benefits. I needed…I needed Weston's hand to *stop* moving up my thigh.

"No, Weston," I said, raising my voice. "I don't want this." He wavered, gave me a hard appraisal, then jammed his hand further up my skirt. "No," I said again, pulling away. "Stop!"

He dismissed my cries. He leaned in and kissed me hard on the mouth, jamming his scotch-soaked tongue down my throat. I tried to push him back, and made a minor success of it, but he overpowered me. I screamed, and he placed his hand over my mouth. I screamed again, but his hand muffled my cries. He stood and pulled me to my feet, kicking his chair to the floor, and keeping his hand over my mouth. My sobs became lost in the palm of his hand. I fought to get free. I thrashed about, and I landed an elbow to his ribs, but it was not enough to escape his hold. He slapped me across the face, a sharp reprisal for the elbow. He spun me around, forced my head onto the table, and lifted my skirt. I shrieked as he bent me over the table, and I shrieked louder when I heard the jingle of his belt buckle becoming unlatched.

Then someone pounded on the door, and Weston and I both froze from fear and curiosity. The person pounded again. "Open the door, Weston," Eric shouted from behind the door. Eric! My heart leapt.

"This doesn't concern you, Eric," Weston panted, trying to catch his breath.

"Help me, Eric!" I cried. Weston grabbed my hair and through clenched teeth told me to be quiet.

"Open the fucking door!" Eric yelled and pounded so hard the hinges bent. "Open the door, or I'm calling the cops."

Weston's slacks were bunched about his ankles. They must have fallen, or he pulled them down without me realizing it. He released me and lifted his pants, fumbling to reattach his belt. I dashed away from him, lowering my skirt with trembling hands. I grabbed my purse and ran to the door and thrust it open. Eric stood outside, heaving, ready to break down the door. We stared at each other for a heartbreaking interlude.

"You okay?" he asked. I nodded, afraid to speak. He studied my face, his expression hardened when his eyes landed on the mark Weston's slap had left. I brought my hand to my cheek and recoiled when my fingers touched the delicate surface.

"Go home," Eric said.

I stifled a cry and stepped past him and into the hall. I dashed to the exit and kept running until I locked myself into my car. My cold hands clutched the steering wheel. Deep, down into the recesses of my stomach, a red ball of emotion was building. It came rushing to the surface, and before I could halt its escape, I bellowed a gut-wrenching scream that filled my car and shattered my being. I screamed and cried and cursed and did not stop until my body exhausted all emotional resources. In the deafening silence that followed, I heard my phone chime. I had seventeen new likes, and I did not care.

CHAPTER 25

Thirty minutes later, I returned home and found my sister and two of her friends scattered about the basement. The hypnotic glow of their phones kept them spellbound enough to ignore my presence. I tiptoed past them and into my room where I replayed the events from the night. A flurry of emotions engulfed me. I wanted to talk to someone, have a shoulder to cry on, a friend to console me, but I had no one—except thousands of online followers I could not confide in.

I paced my room trying to collect my thoughts, trying to make sense of what had transpired earlier. Do I return to work the next day acting like nothing happened? Do I go to the police, and if I did, what would I tell them? That I was raped? I was not. That my boss assaulted me? Would they believe me? Would they listen to the lower-level employee accusing the company CEO of a sexual indiscretion? Eric could confirm my accusation, but would he? He had not seen what occurred, but he must have heard my cries. Why else did he pound on the door demanding Weston open it?

I was disheartened and lost. I needed to clear my head and think outside of my bedroom's confining walls. But above all, I needed a friend. Matt was my only friend; I went to the gym.

From a distance, I watched Matt finish a set of shoulder presses and rack the dumbbells. Our eyes found each other in the mirror. He smiled and waved, and I waved back and motioned towards the exercise studio. He nodded and followed me to the empty room. Right as he entered, I dropped to the floor and cried. He helped me to my feet, and through incoherent, angry sobs, I told him everything.

Ten minutes later we were sitting on the floor, my head resting on his shoulder. "So, what's your plan?" he asked.

"I don't know, but I'm open to suggestions."

At a loss, he shook his head. "You know, you hear these stories, about bosses taking advantage of their employees, but…I guess, as a man, it's something I never worry about."

"I was just an object to him, a conquest. It was the same with Clint."

"Everything is an object with Clint."

"He unfriended and stopped following me after our last date—if you would even call it a date."

"He unfriended you, huh? Well, that'll teach you."

"Sad thing is, it kinda hurt that he unfriended me."

Matt smiled, but I could tell it pained him to do so. "When Derrick left, it broke me," he said. I knew of Matt and Derrick's relationship because they chronicled it on social media, but the details surrounding their breakup was foreign to me. I recalled one day Matt seemed distant and short-tempered. Later that night I noticed he had canceled his social media accounts. I had assumed he and Derrick had broken up, but I never pried because it was not my business. Now I suspected Matt needed me to listen to his tale as much as I had needed him to hear mine.

"Will you tell me what happened?" I asked.

Matt picked at the rough callouses that lined his palms, veritable signs that he spent most his time at the gym. "I spent every second glued to a screen keeping tabs on him," he began. "He posted nonstop, showing the world how great his life was without me. His posts were for my benefit—to hurt me. He assumed I would stalk him, and he was right. When I found the Vegas pictures of him with another man, I knew I had reached my breaking point."

"Did he really go to Vegas, or was it all…" I left my thought suspended, worried I may say something worthy of another ban.

"It was real. Shawn traced his internet activity and confirmed his plane ticket and hotel."

I nudged Matt in the ribs. "You need to stop talking," I whispered. "If you discuss Vicarious Vacations, you will get suspended."

Matt laughed and took my phone and held it to his mouth. "You getting this, Shawn? I know you can hear us." I grabbed my phone, baffled by Matt's audacity, and tapped the Instagram icon. Relief swept over me; I still had access.

"He can't ban me, Paige," Matt said. "I'm offline."

"You're offline?"

"Completely. Instagram, Facebook, Twitter, Tumblr, Tinder, Snapchat, Myspace—"

"Myspace? What's Myspace?"

"It's Facebook for losers. I got rid of all of them, and it was the second hardest thing I'd ever done."

"What was the first?"

"Seeing Derrick live his life from social media without me."

"I'm so sorry, Matt. I didn't know you were dealing with this."

"Don't be. I'm happier now that I'm removed from it. Remember how moody I was a few months ago? How I always seemed on edge?"

"Yeah."

"That was Derrick controlling me through his social media accounts. It sucked because I felt like I had no control over my life."

"I can imagine."

"But I'm happier now that I've logged off. It doesn't control me anymore, and it doesn't determine my self-worth. I enjoy having my privacy. I can go places and be present, live in the moment." He took my hand and kissed it. "You're worse than I was, Paige. I think you realize you have an addiction, and I recognize I am an enabler. I feed your ego and I snap your pictures and I keep my mouth shut as your body gets leaner and your clothes get skimpier. It's sad, and I rationalize it as…just doing my job. If I were a better person, I'd do something else. I love my job, though. I love helping people make healthier life decisions, but it pains me to see that while I get people healthier physically, I'm hurting them mentally. This is most evident with you, Paige."

"What are you saying, Matt?"

He sighed, frustrated that I was not catching his point. "Paige, if you present yourself as an object, you'll be treated as one."

My mouth sprung open, dumbfounded, and offended. "Are you blaming me for what happened tonight?"

"No. I am *not* defending your boss's behavior, Clint's, or any other asshole that will try to take advantage of you. Your boss is a colossal prick, and he should be punished for assaulting you. All I'm saying is, you have more to offer the world than a hot body and fake vacation pics."

For the third time that night, I cried. I cried because Matt was honest and cruel and...wrong. I did not have more to offer. My online persona identified me, and who I was online represented the depth of my ambitions.

. . .

Later that evening, as I pulled into my parents' driveway, I spotted Eric sitting on the porch steps. "Your sister told me you went to the gym," he said as I exited my car and approached my house. "I figured I'd wait."

I tried processing that Eric Vandross was standing on my front porch. His words played back to me. My sister told him I went to the gym, so he met Kelsey? Did she embarrass me? Did they talk about me? If so, what did she say? Did he meet my parents? Oh, god, I hope he did not meet my parents.

"What are you doing here?" I asked.

"I wanted to make sure you're okay."

"I'm fine."

"Are you?"

"I...I...don't know."

"Can you tell me what happened?"

A sincere curiosity blanketed Eric's inquiry. "Are you asking as a friend or a boss?"

"As a friend."

My chin quivered, and my face grew hot under the weight of his answer. "I don't have any friends, Eric."

"You have one," he said. The moment gripped me; I wanted to be in Eric's arms while the world dissolved into a distant afterthought. As if sensing my desire, Eric stepped to me and stopped, unsure how I might react to the physical touch of a man. He held out his arms, granting me the decision to accept or reject his embrace. I fell into him hard, and his arms covered me like a warm blanket.

He held me for a couple minutes and then led me to the bottom porch step. I sat down and wiped my eyes and the cool evening breeze danced on my skin causing small goose bumps to bubble to the surface. I folded my arms across my chest, and Eric, sensing my discomfort, removed his jacket and placed it around my shoulders. The tailored fabric held his scent. I closed my eyes and took him in and prayed he would not ask me to return his coat when he left.

"I do need to talk to you as a boss, however," he said. "I don't expect you to come in tomorrow. Take as much time as you need, but I need to report this to HR. I'm sure your version of events will differ from Weston's. All I know is what I heard, but I'm confident I can fill in the details. I'll do everything I can so that he'll never work at Newage Tech again. If you want to press charges, if you want to go to the cops, I'll go with you. I'm sure you're still processing what happened, but it's best to report this sooner than later. Get the details recorded while the memory is fresh."

I stared ahead, contemplating the decisions I was now forced to make. "I…I just never want to see him again," I said.

"That's understandable, and I'll do what I can so you never do."

"Thank you."

He gave my shoulder a gentle squeeze. "Do you need anything, Paige?"

"I need you to know how sorry I am about Alexis," I implored.

Eric swallowed hard, thrown by my unexpected plead. "Try to get some sleep," he said. "I'll call you tomorrow." He crossed the front yard, stepped into his car, and disappeared into the night.

CHAPTER 26

True to his word, Eric called the next day. He explained that he, Heather, and Weston had a three-hour meeting that morning with HR. He refrained from getting into specifics over the phone but asked to meet later for coffee.

We met at a coffee shop about a mile from the office. I arrived first, settled into a booth, and waited for Eric. He arrived five minutes later, looking spent and defeated.

"Thanks for meeting me," he said, sliding into the booth.

"No problem."

He rested his elbows on the table and thought about how to start. He opened his mouth to speak, but the waitress arrived and asked if we were ready to order. Eric deferred to me, and I ordered a coffee.

"Are you hungry?" Eric asked, and I shook my head. He told the waitress two coffees.

"No food?" the waitress asked. One of her eyebrows crawled halfway up her forehead, wondering why we were occupying a table if we would not order more than coffee. Her silent irritation went undetected, though. Eric was rubbing his eyes, preoccupied with his own workplace irritations. The waitress shrugged and left.

"I'll get right to it," Eric said once the waitress was out of earshot. "Weston is done at Newage. He resigned today."

"Just like that?" I asked. I figured he would put up more of a fight.

"Well, not initially. He...his version of events seemed a little...far-fetched."

"What did he say?"

Eric hesitated. "He said you came onto him."

I gasped. "*I* came onto *him*?"

"No one bought it, Paige. It's a flimsy defense, but it's all he has, so he's sticking to it."

"You heard me screaming, right?"

"Yes. I explained everything—well, everything from my perspective."

"What did you say?"

"I said I overheard you cry for him to stop. More screaming and an obvious struggle. I heard a chair kick over, and I pounded on the door. You opened the door, visibly shaken, and you left."

"What did he say to that?"

"He said I can't prove what occurred inside his office."

I sat back and blinked away the invading tears. "So, it's he said, she said?"

"It's he says, *they* say," Eric replied. "Heather pulled Weston's HR grievance file. He didn't know he even had a file—neither did I to be honest. He's received three sexual harassment complaints in the last eighteen months."

"Are you serious? How is he still working there?"

"Well, he's not now, and it was after we reviewed his file that he agreed to resign."

"What happened with the sexual harassment complaints?"

"Nothing. After the women filed their complaints, they didn't want to pursue it any further. Often women don't want to deal with the headache of going after someone, especially their boss."

"Who filed the grievances?"

"I can't tell you because it's confidential, but I can say the complaints and the women are credible, and Weston knows it."

The waitress arrived with our coffees. She placed them on the table, and Eric rummaged through the sugar caddy looking for a Splenda packet. When he did not find any, he asked the waitress, but she had already left. The potential tip on a six-dollar check drained any workplace enthusiasm she pretended to have. Eric drank his coffee black.

"He's worried you may go after him," Eric said.

"Yeah, I've thought about that."

"And?"

"I'm not sure. What do you think I should do?"

Eric set his coffee down, planted his elbows on the table, and rested his chin on his hands. "Did he rape you?"

"No."

"Did he assault you?"

"Define assault."

Eric stalled. "Did he…touch you inappropriately, forcefully… without your consent?"

"Yes."

"And you told him no?"

"Yes."

Eric nodded without surprise. "He struck you, didn't he?"

"Yes."

"You should press charges. He assaulted you, Paige, and he shouldn't get away with it."

"How do I even press charges? Go to the cops?"

"Yes. You go to the cops, file a report, and you'll need to get a lawyer. Weston already has one."

"What?"

"He's covering his bases."

"I can't afford…how would I prove that he assaulted me? It's my word against his."

"You're right," Eric said. "It is your word against his. Often these situations don't go much further because they are hard to prove. I'm willing to testify what I heard, but he is right. I don't know the specifics."

"Do you believe me? Do you believe it happened the way I described?"

"Yes, I believe you."

Although he offered the answer I most wanted to hear, his response lacked the sincerity I sought. "A part of you doesn't though," I said.

He hesitated, and an uncomfortable pause filled the air. "I believe every word of your account."

"But?"

"Nothing."

"Say it, Eric."

"I said what needs to be said, and I will say it again in front of a judge if it comes to that."

"We're not in a courtroom. Tell me what you're too afraid to say."

Eric took in a deep breath, held it, and exhaled, trying to find the most diplomatic approach to say whatever he was withholding. "I'm curious why you were in Weston's office after hours."

"Why does that matter?"

"It doesn't. Forget I said anything."

"If you didn't want to discuss this, why did you bring it up?"

"You asked me."

"You think I'm…what…easy?"

"No."

"I deserved it?"

"No."

"What do you think?"

"I think a man in a position of power tried taking advantage of you."

"But?"

"But nothing, Paige."

"Don't pander to me, Eric. Say what you're thinking."

Eric massaged his neck, attempting to knead away his stress. "I think…" but he refused to finish his thought.

"Say it."

"It doesn't matter, Paige. What matters is what happened."

"Say it," I demanded. My irritation increased with every second he stalled.

Eric's warm eyes turned intense, and his stare bore right into me as if to say, *Okay, fine. But you asked for this.* "I think you're insecure," he said. "Six months, a year ago, you were fun to talk to and kind and beautiful. Now you're…you're…"

"What? What am I?"

"You're the type of girl that gets asked to stay late," he said. I felt his regret the second he said this. He swallowed hard from the weight of my prodding and refused to meet my frigid stare. His comment hung in the air, silencing us both. I thought to leave, but something kept me glued to my seat.

"What the hell does that mean?" I asked, hoping my voice did not reveal the sudden pain I felt.

"Forget it," Eric said. He pulled his wallet from his back pocket, opened it, found a twenty, and dropped it onto the table. His breathing was heavy, and I sensed he had more to say. I waited, terrified to hear his next charge. Then his body slackened, and all fight drained from him. He rubbed his temples and attempted to stand, but my anger rose to meet his softening manner. I reached across the table and clutched his wrist.

"What else?" I demanded. "What else do you want to say to me?"

"Drop it, Paige."

"Come on, Eric," I goaded him. "You couldn't say anything worse than what you've already said." The fire returned to his eyes, and I shifted in my seat. I released my grip, and he settled back into the booth.

"Why do you think I was still at the office last night?" he asked.

I shrugged. "I figured you were working late."

"No," Eric snapped. "Weston came into my office at lunch asking about you. I said I didn't know much, and I questioned why he was asking. He showed me his phone with your Instagram page loaded and said, 'That's why.' Told me he spent the weekend admiring your Instagram page."

"I'm a fitness ambassador," I said, choking on the title.

"I didn't know you two were meeting," Eric continued. "I was at the elevator ready to leave for the night when I saw you enter his office. I decided to stick around."

"The pictures are for my job," I explained. "My fitness pics average thousands of likes. I get free clothes, and I have to model them for my followers."

"You don't need to explain anything to me."

"I'm an ambass—"

"You've said that."

"It's for my job. I have thousands of foll—"

Eric shook his head. "Unbelievable," he whispered more to himself than to me. He stood. "You have thousands of followers? You get thousands of likes, huh? Are they real?"

"What?"

"How do you know thousands of *actual* people follow and like your photos?" His question mystified me. "My fake honeymoon photo had thousands of likes," Eric said. "Alexis showed me. Half of them were fake."

"What?"

"They manufacture the likes, comments, and friends like they manufacture your vacations. How else can they guarantee how many likes you'll receive for each photo? Hell, Alexis, you could buy a million followers tonight."

"Paige," I corrected him.

"What?"

"My name's Paige."

In his mind Eric replayed his words and caught his error. "Sorry," he said, but I perceived he was not sorry at all. "I guess you remind me of someone."

My phone rang, startling me. I grabbed it and read the screen—Shawn. I panicked. Had I said something incriminating? I needed to answer it, but if I did, Eric would leave. Another ring. I looked up, and Eric was already walking through the diner's exit. I wanted to run after him, but my curiosity why Shawn was calling kept me immobile, so with a shaking hand, I answered my phone.

"Hey, Paige, this is Becky from Shawn Preston's office," a mechanical voice said through the phone. *Oh, no.* "Shawn would like to meet with you tomorrow morning. Can you come by at 9:00?"

"Is something wrong?"

"We'll see you tomorrow at nine." Becky cut the call. I entered my phone's home screen and tapped the Instagram icon. It sprang to life; I still had access. Relief swept over me. I investigated the parking lot; Eric was gone, but his words still rang in my ears. My latest Instagram photo tallied 8,038 likes, and Eric's searing claim forced me to consider how many of those likes may be fake.

CHAPTER 27

I sat in Shawn's office, my hands balled into fists, while I listened to the audio recording—*my* audio recording. Eric's voice interrupted the recording, demanding Weston open the door. I screamed for Eric to help me. He demanded again that Weston open the door, and then Shawn stopped the recording.

Neither of us spoke. Shawn took a pitcher of water from his desk, along with an empty drinking glass, and filled it. "By my count," Shawn began, handing me the water, "you told him no and to stop more than half a dozen times."

I wanted to ask how he had the recording, but I already knew; my contract allowed it. "Why did you show me this?" I asked.

"Your boss is claiming you came onto him, and this proves otherwise."

"Are you always listening to me?"

"Everything is being recorded, but we only listen if it concerns the company."

"How does this concern the company?"

"It doesn't. We have algorithms in place, and certain words are flagged. If you or someone you're with says one of the flagged words, we're notified, and we listen. Yesterday Eric Vandross mentioned Vicarious Vacations, so we were notified and plugged into the audio. Based on that conversation, I went further back to the encounter with Weston Goodman. I figured I'd help your defense. This audio makes your case ironclad."

"I can use it?"

"You'd have to file a subpoena for it. There is some legal red tape, but we'll cooperate."

I took a sip from my water and asked the question I wanted answered above all others. "Are my likes fake?"

My question threw Shawn. "What?"

"My social media likes, are some of them fake?"

"Does it matter?"

"Yes."

"Why?"

"Because...because they're fake."

"So?"

"So...so they're not real."

"Paige, it's social media. None of it is real."

"Yes, it is."

"What's real?" Shawn asked. "You, your friends, their friends...you're all fake. You're all presenting a life that isn't accurate."

"Some of it is."

"Social media is a highlight reel; it's photoshopped living."

"But why give people more likes than they've earned?"

"To keep them addicted. If your picture gets 1,000 likes, you feel good. If it gets 10,000 likes, you feel ten thousand times better. It feeds your addiction, and it makes it harder for you to walk away."

"Is that all that matters to you? Keeping people hooked?"

"Well...yeah," Shawn answered, as if my question were a stupid one.

"What else is fake?" I asked. "What else do you do to keep me hooked?"

"What does it matter?"

"I want to know."

"I don't think you do."

"So, there is something else?"

Shawn flashed a devious grin. "There's always something else, Paige."

"What?"

"You're posting half-naked pictures of yourself on Instagram, Paige. Have you ever been body-shamed?"

"Yes."

"Have you ever been body-shamed since you started taking vacations from us?"

I considered his question. I recalled, during my frumpy days, a handful of comments, always from people I had never met, telling me I was fat or ugly. Those comments had stopped within the last year, but I assumed my new figure had silenced my critics.

"You block shamers?" I asked.

"We block all negative comments. You only see the positive."

"Am I getting body-shamed?"

"Everybody gets body-shamed."

"But I look great."

"Exactly. You're an easy target because you look how most women don't, and they hate you for it. You highlight their insecurities. You present an 'unrealistic' body image because you work out and eat right."

"It's not unrealistic," I cried. "It's my reality and my *real* body! I work hard for it."

"You don't need to convince me, Paige. I get it, but social media trolls get off on bringing people down. They attack what they don't have the skill or discipline to become."

"It's wrong," I said. "Trolling is wrong, and inflating my like total is wrong. Everything you do is wrong."

"Then log off," Shawn said.

This was another challenge, a dare, that he foresaw I would never take. This morning my latest fitness pic had reached 13,000 likes, and the resulting dopamine rush was intoxicating. It validated my existence and gave my life meaning. Did it matter if *some* likes were fake? Did it matter if Shawn sheltered me from trolls seeking to belittle my success for a modicum of their own pleasure? I worked hard for what I had become. Any haters' disdain deserved to land on deaf ears. Their insecurities did not get to exacerbate my own.

"Are you going to press charges?" Shawn asked, returning me from my silent defenses and refocusing on the original purpose of our meeting.

"I don't know."

"Eric is right. If you press charges, you need to file a police report sooner than later."

I waged a brief debate and became panicked when I envisioned what filing a police report entailed. Weston had violated me, and if his HR file proved accurate, it sounded like my incident was not an isolated one. He needed to be stopped, but that meant telling, retelling, *living* my experience over and over again. And what if I lost? What if the people tasked with deciding my fate judged me the same way Eric had in the diner? Even though I had rejected Weston, Eric still speculated my online profile is why he preyed on me. After everything I had endured, Eric's judgement hurt the most. He did not blame me for what happened, but his expression revealed something much worse: disappointment for who I had become.

"Shawn, are we friends?" I asked.

"Friends?"

"Yeah. Are we friends?"

Shawn shifted his feet, uncomfortable with the question. "Sure, Paige, we're friends."

"I mean *real* friends, not social media friends."

"Of course, we're friends," he said, but I divined he supplied his answer because it was what I wanted to hear.

"Do you think I caused this? Did this happen because of the pictures I post?"

"Absolutely not," Shawn answered. *This* I could tell he meant. "A woman can post whatever she wants, and that does *not* grant a man reason to assault her."

"He wanted to sleep with me because of my posts. That's why he asked me to stay late."

"So?"

"So, a year ago it wouldn't have crossed Weston Goodman's mind to have me stay late."

"I still don't see your point."

"I think I caused this."

Shawn kneeled in front of me and gripped the arms of my chair. "Look at me, Paige," he demanded, and I lifted my eyes to meet his. "This is not your fault. Weston can look at your posts, and he can want to sleep with you, but the moment you say no, he must stop. No post, no picture gives anyone permission to rape someone. Being sexy does not give men license to take advantage of women. Do you understand me?" I nodded and averted my eyes. "Look at me, Paige," Shawn said, and I stared back at him. "Do you understand me?" he repeated.

"Yes," I whispered.

Shawn stood. "If you want the audio, have your lawyer contact me."

"Thanks, Shawn."

"By the end of the week, you need to do another fitness post," he said. "You're generating a lot of traffic for us, and people are responding to your story."

"Okay."

"Keep your head up, Paige. You're a strong woman, and you'll get through this."

I smiled weakly and grabbed my purse. Struck with a sudden thought, I turned and asked Shawn: "Do you like your job?"

"I love my job," he said without missing a beat.

"What do you love about it?"

Shawn beamed. "The money." I expected a different answer, a more...noble answer. And although what he admitted appeared shallow, I admired the honesty of it. Even if I expected him to say something less superficial, at least he had the audacity not to pretend to be something he was not. Few people forecast that level of unabashed authenticity.

CHAPTER 28

At 4:00, my alarm startled me awake for my usual morning workout. The previous night I took an Ambien, and the effects were still tempting me with sleep. I texted Matt, and for the first time since he became my trainer, I cancelled a workout session. Moreover, keeping with the theme of uncharacteristic inclinations, I ignored all social media notifications, powered off my phone, and fell back to sleep.

When I woke again, the clock read 6:39. I figured it was 6:39 in the morning. It was not. This reality did not hit me until, while pouring cream into my coffee, I noticed the sun setting when it should have been rising.

The television blared from the other room. I poked my head into the living room and spotted my parents watching an old *Seinfeld* episode. My sister lounged on the sofa Snapchatting with her friends. I returned to the kitchen table with my coffee and stared at nothing. Soon after, the doorbell rang.

I sipped my coffee and pictured my family, perplexed by an uninvited guest, deciding who should answer the door. My mother and sister would, ultimately, defer to my dad. As if on cue, I heard his heavy step shuffling to the door. The predictability warmed me—it was comforting to know some things in my life remained unchanged. My dad pulled open the door, the hinges creaking their familiar tune, before Eric's voice cut into the silence.

"Is Paige home?" I heard him say, and I froze.

"Who are you?" my dad asked.

"My name is Eric Vandross. I work with Paige."

I got to my feet and padded to the wall separating the front room from the kitchen. I rounded my head and peeked into the other room. My father stood in front of Eric, analyzing him with an acute eye. Eric wore a customary work suit with his tie still in place—he must have come straight from the office.

"Well," my dad said, holding out his hand and shaking Eric's. "It's nice to see a man come to the door for my daughter." My dad glanced over his shoulder to my sister. "Kelsey, go tell Paige her date is here."

I closed my eyes with embarrassment. "Oh, no," Eric began. "I…" but he did not correct my dad. He must have detected the disappointment his revelation may cause if he informed my dad he was not there for a date.

So, why was he here?

"What were you saying?" My dad asked Eric.

"Ah…nothing, sir," Eric mumbled. *Sir?* I wish I could have seen my dad's face when Eric addressed him with that formal courtesy; my dad appreciated proper etiquette.

"Kelsey, go get your sister," my dad repeated.

"Fine," Kelsey said in all her teenage entitlement. She stood from the couch and made her way towards the kitchen with her head in her phone. I braced against the wall, motionless. Kelsey walked right past me and down the stairs without ever taking her eyes from her phone.

"Why don't you sit down?" I heard my mom say. I spied my mom as she led Eric to a nearby chair. He sat and took in the room. His eyes wandered until they landed right on me. I retreated behind the wall, but it was no use; I was discovered. Then, as if on cue, Kelsey came trudging up the stairs announcing I was not in my room. As she made this pronouncement, she noticed me huddled against the wall. She looked me over, and her mouth dropped. What did she expect? I had just woken from twenty hours of sleep.

"You're going out like that?" she asked and laughed. "Mom, dad, come look at Paige," Kelsey cried. She lifted her phone and snapped a picture. My mom rushed into the kitchen to evaluate the scene; sorrow filled her eyes the moment she spotted me. "Oh, honey," she whispered. "You can't go out like that."

I began defending myself, explaining in hushed whispers that I was not going out, that I did not have a date, and Eric had shown up unannounced. "Get rid of him," I said through clenched teeth.

"Hi, Paige," Eric's familiar voice said. I turned and looked at Eric. He tried not to smile and failed. This was embarrassing for me and he knew it and he relished it.

"Jeez, Paige," my father said, materializing from behind Eric. "Run a brush through your hair. Did you forget about your date tonight?"

All eyes landed on me. Eric stifled a laugh. "What are you doing here?" I asked Eric.

"I was hoping we could talk."

"Yeah…okay. Can I have ten minutes?"

With reckless abandon, I brushed my teeth, changed my clothes, and tied my hair into a ponytail. When I returned to the front room, my dad and Eric were stooped over the coffee table playing chess. Neither sensed my presence, so I observed from a distance. Eric made a move, taking my dad's queen, and my dad's face tightened. Eric leaned back from the board, satisfied with his strategy, and spotted me across the room. He asked my dad if they could finish their game another time. My dad nodded, disappointed with the postponement, but grateful to be spared the embarrassment of losing. Eric stood and extended his hand, "It was a pleasure sir."

My dad rose and accepted Eric's offered hand with gracious wonderment. "I hope to see you again, young man," my dad said as Eric and I parted.

We exited my house and stepped into the night. "I'm sorry to drop in unannounced," Eric said. "I tried calling, but you didn't answer."

"That's okay. I slept through the day." We were standing on my porch, and I turned and caught my sister spying through the curtains. She squealed with embarrassed delight and pulled the curtains tight.

"I don't suppose you've eaten?" Eric asked.

"No."

"Can I take you to dinner?"

"Dinner? Like…a date?"

Eric shrugged. "Sure, a date. I think we'd have more privacy in a crowded restaurant than we would here." He nodded to the window; Kelsey had returned.

"I'm not dressed for a date."

Eric looked at me as if for the first time. "Don't be ridiculous. You look beautiful." He strode to his car and pulled open the passenger-side door for me. Until that moment, I did not realize that men actually held car doors open for women.

Twenty minutes later we were sitting in a private room, shoeless, reading sushi menus. I had never eaten sushi before, but ten minutes earlier, when Eric asked if I liked it, I told him yes. He made a phone call and reserved a table. The hostess greeted us and led us to a room with paper walls and a table stationed over a hollowed-out space. We removed our shoes and sat around the table, our feet dangling comfortably into the chasm. It was the nicest restaurant I had ever seen.

The menu featured words I could not pronounce. Eric asked me what I liked, but the prices prevented me from giving an answer, informed or otherwise. I placed the menu on the table and told him to order for me to spare me any surprise expenses and embarrassment. He ordered three rolls, and when the waitress exited the room, an uncomfortable silence loomed. Eric took his time breaking it.

"Paige, I'm sorry," he said. "The last time we spoke, I was unkind and unprofessional. I don't know if you've decided what you want to do, but you'll have my backing one hundred percent."

"I'm not going to press charges," I said. Until I said it aloud, I had not decided whether to pursue legal action. Eric appeared surprised; I suspect I did, too.

"You're not?" he asked.

"No. This last week has been hell. Weston has money, and he has connections. I don't even know a lawyer."

"I could help with that."

"With the lawyer or the money?"

"Both."

"I appreciate that, but I just want this behind me. I don't want to fight, and if I pursue this, I'll have to tell and retell what happened. I don't want the…judgment."

Eric nodded. "I can appreciate that."

"As long as he's no longer working at Newage Tech, I'm willing to let this end now."

"He's cleaning out his office as we speak. We made him do it after hours to avoid questions or gossip. I also wasn't sure if you'd be coming in today, and I didn't want to risk any uncomfortable encounters."

"Monday I'll be back."

"I'm glad. It'll be good to have you back." I laughed. "What's so funny?" Eric asked.

"You saying it'll be good to have me back at work," I explained. "That's funny."

"Why?"

"Can I be honest with you?"

"Sure."

"I'm not positive what Newage Tech does. I'm not even sure what my job is."

Eric's face was complete bewilderment. For a dramatic minute, he said nothing, and then he sighed and smiled. "It saddens me to admit that you're not alone."

"I know we sell online security systems, but what does that mean? I'm in marketing, and I'm not sure who I'm marketing to or what the product even is."

"We sell online security for things like identity theft and online fraud. At least, that's the part of the company that makes money."

"What's the other part?"

"Well, I'm trying to…expand our operations."

"With online security?"

"No. Medical innovations."

"What do you mean?"

"Eighteen months ago, we hit our sales quota. The board promised once we did, they'd let me create a Research and Development branch. They're stationed in a warehouse about six miles from the office."

"What do they do?"

"Everything," Eric said. His voice oozed excitement.

"That's broad."

"Right now we're piloting a new topical ointment that can detect skin cancer cells."

"How does it work?"

"As a conduit. It has a CBD base and other recently approved synthetics. Once it's applied to the skin, a doctor or nurse can trace the area with a transducer, and it would flag any cancer cells."

"Newage Tech is doing that?"

"The R&D department is. It works independently from the online security wing."

"Newage must be doing well, huh?"

Eric's excited demeanor turned sour. "Well, truth be told, Paige. If this cancer ointment doesn't work, Newage may not be around much longer."

"What are you talking about?"

Eric thought for a moment, debating whether to disclose whatever weighed on his mind. "We're out of money," he said. "Alexis's father is pulling his funding, and now we've lost Weston's. Our investors are, well…it doesn't matter. The product is taking longer than expected, and if it doesn't work, well, we'll have about six months left."

"Six months? Wow, Eric, I had no idea."

"No one knows."

"So, it's hurting you that Weston had to resign."

"Don't do that," he said.

"It's true though, isn't it?"

"Weston Goodman is… *was* the worst thing about Newage Tech."

"I'm sorry, Eric. I know Newage Tech is your passion project. You built it from the ground up."

"We've had six good years."

"You can't find other investors?"

"I'm trying."

"What about Kenny Waters?" I asked. "I bet he has cash to spare."

"No, I would never do that."

"Do what?"

"Ask a friend for money. Kenny and I go way back. He's one of my best friends, and I won't leverage our friendship for a business proposal, especially one as risky as this."

The waitress arrived with our sushi—three neatly wrapped rolls totaling one hundred dollars. My phone buzzed with an incoming text. Eric and the waitress were conversing, so I checked it. It was from Shawn reminding me I needed to post a fitness picture to my Instagram account by midnight. With all the drama and turmoil consuming my thoughts, I had forgotten to post a picture. I pocketed my phone as the waitress left.

"Everything okay?" Eric asked.

"Yeah, it was a reminder to do something tonight," I said.

Eric positioned his chopsticks with little effort and plucked a piece of sushi from the plate. He dipped it into a puddle of soy sauce and plopped it into his mouth. I gripped my own chopsticks and tried to follow his lead. I failed.

Eric laughed. "Have you ever had sushi?"

"No," I admitted and dropped my head for dramatic effect.

He stood and exited the room. A moment later he returned with a fork. "Try this," he said. I took the fork, dunked a piece of sushi into the soy sauce, and, after inspecting the culinary mystery from all angles, placed it into my mouth. *Wow!* My taste buds begged for more. I had not eaten in over twenty-four hours, and my stomach now reminded me of that. I consumed another piece…and another. It took an effort to *stop* eating.

"So, what do you have to do tonight?" Eric asked.

"Sorry?"

"You said you needed to do something."

"Oh, nothing."

"You don't want to tell me?"

"No."

"Why not?"

"I think you'll…think less of me."

"Now you have to tell me."

I hesitated and said, "I have to post a picture to Instagram tonight."

"You have to?"

"I'm an ambassador for Shredded Fitness. Every Friday I have to post a fitness pic and give an overview about my fitness journey." Eric said nothing. I sensed he had a lot he wanted to say, but he was exercising caution. "Is there something you'd like to say?" I asked.

He studied me for a moment while his lips inched upward into a sly smile. He snatched a piece of sushi with his chopsticks and tossed it into his mouth. "Nope," he said, chewing with a dignified air.

I shook my head and feigned annoyance. "It's part of my job," I said.

"You like telling people you're an ambassador, don't you?"

"What do you mean?"

"Last time we talked you told me you were an ambassador. You said it again a second ago. I can tell it's important to you."

"I will not deny that I enjoy exercising. If I can get paid for it, why shouldn't I do it?"

"You should if you're passionate about it."

"You think it's stupid."

"It doesn't matter what I think."

"It matters to me."

"Why?"

Eric's question was a fair one, and it silenced me. Why did it matter? I had no answer, at least not an answer I wanted to reveal. I could not tell him it mattered because ever since he began dating Alexis, I had been infatuated with him, nor could I tell him my heart stopped a couple nights ago when he held me outside my house or thirty minutes ago when he opened his car door for me. Eric was kind and warm and out of my league—that is why it mattered.

"It doesn't matter," I said. "You're right."

"Can I ask you something?"

"Sure."

"The picture you take tonight, what will you be wearing?"

I searched for any hidden derision in his question, hoping to foresee his point, but came away empty. The way he looked at me, convinced me that he was just curious. "I don't know," I answered. "Shredded Fitness sends me outfits, but I haven't decided on anything yet."

"May I suggest something?"

"Sure."

He fished his phone from his back pocket, opened his camera, aimed it at me, and snapped a picture. "What are you doing?" I protested. Eric ignored me, typed something into his phone, and then my phone buzzed with an incoming text.

"Check it," Eric said.

I retrieved my phone and checked the message. It was the picture Eric had just taken. My large, perplexed eyes shone straight into the camera, and a confused frown pursed my lips. It was an unflattering, honest photo in need of a filter and better lighting.

"Post that," Eric said.

"I couldn't."

"There is no picture on your Instagram more beautiful than that one," he argued.

"You don't know that."

"Yes, I do."

I looked back at the photo. I appeared so...ordinary and so...common. Yet somehow, while analyzing my average features, I never felt more beautiful.

CHAPTER 29

After my dinner with Eric, I retreated to my room to take a picture for my Instagram fitness post. I stripped down to a sports bra and matching booty shorts compliments of Shredded Fitness. I stuck out my butt and puckered my lips and snapped three selfies. My bloated, sushi-filled stomach stared back at me. It was late, and I lacked the patience to wait for my food to digest. I sat on the edge of my bed and thumbed through my saved pictures searching for one worthy to post. Save for two selfies, I had already uploaded almost everything archived in my phone. I had taken the selfies months ago in response to photos Clint had sent me.

One night, without warning, he sent me a shirtless pic. The lighting highlighted his chiseled arms and rock-hard chest. I responded with the expected excitement, interjecting several fire and tongue emojis into my reply. He asked for a nude photo; I declined. He persisted and sent another shirtless photo—this one, cropped right above his pubic region, offered more skin. He told me I needed to do the same since I now owned two shirtless pics of him, and he did not have any of me. The request stroked my ego, so I sent a bra and thong picture. He replied with a thread of eggplant emojis and told me to lose the bra. I did, but I covered my nipples with my arms while pushing up my breasts to help them appear larger. The photo was meant to tease, and it did. More eggplant emojis followed. His flattery did wonders for me. A moment later he sent another picture. He was naked and holding his erect penis in his clenched hand.

The picture did little to excite me, but it represented more; it was a dare—an invitation to raise the stakes, a challenge to respond with my own provocative photo. I took down my underwear and laid on my bed. I crossed my legs, using them as a teasing concealer to hide the parts of me I wanted to keep hidden. I draped my hair over my shoulders to cover my breasts. It took five minutes to get the pose and placement of everything right. I snapped the picture and studied it. It was tasteful yet sinful. I blushed at the result and ran the picture through a series of filters, choosing the one that best showcased my assets and hid my flaws. I took a deep breath and sent it. For the next thirty minutes, I clenched my phone, waiting for a reply that never came. The next time I saw him, which was our third and final date, I asked him why he never responded to my artful picture. He answered: "'Cuz, I already busted my nut."

Now, as I revisited my tasteful, nude pictures, I debated whether to post them. If other women's fitness profiles offered accurate metrics, I projected my semi-nude photos harnessing 30,000 to 40,000 likes. The estimates excited me, but did I dare expose so much of me to the world? Once I crossed that bridge, my followers might expect nude pics weekly. The creative tactics needed to execute those expectations might prove stressful beyond words. However, the payoff…I needed more time to weigh the benefits.

While I did so, I reflected on my night. I recalled the picture Eric had snapped of me at dinner. He told me it was more beautiful than anything I had ever posted to Instagram. This was conjecture since he did not have an Instagram account, but he said it with so much sincerity, that his conviction made me wonder if he was right. The photo was so plain, so…authentic. Maybe that was what my followers needed. Often celebrities posted unfiltered pictures of themselves to show everyday people that, once the glamour and glitz got stripped away, we are more similar than we admit. My followers might appreciate the blemished, human side of me as well as the provocative one. After all, Eric did.

I uploaded the unaltered photo, wrote a brief message describing what it means to be true to oneself, punctuated it with my discount code, and went to bed.

· · ·

My photo had 403 likes. I had just woken and checked my Instagram page. 403 likes. I was baffled and disheartened. My previous photo featuring me in a pair of Shredded Fitness booty shorts had over 15,000. The tally must be wrong. I refreshed the page; the number did not change. Another refresh with the same results. I read the comments— there were not many. A few applauded my bravery for posting something so genuine and simple, but most asked when to expect another thong picture. Was the value of my backside 14,597 times more likable than my unadulterated face?

I tried making sense of my followers' proclivities when, without warning, the nude photo saved to my phone appeared on my Instagram page. Mystified, I clicked on the photo. Someone, assuming my identity, had written: "I heard your requests loud and clear. Enjoy! Don't forget to visit Shredded Fitness and use the discount code: "Paige15" to receive 15% off your personal fitness program." Someone had access to my account; someone had access to my photos. Shawn.

Did my contract allow him access to *everything* on my phone? Besides listening to my conversations, did he have permission to view and upload any photo I had archived? I tried to remove the photo but could not. I tried to delete the message Shawn had written. That too was impossible.

My phone chimed with a new text message from Shawn: "People don't want authentic photos. They want sex appeal. This photo will earn 50,000 likes. You're welcome."

I was now on full display to the entire world, and I was powerless. All my accounts were at the mercy of Shawn's whims. I shuddered and watched as people began, en masse, to like my picture. The familiar dopamine rushes I had grown accustomed to were not comforting me. My drug no longer produced its same potency. Had I developed an immunity to the effects?

. . .

I powered off my phone and hid it in my purse. I put my purse in my filing cabinet and locked the drawer. From my work computer, I retrieved the email I forwarded to myself—a PDF of the contract I had signed that granted Vicarious Vacations complete control of my online accounts. I printed the thirty-six-page document and walked straight to Eric's office and knocked on his door. "Come in," he said through the door. I entered and asked if he had a free minute; he did.

I approached his desk and handed him the contract. "What's this?" he asked, taking the small stack of papers.

"That's my contract from Vicarious Vacations. All clients now sign that when they create an account."

Eric skimmed the first page and flipped to the second. "Why are you showing me this?"

"Jump to page twenty-nine, paragraph three."

"Why would anyone agree to this?" Eric asked, reading the section I outlined.

"Because nobody reads contracts."

"This gives them unlimited access to everything," Eric said, still reading. "Anything you search for online, your credit card information, your bank statements."

"Yeah, and they can access any photos you save to your phone. And they can upload them to your social media accounts without your consent."

Eric stopped reading and looked at me. "What happened?"

"Pull up my Instagram account."

"I don't have an Instagram account."

"It doesn't matter. Just google 'Paige Reynolds Instagram' and you'll find it. I don't have it set to private."

"Why wouldn't you have it private?"

"Because…"

"Because you're a fitness ambassador?" Eric jeered.

"Just do it, Eric."

Eric typed my name into Google. He clicked into the top hit and found himself staring at a nude photo, *the* nude photo, of me. Embarrassed, he averted his gaze.

"I saved that photo to my phone," I explained. "Vicarious Vacations uploaded it without my consent."

Eric stole a second glance at the photo; I wondered if he liked what he saw. "Well," he began, picking up the contract and thumbing through it. "You gave consent. If you signed this, you agreed to let them access all your data, photos included."

"But I don't want that online!"

"Why?" he asked, returning to the photo and reading the like tally. "Your picture has 55,000 likes. Isn't that the point of this?"

It *was* the point, and I would be lying if I pretended not to appreciate the photo's popularity, but I did not like that Shawn had unrestricted access to my personal photos. The power my negligence granted him irked me.

"Could you please not belittle me right now?" I asked.

"Why bring this to me?" he asked, holding up the contract.

"This is what Newage Technology does, right?"

"Hack people's phones and post their naked pictures online?"

"No," I said. "Cyber security. Protect consumers from online predators."

"Well, yeah, but…"

"But what?"

"But you gave them permission. We can't protect your identity and your privacy when you give a company permission to infiltrate your personal devices."

"But I didn't give them permission."

"Yes, you did."

"Not knowingly."

"Legally, you did."

"Can't you do something?"

"Like what?"

"I don't know!" I cried. "Something! You're worried about funding, right? Well, solve this problem. I'm sure you'll make a fortune because I can't be the only one dealing with this. People agree to let Vicarious Vacations take over their lives without realizing it. Find a loophole and create a service that supersedes the parameters of the contract."

Eric scratched his day-old stubble, ruminating on a solution. "I'll look into it," he said. "I'll run it past some people and see if there's a way around it."

"Thank you."

"So...this is what it means to be a fitness ambassador, huh?"

"No," I said. "I don't want that picture online."

"Then why is it?"

"Because they tricked me."

"And why were you tricked?"

"I already told you why."

"And why were you tricked?" Eric asked again, trying to prove a point that eclipsed me.

"Because I didn't read—"

"No," Eric interrupted. "That's not why. They didn't trick you; they tempted you, and you took the bait."

"Is this what we do now? Every other encounter you go from being a friend to a prick?"

Eric's condescending grin vanished. "I'm sorry," he said, and he sounded like he meant it.

"I just want to matter, Eric. Can you understand what it's like not to matter to anyone?"

"Yeah," he said, "I can." He did not elaborate, and I lacked the energy to pursue a more detailed explanation. I stood and moved to the door.

"Hey, Paige?"

"Yeah?"

"Kenny is leaving town tomorrow. He and his girlfriend invited me to dinner tonight. Would you like to come?"

I was dumbstruck. "When you say Kenny, are you talking about Kenny Waters?"

"Yeah."

"And when you say his girlfriend, are you talking about Paisley Evans?"

"Yes."

"Kenny Waters and Paisley Evans, the movie stars?"

"Yes."

"You, Eric Vandross, are asking me if I will go to dinner with you and your movie star friends?"

"Yes."

I burst into laughter. Eric jumped, frightened and perplexed. "Okay," I said and then launched into another fit of hysteria.

"I'll pick you up at seven," Eric yelled as I closed the door behind me.

I wandered back to my cubicle in a haze, trying to compartmentalize the night that now lay on the horizon. When I checked my phone, a message greeted me: "Dear Paige Reynolds, all social media accounts are hereby suspended for thirty days. Cause for suspension: breach of contract. If you have questions, please visit the Vicarious Vacations website."

CHAPTER 30

I tried calling—no answer; I sent texts—no response. Shawn was avoiding me. I ran to my car and drove to his office. His secretary told me he was with a client, but I did not care. I hurried past her, (she gave me a curious stare) ready to burst into Shawn's office and begin my accosting.

But the door was locked.

I had not expected this. In movies where someone needs to confront another, the disgruntled party can always rush into an office unannounced and unimpeded. I tried the handle again to no avail. "I guess I'll wait," I told the secretary. She pointed to the sofa.

Twenty minutes later a couple exited Shawn's office. They held hands and smiled like they were auditioning for a Viagra commercial. Shawn must have sold them an exotic vacation with the promise of thousands of likes.

He escorted the lucky couple from his office and noticed me waiting on the edge of his sofa. My presence did not surprise him. He shook hands with the departing couple and turned back into his office, leaving the door open for me to follow.

"You violated your contract again," Shawn said the moment I entered his office.

"How?"

"We heard your conversation with Eric."

"How? I didn't have my phone."

"Eric did."

"Eric? He has a contract with you?"

"No, but Alexis does."

"That's…illegal," I said.

"Not if they're on the same phone plan."

"She's dead!"

"Their phone plan isn't."

"How can…you're listening to people without their knowledge."

"We only listen when we are discussed. Eric is not that interesting, and neither are you, Paige, but when you run your mouth about our business operations, per your contract, we have every right to intervene and institute penalties. Your negligence threatens our business. You need to understand that, chances are, we're always listening. Our base is growing every day, and the more clients we sign, the more ears we get."

"Please don't ban me," I pleaded. "I'm sorry. I didn't know—"

"You didn't know we were listening," Shawn interjected. "So, what, I should practice leniency because you thought you weren't being heard? That's ridiculous. You're contrite because you got caught."

"I can't go a month. It'll kill me."

"It will be difficult."

"Please, Shawn. I promise I'll never say another word."

"I have no reason to trust you, Paige. You told Eric about your contract, and now you're looking for a loophole to get out from what you agreed to."

"You posted a picture without my consent."

"That's not true. Your contract—"

"I didn't read my contract! I didn't know it allowed you to go into my phone and take any picture. That photo is private."

"It's a tasteful photo. Besides, you should be thanking me. It's your most-liked photo."

"Yeah? And how many are real?"

Shawn displayed a telling grin. "The photo *you* posted, the one with no makeup, the one with no skin, the one that Eric took and sold you the ridiculous premise that you were beautiful, *that* photo—all those likes are real. All 436."

"I'd rather have 436 real likes than 50,000 fake ones."

"No, you wouldn't," Shawn said. "Your phone, all phones, have dopamine detectors. Whenever you're holding your phone, it's recording and calibrating your level of enjoyment. When you first checked your phone after posting your latest pic, your stellar 400-like pic, you didn't get a dopamine rush. In fact, you were disappointed, and your depression spiked. When I posted your nude photo, you experienced a plethora of emotions: confusion, anxiety, frustration…at first. But once the likes started eclipsing even *your* expectations, you felt pleasure. Your dopamine levels were off the charts, and that picture has made you feel better than any other picture you've posted."

"You're lying."

"The data doesn't lie, Paige, so you can stop your bullshit crusade. You're not mad I posted it. In fact, you love that *I* posted it instead of you because it allows you to pretend you're upset. You can play the saint even though you are reaping the benefits of being the sinner."

"But if the likes are fake, what's the point?"

"You tell me. Why are you getting off on fake likes?" I had no answer, so Shawn answered for me. "Delusion," he said.

"Delusion?"

"You, like everyone else, delude yourself into thinking *your* likes aren't fake. We never believe negative things, deceptive things, about ourselves. They only apply to everyone else. Do you remember the Dark Days of Instagram?"

Yes, I remembered the Dark Days of Instagram. Instagram opted to hide the number of likes a post received from followers. Only the account holder had access to a post's popularity. Instagram believed this might help combat users' depression and anxiety.

"Yeah, I remember the Dark Days," I said. "What about them?"

"At the height of Instagram's popularity, it received a lot of push back from the public," Shawn explained. "People were dying, literally, because when a user saw that her post received twenty likes, but her friend's post received 100, the user with the fewer likes got depressed. The depression led to anxiety, and the anxiety exacerbated her insecurities. That triggered her and then she needed a safe space. When you combine those things, people died, often from suicide or mass shootings. So, Instagram hid the number of likes. It made sense. If users can't see how well-liked their friends' posts are, there's no reason to get depressed. And that's what happened. Teen and young people's suicide rates declined, but do you know what else did?"

"What?"

"Instagram's bottom line and the drug companies peddling antidepressants and anxiety medications. People started logging off and some even canceled their accounts. Turns out people want to see how many likes their friends receive. They like the competition. So, Instagram, influenced by the powerful drug lobbyists, brought the feature back. How much joy do you get knowing your photos have become more popular than Alexis's? How much do you love flaunting your 'Instagram influencer' rank or your ambassador status? You like the perks that come with being relevant online while your friends wallow in obscurity. You don't care if your likes or followers are fake because you know that your friends and followers see the number of likes you're receiving, and they have no idea what's real. All they see is that you posted a 50,000-liked photo. You savor that they recognize how important you are. It elevates your status because we gauge status by one simple metric: popularity."

Shawn took a remote controller from his desk and pointed it to the screen on the far wall. "Do me a favor," Shawn said. "Take out your phone." I reached into my purse and grabbed my phone. "Just hold it," he said. He hit the power button on the remote. My Instagram page sprung to life on the TV. My nude photo filled the screen. "Look at your like total," Shawn said. It had 56,221. The total started increasing, slowly at first and then settling into a steady uptick. After two minutes the likes plateaued. The final tally: 60,222 likes.

"Now," Shawn continued, "read the comments." The comments were a carnival of eggplant, tongue, and fire emojis. Shawn scrolled through the thread for a couple minutes and stopped. He counted to ten and pressed another button on the remote. The screen changed to a graph. Running vertical were numbers ranging from zero to one hundred. The horizontal axis calibrated timestamps measured into fifteen second increments. "This is your phone's dopamine detector," Shawn said. "You see that spike?" The "spike" Shawn referenced shot to sixty-seven on the horizontal axis and peaked at ninety. For two minutes the line hovered between sixty-five and eighty.

"That's how your body reacted while you watched your likes increase. That second spike is when you started reading your comments. You'll notice that the blue line is still, while we're talking, crawling across the graph in real time. It's a nice and steady crawl with no dopamine spikes. That's because it's gauging your levels right now, and you're not excited. You're not excited because you're staring at a graph and not your naked picture."

I dropped my phone into my purse and the blue graphing line disappeared.

"Just say the word, Paige, and I'll discard the photo right now. If that's what you want, I'll do it. I will remove your most-liked photo, but I need you to tell me to do it." I remained silent, choking on my inability to fathom a modicum of virtue. "That's what I thought," he said. "Let yourself out. I have an appointment at 11:00."

"Please don't ban me," I said.

"You violated your contract."

"You've seen how addicted I am, Shawn. Your graph proves that. A thirty-day ban will kill me."

"It might."

"What can I do so you'll drop the suspension? Please, I'll do anything."

"You can learn to keep your mouth shut. Now leave. I need to prepare for my next client."

I walked to the door, but before I stepped outside, Shawn said, "Enjoy your dinner tonight. Too bad you're suspended. Imagine the reaction if you posted a selfie with Kenny Waters and Paisley Evans."

I tried to respond, but my voice got lost in my throat. Of all of Shawn revelations, his last comment, saturated in truth, stung the most.

CHAPTER 31

"So, Paige, what do you do?"

Kenny Waters had asked me a question. I watched his lips move, and I heard him say my name, but I was not sure what he had asked, so I just stared at him. When I was not staring at him, I stared at his girlfriend, Paisley Evans. Who could blame me? I was having dinner with two of the world's biggest celebrities. Staring was the appropriate reaction.

Eric grazed my elbow, breaking my reverie. "You okay?" he asked.

"Yeah," I said. "Why?"

"Kenny asked you a question, and you're just staring at him."

"I'm sorry," I said. "What did you ask me?"

"I asked what you do," Kenny said.

"Oh, I work with Eric."

"Doing what?" Paisley asked. Her beauty stunned me silent. Her hypnotic green eyes, dark skin, and all her other desirable features contrasted nicely with my insecurities.

"I work in marketing at Newage Tech," I answered.

"What is Newage Tech?" Paisley asked. "What do you do?"

Eric cleared his throat and said, "Well, right now we lose money." Kenny and Paisley laughed. I examined their teeth and wondered if they had braces as children. "We monitor online fraud," Eric said, once the steam from his joke dissipated. "Protect consumers from identity thieves. We've been undergoing some other ventures—medical research."

"What type of medical research?" Paisley asked.

"Is it the thing we talked about a couple months ago?" Kenny asked Eric.

Eric nodded to Kenny and said to Paisley: "Cancer prevention and treatments."

"That sounds…heavy," Paisley said.

"Well, I'm hoping we're on the edge of making a breakthrough."

"Eric has assembled an entire team to create a cancer ointment," Kenny explained. "It somehow grants doctors a less…invasive way to detect cancer cells."

"Yeah," Eric interjected. "We're getting ready to pilot it."

"That sounds…life-changing," Paisley said.

"I hope so," Eric said.

"It's admirable, man," Kenny added.

"Only if it works."

"How are things…in the money realm?" Kenny asked. I sensed this was not the first time he and Eric had discussed money concerning Newage Tech.

Eric shrugged. "I'll figure it out."

"Are you looking for investors?" Kenny asked. "I heard Hank pulled his funding."

Eric shifted in his chair. "Who's Hank?" Paisley asked.

"Alexis's father," Kenny whispered loud enough for the entire table to hear. Kenny's revelation appeared to further confuse Paisley. "Alexis is…was…Eric's wife," Kenny explained.

"Oh, yeah," Paisley said, remembering. She frowned and tilted her head. "Kenny told me. I'm so sorry. That is the saddest story."

Eric cleared his throat and took a drink. "It's fine," Eric said. He turned to Kenny and said, "And, thank you, but I'll manage. I've approached other investors, and a few seem interested." Kenny sensed Eric no longer wanted to discuss Newage Tech's financial situation. He took the hint and decided to shift the conversation to me.

"So, Paige," he said. "Tell us about yourself."

"Huh?"

"Tell us three things about yourself."

I turned to Eric, looking for help. He stared back at me, expecting to learn something new about me, too.

"I…ah…I don't know."

"Tell me your favorite movie," Kenny said.

"Don't ask her that," Paisley said.

"Why not?"

"Because she'll lie," Paisley answered. "She's sitting with two actors."

"She doesn't have to say one of our movies," Kenny retorted.

"You mean she doesn't have to say one of *yours*," Paisley teased.

"Okay," Kenny said. "We won't discuss movies. What's your favorite book?"

My favorite book? I had not read a book since…

"I can tell you what her favorite book isn't," Eric said. "*The Great Gatsby.*"

"You don't like *The Great Gatsby*?" Kenny asked with glaring offense.

"I…"

"I gave it to her over a year ago, and she never touched it," Eric said.

"Oh, man," Kenny groaned.

"I don't blame you, Paige," Paisley said, coming to my defense. "I read it in high school and hated it."

"What?!" Kenny and Eric said together, each shooting accusatory stares at Paisley.

"I didn't like it," she said, standing her ground. "It was boring."

"Wow," Kenny mouthed.

"What?" Paisley asked.

"This is it," Kenny told the table. "This is the breakup. When the tabloids ask, tell them your poor taste in literature did it."

"It's overrated," Paisley said.

"Stop saying things right now," Kenny teased. "You're embarrassing me in front of my best friend."

Paisley lifted her wine glass to me for a toast. "To not reading *The Great Gatsby*," she said. I reached for my wine glass.

"Don't you dare toast to that," Eric said. He was overlaid with joy and warmth and consumed with the table's banter. Flaunting a defiant smirk, I raised my glass and touched it to Paisley's and took a drink. Kenny and Eric looked at each other, both defeated, both enjoying their defeat.

"We need to go find better dates," Kenny mused.

"I saw two women walk into the bathroom," Eric said. "Should we follow them?"

"Were they hot?" Kenny asked.

Eric regarded Paisley and then me. We both displayed threatening scowls that did little to hide our mirth. "Meh," he answered.

"See," Paisley said. "Eric knows."

"Knows what?" Kenny asked.

"You're already with the two hottest women in this restaurant," Paisley said.

Kenny raised his glass, armed and ready to offer his own toast. He looked at each of us, and we all lifted our own glasses. "To dating the hottest women in the restaurant," he said, and we clinked glasses. It was the perfect toast, and it broke my heart that I could not capture it with a picture. Engaging in a toast with Eric Vandross, Kenny Waters, and Paisley Evans! That would be a photo worth a million likes!

•   •   •

"Did you enjoy yourself?" Eric asked. We were standing on my porch. The night breeze cooled the evening and chilled my skin. Eric removed his jacket and placed it over my shoulders. This was the second time he had given me his jacket. The thoughtfulness of the gesture moved me, and I wondered how many times he had performed it for Alexis. Did he give all his dates his jacket when he suspected they were cold, or was I the exception? I wanted to believe the latter but understood Eric's chivalry likely extended beyond me.

"Yes, I enjoyed myself," I told him.

"You didn't say much."

"I was afraid I'd say the wrong thing."

"Were you a little star struck?"

"I was a lot star struck."

"Kenny is a great guy. Don't let his fame blind you. He's just like us."

"He's nothing like us," I said, and Eric frowned. "What?" I asked.

"I don't understand the infatuation with movie stars," Eric said.

"You don't?"

"All they do is recite lines they weren't clever enough to write, and if they screw up, they get to do it again. They get as many tries as it takes to get it right. I don't know of any other profession that allows infinite do-overs?"

"I never thought of it that way," I said.

"Don't get me wrong, acting takes talent, and Kenny is one of the best in the world, but it's sad actors are so revered. Too bad teachers, doctors, cops, and farmers don't get the same level of fame celebrities do. A scientist creates a cure that saves millions of lives, and we don't care. But if a pop singer shows her breasts, the world goes crazy."

"Are you talking about Quinn Hayes?" I asked.

"Was that her name?"

"Yeah."

Quinn Hayes, the legendary pop singer, attended a PETA rally nude. It was part of a music video. The video went viral and almost broke the Internet. At last count, her music video had close to fifteen billion views. At least a hundred were mine.

"Thanks, by the way," Eric said.

"For what?"

"For not asking Kenny and Paisley for a picture. The first time Alexis met Kenny, she asked for a selfie before they had finished shaking hands."

"I don't remember her posting a picture of her and Kenny."

"That's because I wouldn't allow it. We got in quite the fight. She kept telling me how many likes she'd get."

I wanted to ask Kenny and Paisley for a picture, but because of my suspension, I could not have posted it for thirty days. Had I taken one and saved it to my phone, Shawn might have uploaded it without my knowledge. The not knowing would have driven me crazy, so I figured it best to avoid the entire dilemma.

"Eric, why did you ask me to go with you tonight?"

"What do you mean?"

"I mean…I'm everything you despise."

"What do you mean?" he repeated.

"I've watched that Quinn Hayes video a hundred times. I'm a fitness ambassador who's required to post photos every week, and the reason I didn't ask Kenny for a picture is because I'm banned from social media for thirty days."

"You're banned?"

"Yeah."

"Why?"

"Breach of contract."

"When did you—"

"When I talked to you about my contract in your office."

"They banned you for that?"

"Yes."

"For thirty days?"

"Yes."

"That's funny…and brilliant," Eric said.

"It's neither of those things. It's hell."

"More than anything it's sad, but not for the reasons you're thinking. But it *is* brilliant."

"How so?"

"They figured out a way to control their clients by taking away the thing they love most."

"It will be the hardest thirty days of my life," I said. Eric scorned my hyperbolic assertion. "Listen, Eric," I began, "I'm not smart. I don't read books, and I can't talk to you about politics. Hell, I can't even explain the differences between republicans and democrats. Healthcare reform? That's a foreign language to me. I've never listened to a podcast. Sam Harris, Ben Shapiro, Eric Weinstein—I don't know those people. All the things you guys were talking about tonight…I had nothing to offer."

"What can you talk to me about?" Eric asked.

"Stuff that doesn't matter, stuff that will not improve the world or save lives. Do you want to know what Paisley wore to the Golden Globes last year? A yellow Versace gown. Do you have any idea how many Twitter followers Kenny has? Over seventeen million. None of that matters, but that's what I know. I can show you how to upload a YouTube video or airplay a movie. Other than that, I'm…nobody."

"Do you like who you are?" he asked. I pondered his question, and the harsh reality struck me; I was a twenty-six-year-old anxiety-ridden depressant still living at home whose primary worry was whether I had enough Ambien to get me through the next thirty nights.

"No," I whispered. "I don't like who I am."

Eric stepped closer to me. "Then change who you are," he said. He took my head in his hands and kissed my forehead. Before he could pull away, I snaked my arms around his shoulders and pulled him into me. For a second he stiffened, unsure what to make of my sudden gesture, then his body relaxed, and he wrapped his arms around me, too.

"You avoided my question," I said, still holding him. "Why did you ask me to come with you tonight?"

"I missed my friend," he answered. I held him for another moment and then released him. He stepped back and gazed deep into my eyes, ready to answer any other questions I may have. But I had nothing else I needed answered.

We stood in the night's silence, present and content. I guessed he did not imagine kissing me. The dynamics of the evening did not lend itself to such an act, but I wondered if he at least *thought* about it. Did he wonder, as I did, how his lips would feel on mine? I hoped that he did, even if the fantasy would always elude us.

A sudden breeze pierced the night, chilling us. Eric took it as a sign for his departure. He flashed a departing heartfelt smile and walked into the cool night. "Have a good night, Paige," he called over his shoulder.

"You too, Eric."

While he drove away, I turned to go inside, thought better of it, and sat on the porch. I heard the front door open and a moment later my dad was sitting on the porch next to me. For a moment we remained silent, neither of us wanting to disturb the night's tranquility. I expelled a soft yawn, and my dad asked about my date.

"It was...heartbreaking," I answered.

"Why?"

"He's an amazing man, and I'm an...average girl."

"What makes him amazing?"

I reflected for a moment. "The world is better because he's in it."

"And what makes you average?"

It took me longer to contemplate this. "I'm only as good as the people who like me," I said.

I expected an obligatory rebuttal from my dad that never materialized. He stared into the night sorting his own thoughts. I stood to go inside.

"My co-worker showed me your latest Instagram picture," my dad said, refusing to look at me. "Your mother hasn't seen it, but I suspect your sister has. I wish I hadn't."

I considered explaining that I had not consented to the post, but I suspected any explanation would lead to more questions. There was no point in justifying what I had come to accept—my online persona reflected who I had become. "I'm sorry, dad," was all I said before going inside.

CHAPTER 32

I crept into my parents' bathroom and opened their medicine cabinet. A surplus of prescriptions lined the shelves. I read the labels, looking for, but not finding, the Ambien. Heart meds, expired pain pills, hypertension scripts, anxiety, and depression meds I already had. My parents appeared to have it all—except what I needed. I had taken my last Ambien the night before, and I was only three days into my ban. I needed at least twenty more pills if I expected to reach thirty days.

"You won't find them," a voice behind me said. My mom stood in the doorway.

"What?"

"The Ambien," she said. "You won't find them."

"I'm not—"

"I hid them."

"Why?"

"Because several disappeared."

"I didn't—"

"Yeah, you did. It wasn't your father or your sister."

"Maybe someone—"

"What? Broke in? Someone broke in and stole the Ambien? They ignored the Percocets and the Lortabs and only took the sleeping pills? Come on, Paige."

"I need them, Mom."

"Are you taking your Cymbalta?"

"Yes."

"And your—"

"Zoloft," I interrupted. "Yes. I'm taking my meds, mom."

"All your meds?"

"Yes."

"And you still can't sleep?"

"No."

"Are you taking uppers?"

"Uppers?"

"That's what Kelsey calls them."

"No, I'm not taking uppers," I said.

"Well, you've lost so much weight."

"That's because I spend two hours every day at the gym."

"Doesn't that make you tired?"

"It does, but I need something stronger."

"We can go to the doctor, sweetie."

"I don't want to go to the doctor," I snapped. "I just need help getting through the next few weeks. Can't you give me a couple pills?"

"I need them, honey. I only have seven left, and Dr. Bennett won't call in a refill."

"What about Nyquil?" I asked. "Do we have any of that?"

"Are you sick?"

"No, mom, I'm not sick. I'm…I need to sleep. I need to not be awake."

My mom stepped into the bathroom to better examine me. "Sweetie, are you okay?"

I stared into my mom's inviting eyes. "No," I answered.

"What can I do?"

"You can give me an Ambien."

"I won't do that."

"Then nothing, Mom," I answered. "No one can do anything." I exited the bathroom and strode downstairs. Kelsey sat on the sofa watching YouTube videos on her phone. "Did you tell mom I'm on uppers?" I asked.

"No," Kelsey answered, too preoccupied with her phone to pay me much attention.

"What did you say to her?"

"She said you've lost a lot of weight, and I said *maybe* you were on uppers."

"I'm not on uppers."

"Okay," Kelsey replied, keeping her nose in her phone.

"You're addicted to your phone. Do you realize that?"

"So are you."

"Do you see my phone right now?"

She glanced at me, shrugged, and stared back at her phone. "You're probably going in your room to get it."

"No, I'm not."

"Okay."

"I'm going for a run."

"Okay."

"Do you want to come?"

"No."

"Do you want to go for a walk?"

"What for?"

"To get out of the house."

"That sounds lame."

"Have you looked at my Instagram or Twitter accounts today?"

"I can't. You blocked me, remember? You didn't want me to show dad pictures of your ass."

"Why did you show him my pictures?"

"Why not?"

"He doesn't want to see that."

"Then why are you posting them?"

"I'm an ambass...never mind."

"Whatever."

"Do you want to go to a movie?"

"No."

"Do you want to go get something to eat?"

"No."

"Do you want to do anything?"

"I want you to leave me alone."

"I had dinner with Kenny Waters and Paisley Evans a couple nights ago."

"Bullshit," Kelsey said, but she averted her eyes from her phone long enough to gauge the validity of my claim.

"I did."

"Prove it."

"I can't."

"You're a liar."

"Forget it," I said. I retreated to my room and closed the door. I checked my phone—no messages or notifications. I tried to log into Instagram. Nope. Facebook, Tik Tok, and Twitter—all denied. Even Pinterest blocked me. I threw my phone on my bed and paced my room. I needed stimulation, a distraction from my boredom. *Constant overstimulation numbs me. Boredom's not a burden anyone should bear.* I remember my high school chemistry lab partner reciting that to me whenever anyone in class complained of boredom. Once I asked where he heard it. He shrugged and said, "In a song." The words did not hold much weight then, but given my current predicament, I doubt a more relevant maxim existed.

I needed a distraction, something to keep my mind from dwelling on my suspension. Was this what addicts endured when they detoxed? I opened my nightstand drawer searching for a piece of gum. Maybe the chewing could alleviate my boredom. I spotted a pack of Trident, removed a piece, and tossed it in my mouth. Then I noticed, forgotten inside my drawer, Eric's copy of *The Great Gatsby.*

I retrieved the book and studied the cover, remembering when Eric gave it to me. He compared Alexis to Gatsby. The comparison eluded me. Was Gatsby a person? A place? An idea? He lent me the book hoping I would read it, giving us something to talk about later. I pictured us discussing the similarities between Gatsby and Alexis, laughing about their commonalities, dissecting their differences. In the throes of our analysis, Alexis would enter the breakroom, sabotaging mine and Eric's merriment. She would combat our joy with a passive aggressive comment or action—something like blocking me on Instagram or calling me frumpy. It would have been a great memory had I been gifted with the mental fortitude to read the book.

I weighed the novel in my hands and flipped it over. It was not too long. I recalled one of my college professors assigning a 500-page novel the last month of the semester. The audacity to expect his students to read 500 pages in four weeks! I shoved the book in my backpack, came home, and read the SparkNotes. I got a C on the final and the course. The coincidence of my current situation was not lost on me. Like my past college semester, I had four weeks until my suspension ended. Here I had another book, albeit a much shorter one, beckoning me to read it. I opened to the first page and began.

CHAPTER 33

I spent the weekend with Gatsby, analyzing and dissecting the similarities between him, Alexis, and myself. Most seek popularity and acceptance from those we want little to do with. We want the perception of mattering, the illusion of relevance, and in the end, what do any of us have to show for it? Gatsby and Alexis became victims to their own vices. Superficialities drenched Gatsby's unrequited love, while artifice layered Alexis's unabashed envy. Was I destined to face a similar doom? Which friends or followers would come to my funeral? Sure, I would have a greater audience than Gatsby, but would my mourners come to mourn or for the photo opportunity, much like Alexis's "friends"? I struggled with the novel's honesty and its challenge for self-discovery. But I loved it for its brutality. I contemplated this while sitting in the breakroom Monday afternoon—day seven of my suspension.

I had googled: "Books like *The Great Gatsby*" and found a list of ten books that promised, "If you loved *The Great Gatsby*, you'll love these." I printed the list and escaped to the breakroom for an afternoon coffee. Eric entered soon after. He approached my table and asked if I wanted company.

"Sure," I said. He sat down, and I slid the book list across the table to him. "Have you read any of those?" I asked.

He consulted the list. "I've read these," he said, pointing to six of the ten books. I asked which was the best, and he told me. "Did you read *Gatsby*?" he asked.

"Yeah."

Eric appeared surprised. "Why?"

"Because I needed something to do."

"And?"

I told him I understood why he made the comparison to his late wife, and I told him I saw a lot of Gatsby in me, too. "It's funny," I said. "My entire life I wanted to be like Alexis, and now that I am, I'm not sure I want to anymore."

Eric gave me a reflective glance. "Well, I can tell you one difference between you two." I raised my eyebrows and waited for his elaboration. "She never read *The Great Gatsby*." He meant this as a compliment, but it hurt more than it praised.

"I have a question, but I'm afraid to ask it," I said.

"What is it?"

"Did you love your wife?"

"Of course I did," Eric answered without even taking, *needing*, a moment to digest the question.

"You talk like you didn't."

Eric cast a forlorn gaze and sighed. "Well, that reflects my character more than hers."

"What did you love about her?"

"The moments when she put her phone down and allowed herself to be present. We had several of those when we first started dating. With each year into our relationship, they became less frequent. By the time she died, they were nonexistent." Eric reached back far into his marriage, recalling the times when just having each other seemed to be enough. His nostalgia was short lived, however, for his eyes sharpened and his face became inscrutable. "For our last anniversary, she posted a long tribute about me on her Facebook and Instagram pages. She professed her love, telling the world that, besides being the perfect husband, I was also her best friend. It was a beautiful tribute, but I didn't even know about it until after she died. I found it when I logged into her accounts to delete them."

"I remember it," I said. "It moved me. Made me so jealous of your marriage."

"Yeah? Should I tell you how we spent that anniversary? I made dinner reservations and booked a honeymoon suite downtown. It was a surprise. When I got home, she'd already showered and changed for bed. She was on the sofa eating Chinese takeout and watching TV. It wasn't even 5:00 yet. When I told her I made dinner reservations, she said, 'That's so sweet, but I don't feel like going out tonight. I'm exhausted.' I was perplexed. She had left work early to go shopping—I assumed to buy an anniversary gift. She spent the afternoon with that other guy, the one she was messaging on Facebook. We were in bed by 8:00, didn't even kiss her goodnight." The depth of the moment stalled Eric. He gave a half-hearted, somber chuckle and finished his thought. "She told everyone how much she loved me except me. It's like social media has a checklist of annual required posts: Anniversary—profess your love for your spouse. Child's first day of school—post a picture explaining how fast kids grow. Halloween—model a slutty costume. Mother's Day—write a tribute to mom. All of it is so generic."

"I'm sorry, Eric," I said.

He shrugged away my apology. "Don't be. I told you because you thought we had the perfect relationship. Hell, after going through her social media accounts, I started questioning if it was better than I remembered it, but no, I remember it for what it was. Her posts were for show, to make people jealous of a life she didn't even live. If we loved those we pretended to, it would be enough to tell them, not the world."

"Can't people do both?"

"Sure, but if you have to share it with the world, it's not because you love your spouse, it's because you love yourself."

I nodded, unable to deny the truth to his claim. "I don't want to be like Gatsby," I said.

He considered this and replied: "Then don't." He tipped his coffee and exited the breakroom.

CHAPTER 34

I sat at my desk going over spreadsheets when Eric entered my cubicle. He handed me a book—*1984* by George Orwell. "What's this?" I asked.

"*That* is the book you need to read," Eric said. "It's our world today."

"Okay," I said, thumbing through the novel. "Thanks."

"I'm running across the street for a cup of coffee. Meet me outside in ten minutes."

"Okay."

"And…" Eric leaned closer to me and whispered, "leave your phone."

Ten minutes later I met Eric outside. "What's going on?" I asked.

"Did you leave your phone inside?"

"Yeah."

"I may have found a hole in your Vicarious Vacations contract."

"Where's *your* phone?"

Eric padded his pockets and came away empty. "I must have left it in my office."

Relief swept over me. "Okay."

"Why?"

"They can listen on your phone, too."

"I don't have a Vicarious Vacations account."

"Yeah, but Alexis did."

"So?"

"That's how they got me. They can listen on anyone's device that has signed a Vicarious Vacations contract. I got my thirty-day expulsion because they heard our entire conversation through your phone."

"How? I've never signed a contract."

"Alexis did, and you're on the same cell phone plan."

"Yeah, but…" Eric paused as the information flooded his head, and the pieces took shape. "Holy shit," he whispered, still contemplating. "But you signed your contract after Alexis died, right?"

"Yeah."

"It's the updated contracts that allow them to listen on users' cell phones. Alexis couldn't have signed an updated contract."

"You must have," I said.

"But I didn't."

"When did you last update your phone?"

"I don't remember. A month ago."

"Did you read the terms and conditions for the update?"

"No," Eric said. "No one reads those." I lifted my eyebrows and offered a disappointing smile. "They hid it in the update?"

"Yes," I said. "They sent all users an update, and it grants Vicarious Vacations complete access to their devices. If you say anything inflammatory about them, they can suspend your social media accounts."

"They delete them?"

"No. My accounts are still active, but I can't access them. Only Vicarious Vacations can, and they can post whatever they want without telling me."

"But you can still see your accounts, right?"

"No. I can't log in."

"What if you logged in from a different device?" Eric asked. "What if you used my phone or computer?"

"It would recognize my fingerprints."

"What if I logged into Instagram and searched for you? I could see what they've posted, right?"

"Yeah, but you don't have an account."

"Hypothetically speaking."

"Yeah. You could."

"So, what if you were standing over my shoulder?"

"All devices now have retina scanners, so I couldn't look unless I was out of the scanner's range."

"Wow," Eric said. "They've thought of everything, huh?"

"Yeah," I said. "It sucks.

"Big Brother *is* always watching, I guess," he said, offering a reference that eclipsed my understanding. "What day is this?" he asked.

"Eleven."

"How are you handling it?

"I'm miserable, Books have helped, though. I never would have guessed."

"My patent lawyer looked over your contract. He said it's ironclad, but he found something that may be helpful. Per your ambassador clause, you're required to post a picture with your Shredded Fitness discount code every seventy-two hours. If you cannot do so, Vicarious Vacations can post one for you."

"Yeah," I said. "That's why they posted the nude photo of me."

"But you posted a picture within the required timeframe. You posted the picture I took of you at the restaurant, remember? You included your discount code with the picture, so that counted as a Shredded Fitness post. They didn't wait seventy-two hours to post the nude picture; they only waited eight."

"So, what are you saying?"

"I'm saying they posted it without your consent. Legally, they have to remove it if you ask them."

I pondered this, and asked, "Because they violated that part of the contract, does it deny them further access to my photos?"

"No," Eric said. "All you can do is demand they remove the photo. They'd have to comply." He paused and waited for me to respond, but I said nothing. "Isn't this what you wanted?" he asked, sensing my uneasiness. I attempted to comment, but my words met a roadblock. The truth was I wanted the picture to remain on my feed—it was my most well-liked photo. Eric divined what I could not vocalize. "You don't want it taken down," he said. The realization almost broke him.

"It's receiving so many likes," I justified.

Eric placed his elbows on his knees and rubbed his eyes. "Unbelievable," he muttered. "Why did you ask me to help if you weren't serious?"

"I want out of the contract. I don't want them to have access to my phone and run my accounts, and I don't like that they can hear my conversations."

"But you're okay with them posting naked pictures of you if you get a lot of likes?"

"I'm not naked."

"Yes, you are."

"But you can't see anything."

"What the fu—" Eric sprung to his feet. "Listen to yourself, Paige. They violated your privacy, and they posted a photo without your consent. Doesn't that bother you?"

"Yes," I said. "I agree that what they did is wrong, but…"

"But thousands of people like the photo," Eric said, finishing my thought. I stared at the ground. "You're…pathetic," Eric muttered.

"I know," I said. "I can't beat this, Eric. It's an addiction."

"Don't ask me to help you anymore," he said. He strode across the street and into the office building. I stayed on the bench for thirty more minutes, trying to understand why I let something that was destroying my life, continue to control it.

It must have been close to 5:00. The sudden charge of excitement that accompanies the end of the workday filled the office. I thumbed a couple pages in *1984,* searching for the last page of the chapter. Five more pages. I leaned back in my chair and continued reading.

"What are you reading?" an unfamiliar voice asked. Ryann stood in my cubicle, her work bag slung over her shoulder. I raised my book showing her the title. "I read that in high school," she said.

"Did you like it?"

"I can't remember it that well. It had something to do with rats."

"Rats?"

"Yeah."

"Must be later in the book. I just started it."

"It's nice to see you reading something that isn't on your phone," Ryann quipped. I forced a smile. "So...I've been meaning to ask you something," Ryann began, appearing tense and worried.

"What?"

"I've seen you talking with Eric."

"Yeah..."

"Are you guys...dating?"

"No."

"Oh," Ryann frowned.

"Why would you ask that? Are people saying we're dating?"

"No, it's not that. I was...well, I was wondering if you knew why Weston Goodman isn't working here anymore?"

"Weston?"

"I thought maybe Eric said something."

"Like what?"

"I don't know. Anything."

I dropped *1984* on my desk. "Did something happen between you and Weston Goodman, Ryann?"

"I heard there've been complaints."

"Complaints?"

Ryann made sure no eavesdroppers were within earshot. "I made a complaint about him."

"What type of complaint?"

"He said...inappropriate things."

"To you?"

"Yeah."

"What did he say?"

"I'd rather avoid the specifics. Let's just say they were of a...sexual nature."

"You're one of the three?" I whispered, recalling that three women had filed sexual harassment grievances with HR.

"Excuse me?"

"Three women filed sexual harassment grievances against Weston."

"Did Eric tell you that?"

"Ah..."

"What did he say?"

"I…I can't…I'm not supposed to say anything," I said. "Eric hasn't told me why Weston resigned."

"He resigned?" Ryann asked. "He wasn't fired?"

I hesitated, unsure what I could share. "It was a…forced resignation, I believe."

"Well, I'm glad he's gone."

"Yeah. Me, too."

Ryann checked her watch. "Well, it's after five," she said. "Sorry to pry. I just thought maybe you knew something. I'm glad that prick is gone. Have a good night, Paige." She started down the hall. Then, before reconsidering my next move, I jumped to my feet and called after her.

"Hey, Ryann. You want to go grab a drink?" I asked. My invitation confounded Ryann. We had never socialized outside of work. We had never socialized inside of work, either. Her inquiry regarding Weston was the most we had ever spoken to one another. "Never mind," I backtracked. "I didn't mean to—"

"Sure," she said. "A drink sounds nice."

CHAPTER 35

Day twenty-nine of my suspension. In less than twenty-four hours, Shawn would lift the ban. Today would be the longest day of my life.

I read four books in the last twenty-nine days. I was now halfway through my second reading of *1984*. Orwell's prophetic cautionary tale frightened me. What frightened me most was how society ignored his call for action. He had asked the world to wake up, only to have the masses hit snooze, and I had been the heaviest sleeper. Now, I was waking up, and yet by this time tomorrow, I would be right back into bed.

I was six days removed from my last dose of medication. Surprisingly, I felt great. I woke every morning and meditated. (Matt recommended a 10-minute meditation app that helped him cope with his breakup.) After meditating, I hit the gym. I warmed up on a bike, lifted, and finished with interval training. When I was not talking with Matt, I listened to audiobooks—another new coping luxury courtesy of Matt. Books were a pleasant respite from the constant gym chatter that used to penetrate my impressionable ears.

My body was fit and my mind sharp. I slept through the night without narcotics. At work, I now focused during meetings and even volunteered, to the surprise of Ryann, for a new project. Often, I even left my phone behind when I went to lunch or attended work meetings. I became present to the world around me. I interacted with colleagues— the few that did not use their phones as buffers to avoid human interaction—and Ryann and I were making a habit of going out for drinks every Wednesday after work.

And yet tomorrow, once Shawn lifted my ban, I would return to social media. I still craved it, yearned for it. What had I missed in the last twenty-nine days? What, if anything, had Shawn posted on my accounts during my absence? The deadline, now so close, occupied all my thoughts. Twenty-nine days clean, but I foresaw my relapse waiting on the horizon. I was like the inmate approaching the end of a sentence and already planning the next heist.

Day twenty-nine landed on a Thursday. It was five minutes to five, and the office buzzed with co-workers eager to go home for the day. I sat at my computer analyzing my third quarter numbers and weighing them against my fourth quarter projections. The improvements were obvious, and I wondered if they were obvious enough to warrant a raise.

Ten minutes later and the office was a ghost town. I closed my computer, gathered my things, and headed for the exit. The nearest exit stood less than thirty feet from my cubicle. On the opposite side of the building, near Eric's office, was another exit. I had developed the habit of traversing the maze of cubicles and leaving through the exit nearest Eric's office. My habit was borne from the hope that he may notice me and ask to talk. About what? Anything.

We had not spoken since he informed me of Vicarious Vacations' breach of contract. I took that information and did nothing with it. Eric made it clear he did not want me bothering him anymore. He had done me a favor, only to call my bluff on it. He had no interest in cultivating a friendship with someone suffering from a social media co-dependency problem. Alexis showed him the pitfalls that accompany those relationships. So, I gave him his space, and he, to my disappointment, reciprocated the behavior. God, how I missed him.

His blinds, as usual, were drawn, but I deduced from the slice of light underneath his door he was still inside. The office rumors speculated he logged sixteen-hour days. Most assumed his new work schedule was a means to tie off any loose ends left by Weston Goodman's resignation. (Thankfully, no one appeared to know the cause of Weston's abrupt departure.) A few speculated Eric was working on a project that had serious financial implications for the company. I knew the truth that lived in this rumor, and I kept my mouth shut about it.

I slowed my gait while passing Eric's office, allowing him a longer window to open the door and catch me passing. My step resumed its natural pace once I crossed his threshold and was forced past Weston's now-abandoned office. Heather's office, the other CEO, came last. Her blinds were opened, her lights were out, and she was nowhere in sight. I had never seen her past closing time.

I made it to the exit unimpeded, and accepting disappointment, pushed through the door. Then I stopped, and before reconsidering my impulse, I retraced my steps to Eric's office. I knocked three times and waited. A minute later, I knocked three more times and waited again. My fist was raised to knock again when he thrust opened the door.

We stared at each other, unsure what to say. I suspected it fell to me to speak first since I had knocked on his door.

"Hey," I said.

"Hey," he said. He waited for me to say more; I waited for him to do the same. "What do you want?" he asked.

"I don't know," I said.

More silence. "Did you need something?"

"No."

"Okay."

"Okay."

More silence. "Did you want to come in?" he asked.

"What for?"

"I don't know. You are the one that knocked on my door."

"I miss you," I said, giving voice to the lone thought bouncing around my head.

Eric leaned against the door frame and exhaled a long, defeated sigh. "Maybe you should come in," he said.

"Okay," I said and stepped past him and into his office. He closed the door and rubbed the back of his neck. He appeared tired and spread too thin. I perceived my intrusion was a welcomed respite from work. He straightened his shoulders and sat behind his desk. We held each other's gaze, unsure what to say, yet content with not saying anything.

"I read *1984*," I said, breaking the silence.

"Yeah?"

"Yeah."

"And?"

"And I'm reading it again, and I hate it. I hate how accurate it is, and I hate how much of myself I see in it."

Eric considered my hatred, seemed to agree with it, and said, "Did you ever think about returning it?"

"I have. I've thought of returning *Gatsby,* too. And your two sport coats."

"So, why haven't you?"

"They're all I have of you," I said. Eric shifted in his seat; my answer, soaked in so much unrequited honesty, caught him off guard. He was not sure what to make of the naïve girl sitting across from him laying her heart on the line. I was a few hours from my inevitable relapse; what risk was I taking if I now said the things I had kept secret for so long?

"Well, keep them as long as you need."

"I don't want them as much as I want you," I said. Eric considered my admission. Did my forwardness frighten or excite him? My greatest fear was he felt indifferent. "My suspension ends tomorrow," I said, changing the subject.

"Well, you made it," he said. "Congratulations."

"You think I'm pathetic."

"Paige, you have no idea what I think."

"I've been on social media since I was twelve. That's more than half my life. Yes, it's dumb, and I recognize it's bad for me. I recognize the more friends I have online, the fewer friends I have in real life. How many likes a post gets, defines my self-worth. I've objectified myself in this pursuit. I realize this, and I want to stop, but I'm not strong enough." I paused, hoping Eric had something to offer. He scrutinized me with expressionless eyes. "I feel like a junkie who's getting out of prison tomorrow, and all I can think is where I can get my next fix."

Eric leaned forward, his eyes locked on mine. "What do you want, Paige?"

"I want a reason not to log on tomorrow."

"Not wanting to log on is your reason."

"You can't understand," I said. "This doesn't control you the same way it controls me. You're asking me to surrender my identity, to release my connection to the world."

"It's a fake world."

"Yes, but it's the only one I have."

"No, it's the only one you've chosen," he countered.

"Eric, you don't understand."

"You're right, Paige. I can't empathize with you, and I can't understand why you *want* to get back on the thing that makes you feel lousy."

"That's because you never fell for it. As a kid my parents gave me a phone and told me to entertain myself. I got lost in a superficial world. It's the world I've known for the past fifteen years, and I'm at a loss about how to defeat this."

"How did you get through the past thirty days?" Eric asked.

I replayed the past month in my head. "I worked out," I said.

"You did that before. What else?"

"I meditated, read, focused on my work, hung out with friends. I even played Scrabble with my parents."

"You hung out with friends?"

"Ryann," I said. "We've been getting drinks after work. Matt comes, too. He's my trainer."

"And how does it feel connecting with people instead of a product?"

"It feels great," I admitted.

"So, the last thirty days you've interacted with people, you've read, meditated, exercised, you...lived?"

"Yeah," I said. "I lived. I lived for one month, and it has been great, but I have almost fifteen years of an addiction knocking at the door knowing that it can get in tomorrow."

"So, end it all," Eric said.

"What do you mean?"

"Do you want to quit social media?"

"Yes."

"No, I mean do you *really* want to quit? Don't tell me what you think I want to hear. Tell me the truth. Do you want to quit social media?"

"I want to be someone you're proud of."

"How about being someone you're proud of," Eric replied.

"I want that, too."

"This isn't about me, Paige. It's about you."

"I want to be a different person. Someone who doesn't need outside affirmation."

"That's what you want?"

"Yes." Eric's eyes told me he did not believe me. "It's what I want, Eric."

"Okay. Break your contract again."

"What?"

"Break your contract. End it all. If you break your contract, you'll receive a lifetime ban."

"Oh, no," I gasped. "I couldn't. I can't—"

"Why?"

"You don't understand what you're saying."

"What will you miss if you can never log on again?"

I opened my mouth to explain, but a blockage formed, preventing me from voicing an argument. Thoughts bubbled to the surface, each one, when recited silently, sounded more ridiculous than the one before it. What would I miss—everything! Social media operated the world. People communicated and connected through social media. It was unthinkable to throw that away. I already lived in constant fear because I had two strikes against me. The rest of my life I would be on edge, worried I might slip and reveal something worthy of a lifetime expulsion. I shuddered at the thought. A life void of social media was not a life; it was a prison sentence, solitary confinement, locked away from the rest of the world. I wanted to explain this but sensed Eric would disregard any justifications I presented. I shut my eyes and practiced a mindfulness technique I had learned two weeks earlier.

My thoughts slowed, and the panic dissipated. Eric's question stopped ricocheting inside my head and just hovered there, waiting for me to dissect what it *really* meant to live without social media. What would I miss? Living my life by *not* living my life? Go to Niagara Falls instead of pretending to? New York City may become a reality, not a clandestine stay in a crummy hotel room. If I no longer manufactured fake love on social media, I must learn to love in real life, with an actual person. What did it mean to never log into social media again? It meant living my life for me instead of pretending to for everyone else. And yet, through my newfound understanding, something kept me silent.

I opened my eyes; Eric stared back at me. His question still needed an answer. I did not have one, though. I realized what I should do—I realized what I wanted to do—and I knew I would not do either. Eric's eyes implored me to do the right thing. My heart raced. I stared at him and mouthed the words: "I'm sorry." Eric's pleading stare begged me to reconsider, begged me to stay and not walk out the door. But walk out the door is what I did.

CHAPTER 36

I sat on my bed and stared at my phone. The notification arrived seven minutes ago. It read: "Your thirty-day probation has ended. Welcome back, Paige!" I just needed to tap the notification. One tap would transport me to my Instagram page, back on the social media grid, granted access into the most inclusive club on the planet. One simple thumb movement would reunite me with the world of celebrity selfies and countless cat videos. But I did not tap the notification. Once I returned, I would be lost, once again consumed in an artificial world. Was the latest celebrity tweet worth thirty days of sobriety? Thirty days down the toilet to see Kylie Jenner's ass, or so I could post mine? *Thirty days...thirty days...thirty days*, I recited. I had to make it to thirty-one.

With a shaking hand, I placed my phone on my nightstand, grabbed my gym bag, and shuffled out the door. Ten minutes later, I arrived at the gym. Matt greeted me at the entrance wearing a concerned expression. "Did you log in?" he asked.

"Not yet," I answered. "I left my phone home and came here for a distraction."

"When you go home, will you log in?" he asked.

"I don't know."

"Want me to grease the rails? Give you an incentive to stay off the grid?"

"I'm listening."

"From now until the day you log in, all workouts are free."

"Are you serious?"

"Yes, but the day you log in, you must tell me, and I charge you again."

I judged the parameters of the bet, searching for any overlooked fine print. "Okay," I said. I held out my hand to solidify the agreement.

"Great," Matt said, releasing my hand. "Let's get started."

"Matt, why would you agree to this?"

"You don't need me to train you anymore, Paige. You know how to exercise and diet."

I had already considered this months ago, but I enjoyed working out with Matt. He was my friend, and I did not have many friends. "So why not drop me as a client?" I asked.

"You're not a client to me anymore, Paige. You're a friend."

The lump Matt's comment caused stayed stuck in my throat. I almost expected cheesy background music to kick on to outfit the scene. It was like I had entered my own *Full House* episode.

I would make it to day thirty-one.

Three hours later, I entered Newage Technology. My phone rested inside my purse; the unopened notification still emblazoned on the home screen. I powered on my computer and eased into my chair. I began typing:

> *Dear Newage Technology Co-workers:*
> *My name is Paige Reynolds. I've worked at Newage Technology for three years. Some of you know me; most of you do not. If you follow me on Instagram, Twitter, Facebook, Tik Tok, or any other social media platform, you've likely seen that I have traveled to Niagara Falls, New York City, and Costa Rica this year. I have not. There is a company called Vicarious Vacations. They manufacture fake vacations for people with the promise to upload fabricated photos from the vacation(s) to help gain social media popularity. My social media persona is a lie. I am sending this email to inform you I will no longer be on social media, but if any of you want to get a cup of coffee or talk or make a new friend, stop by my cubicle anytime. Thank you for your time.*
> *Paige Reynolds*

I added Matt and Shawn's email addresses to the CC box and sent the email. I took my phone from my purse and unlocked the screen. The notification appeared, and I tapped it. My Instagram page flickered for a moment and then turned black. A new notification appeared. Vicarious Vacations had initiated a lifetime expulsion from all social media accounts for breach of contract. All social media services were suspended indefinitely. I dropped my phone into my top desk drawer and strode down the hall to Eric's office. I knocked on his door and let myself in without waiting for an answer. He sat at his desk reading my email. His mouth hung open in bewilderment.

"Hey," I said.

"Hey," he said.

"Do you have plans for tonight?" I asked.

"No."

"Neither do I."

He stared at me, and I stared back, waiting for him to gain some clarity. It arrived in waves, pulling the corners of his mouth into a pleasant grin. "Would you like to go out tonight?"

"I'd love to," I said. "Pick me up at seven."

I closed the door and marched back to my cubicle where Ryann was waiting for me. "What is Vicarious Vacations?" she asked.

"Buy me a coffee, and I'll tell you about it."

"Let's go," she said.

"Great. Just let me grab my phone." I wanted Shawn to hear everything I had to say.

CHAPTER 37

I sat with my feet, free from the confines of my high-heeled shoes, propped up on Eric's desk. I ate from a Chinese takeout cartoon. Eric sat next to me, eating from his own container. "Is this your daily lunch routine?" I teased. "You sit in here with your feet propped up, eating takeout while the lowly serfs outside your office jockey for any scraps you may leave behind?"

Eric laughed at my astute observation. "Lowly serfs?" he asked. "Is that how you see yourself?"

"Is there any other way?"

"Well, if you're throwing out labels, what's mine?"

"You're the king," I answered.

"Wouldn't that make you the queen?"

"No."

"Why not?"

"We're not married. Heather's the queen."

"Heather?"

"Yeah. She's the other CEO."

"But we're not married."

"But she has power."

"Your logic makes no sense."

"Let me dumb it down for you. I work in a cubicle; Heather has an office. You have an office, too. You're the king, she's the queen, and I'm a serf."

Eric opened his mouth to offer his rebuttal, but Heather's sudden appearance stifled him. She smiled at me, no longer unaccustomed to my presence in Eric's office, before shifting her gaze to Eric. "Let's talk after lunch," she said.

"It didn't go well?" Eric asked. Heather shook her head. "How long do we have?"

"Three months," she said. Eric plunged his fork into his ham fried rice and placed the carton on his desk. I lowered my feet and put a consoling hand on his knee. He closed his eyes for a second, mulling over his options. When he opened them, he appeared to have aged ten years.

"Maybe it's time you talk with Kenny," Heather said.

Eric rubbed his chin, scratching his palm with his five-day-old scruff. "I don't want to do that," Eric said.

Heather shrugged. "Without new investors, we have three months."

"R&D needs at least another year," Eric said. "They're close, but they need more time."

"We don't have a year."

"Heather—"

"I hear what you're saying, Eric," Heather said, cutting him short. "But you need to hear what I'm saying. We can keep the company solvent for three months. Perhaps make it a year if you halted your passion projects. They're killing us."

"That's not fair," Eric said. "I did nothing without first consulting you."

"This isn't about that," she said. "I support what you're doing, but we can't afford it any longer. If you want to lay off half the staff, we could stretch our funding to six months."

"We can't lay off half the staff," Eric said. "We'd lose clients and revenue."

Heather knew this; she had to because I knew it. "I've tapped all my resources," she said. She waited to see if Eric had anything else to add. He did not. "Call Kenny," Heather said and closed the door.

Silence permeated the office. "I think Kenny would help," I said.

"Yeah…" he sighed.

. . .

I stood over Eric's bathroom counter applying my makeup. Eric was in the bedroom getting dressed. My phone dinged with a new text message from Matt. "Look who came into the gym?" it read. Attached to the text was a picture of himself and B-minus action movie star Oliver Lukas. I laughed and typed, "Awesome! See who can bench more!"

"Who's that?" Eric asked as he entered the bathroom.

"Matt," I said and showed Eric the photo of Matt and Oliver.

"Is that Oliver Lukas?"

"Yeah. He came into the gym today."

"When did he last make a movie?" Eric asked.

"I have no idea. I remember my dad watching his movies when I was a kid. They were awful."

"Matt must be a big fan to ask for a picture."

"He loves him. He was Matt's childhood crush."

"I bet they get so tired of that," Eric said.

"What?"

"People always asking for pictures."

"I think celebrities love the attention."

"Not as much as the fan who posts it," Eric said. A tinge of pain invaded my heart. I had not been on social media in three months, but it still stung every time I thought of a missed Instagram opportunity. "Tonight you should get a picture with Kenny and Paisley," Eric said. "You can one-up Matt."

I laughed and began applying my lipstick. "If Matt suspected I was having dinner with Kenny Waters and Paisley Evans, he'd be at the restaurant before we got the check." I lowered my lipstick, struck with a sudden thought. I looked at Eric. He finished tying his tie and found me eyeing him in the mirror.

"What?" he asked.

"I think I just found your new investor."

CHAPTER 38

Shawn's secretary kept shifting her gaze from Kenny to Paisley. I spied her take her phone and snap a quick picture. "The receptionist just took a picture of you two," I said loud enough for everyone to hear. The secretary pretended she had not heard me even though she blushed from my telling. She swiveled to her computer and lowered her head to avoid my prying eyes.

"How about a selfie?" Kenny asked.

The receptionist straightened. "Are you serious?" she asked.

Kenny nodded and turned to Paisley. Paisley appeared annoyed but stood, ready to fulfill her celebrity duty.

"I can take it," I offered.

The receptionist came running from behind her desk. She handed me her phone and stood between Kenny and Paisley. I snapped a couple pics and handed back her phone. "What's your name?" I asked her.

"Becky," she said, annoyed that, after the better part of a year, I still had not learned her name.

"Make sure you post that, Becky," I told her. Kenny and Paisley smirked, privy to my plan. Eric put his head in his hands and rubbed his temples.

Shawn's office door opened, and Shawn stepped out. His eyes, cold and unforgiving, fell to me at once. My office email created a PR headache for Shawn, and he still hated me for it. After I revealed what Vicarious Vacations was with my co-workers, Shawn, hoping to implement damage control, asked to meet. He promised not to post anymore pictures to my account without my consent if I stopped discussing how Vicarious Vacations operated. I insisted his guarantee go into an updated contract. He agreed, but I had to resign my position as fitness ambassador. As part of the resignation, he consented, to my dad and Eric's merriment, to dissolve any photos I had posted during my tenure as fitness ambassador.

I figured I had seen the last of Shawn Preston, and so did he. When I called to arrange this meeting, he reached deep into his lexicon to uncover the most colorful language possible to tell me he was not interested. When I mentioned Kenny Waters and Paisley Evans, he suddenly was.

Now as his vengeful gaze bore into me, it was clear he still harbored suffocating resentment. When he spotted Kenny and Paisley, his expression changed. He greeted them in pure, unadulterated Shawn Preston fashion and invited us into his office where a fruit tray and a platter of avocado on toast greeted us.

Kenny assailed the fruit, while Paisley helped herself to the avocado and toast. Eric and I, determined not to accept anything from Shawn, sat down empty-handed. I gripped his thigh, giving it an affectionate squeeze. He took my hand and serviced a smile, but he would have rather been anywhere else at that moment.

"So," Shawn began once everyone had settled into their chairs, "I'll admit you've piqued my curiosity. What is the purpose of this meeting?"

I glanced at Eric. He nodded, deferring to me, and then studied the far wall with a hollow expression. I cleared my throat and began. "Newage Technology would like to go into business with Vicarious Vacations."

"Why?" Shawn asked. "Newage Technology is an online security service."

"That's one branch of what we do. We're also developing advancements in the medical field."

"Okay, so what does that have to do with Vicarious Vacations?"

"Newage Tech is expanding its client base."

"In what capacity?" Shawn asked.

I reached into my bag and pulled out a folder and handed it to Shawn. "The data is clear," I said as Shawn removed the stack of spreadsheets from inside the folder. "There are three types of photos that gain the most attention on social media. Vacation posts, provocative photos, and celebrity encounters. You only offer services for two of these three demographics."

Shawn regarded me and placed the folder on the table. "I'm guessing this is why you're here." Shawn said, addressing Kenny and Paisley. Kenny nodded and tossed a piece of watermelon into his mouth.

"We want to do with celebrities what you already do with vacations," I said. "For example, next month is the Oscar Vanity Fair party. Kenny and Paisley will be there."

"Along with hundreds of other high-profile celebrities," Paisley interjected.

"We want to give everyday people the opportunity to 'attend' the party," I said. "Vicarious Vacations will provide this service, meaning your clients can post pictures of themselves with the world's hottest celebrities."

"You'll allow my clients access to the Oscar Vanity Fair party?" Shawn asked.

"In spirit, yes," I answered. "But they won't actually be there."

The wheels in Shawn's head were spinning. It did not take long for the dollar signs to appear. "You mentioned hundreds of celebrities," Shawn said to Kenny and Paisley. "My clients will have access to more than you two?"

Paisley reached into her purse while Kenny retrieved his wallet. Together, they tossed two business cards in Shawn's direction. He took the two cards, careful not to bend them, and admired their design.

"Johnathan Myers is my agent," Paisley said. "That's his card. He represents the biggest names in Hollywood."

"Yeah, I've heard of him," Shawn said.

"Carrie Iverson represents me," Kenny said.

"I know Carrie," Shawn said.

"You know her, or you know *of* her?" Kenny asked, seizing the opportunity to put Shawn in his place.

"I know *of* her," Shawn stuttered.

"Their agents want to work with you," I interjected. "They will give you access to the biggest names in Hollywood."

"How?"

"You'll have their schedules," Kenny explained. "Their whereabouts."

"Once you know their schedules, you can create fake encounters," I explained.

"And these celebrities are on board with this?" Shawn asked. "They will let me create fake pictures using their images?"

"Yeah," Paisley said. "When movie stars take pictures with fans, it gives them a more…down-to-earth image. This allows them to reap the benefits of engaging with fans without having to interact with them."

"I think I understand what you're saying, but spell it out for me so I'm not blindsided with some frivolous lawsuit later," Shawn said.

"Suppose," I began, "a client buys a vacation to Bermuda, and you know that pop singer Larry Kingston will be in Bermuda at the same time. You sell your client a trip, and for an additional fee, they can get a photo with Larry Kingston—who, coincidentally, is 'staying' at the same resort. Suppose one of your clients is waiting in line at Chipotle when international supermodel Samantha Johns walks in and gets in line behind your client. They snap a selfie, and the likes and comments accumulate. Just like your vacations, it's all fake. Your clients never actually see any celebrities. They never bump into them while waiting for an Uber or jet skiing in Belize, but no one will know the truth. You can sell celebrity encounters the same way you sell vacations. A movie premier goes for x-amount of dollars, a chance encounter at a restaurant goes for a little less."

Shawn contemplated my proposal, and for dramatic effect, pretended the idea may be too risky to undertake. But under his facade, he realized this was a goldmine. "So, what's the financial breakdown?" he asked.

"We cut it three ways," I said. "Newage Tech gets a cut because they will provide the online security of these accounts." Shawn opened his mouth to speak, but I cut him off before he could say anything. "That is non-negotiable," I said. "We now get to run the security end of Vicarious Vacations."

"Okay, but how are we cutting this three ways?" Shawn asked. "Equal shares?"

"Not for celebrity encounters," I explained. "Newage Tech takes forty, the agencies get twenty each, and you get—"

"Twenty?" Shawn said. "That's ridiculous."

"All you're providing is the platform," Eric interrupted. Shawn turned to him as if seeing him for the first time.

"I have the clientele," Shawn retorted.

"You don't have the celebrities," Eric countered.

"You just added twenty percent to your bottom line today, Shawn," I said. "Twenty percent without even lifting a finger. We think that's generous."

Shawn stood and paced the room. "I'll need to think about it," he said.

"Go into Becky's Instagram page," I instructed. "Put it on the TV."

"Becky?" Shawn asked.

"Your secretary," I answered.

Shawn took his tablet from his desk, entered Becky's Instagram page, and projected it onto the TV screen. Becky's most recent photo, the one taken ten minutes earlier in Shawn's waiting area, filled the screen. The photo already had over 7,000 likes.

"7,000 likes in ten minutes," I said.

"You know some of those likes are fake," Shawn said.

"And you know that doesn't matter," I said. "What matters is Becky has received 7,000 hits of dopamine. The addict is getting her fix. But what matters most is her followers will see those 7,000 likes, and it'll spark a rage of jealousy. Next thing you know they'll be knocking on your door asking if you can create a photo with their favorite celebrity."

Shawn could not dismiss my argument. We were all businesspeople, and that was why even Eric had, reluctantly, agreed to my idea. He did not want to partner with a faux vacation service that perpetuated social media addictions and catered to society's lowest common denominators. But he also did not want his business to fold. Allowing consumers the illusion of relevancy through celebrity encounters would generate enough funds to continue his medical research. Partnering with Vicarious Vacations would grow Newage Technology exponentially. He would have to double his staff. "This must be how Tom Walker felt," he had said when Kenny and I convinced him to let us bring the concept to Shawn. I did not recognize the reference; it was not necessary. Eric's uneasiness was tempered because he understood he had to compromise his morals now if he hoped to redeem himself later.

"Okay," Shawn said. "Let's do it."

CHAPTER 39

I searched the departure listings board and found our flight. Eric left in pursuit of a bathroom and coffee. I sent him a text telling him the gate and made my way toward it, towing my carry-on. At the gate I found two empty chairs. I sat in one and placed my carry-on in the other. I yawned, suffering the effects of booking a 6:00 AM flight. My coffee could not come fast enough. I kept an eye out for Eric and spotted him walking down the concourse. His old college backpack, which needed to remain in the back of the closet where neglected belongings belong, hung loosely over his broad shoulders. He carried two coffees. I smiled as he approached.

The past twelve months had comprised the best year of my life. I had earned enough money to get my own place. I found a two-bedroom townhome, lived in it for six months, and sold it the day after Eric asked me to move in with him. Eric's medical research was undergoing tests to get FDA approval, and our partnership with Vicarious Vacations generated so much revenue, that we opened a second office. When Eric told me about our expansion, he suggested we celebrate. "What do you have in mind?" I asked, and he handed me a shoebox containing a brand-new pair of running shoes. Inside each shoe was an entry, one for each of us, for the Easter Island marathon.

A month earlier we each made our own bucket lists. "Let's check them off now while we're still young," he said. Easter Island occupied my first spot. (I had inadvertently discovered the secluded island while shopping for townhomes—do not ask me how.) Running a marathon checked in at my second spot, which also made Eric's list at number five.

"I figured you could cross your top two off in one trip, while I knocked out number five on mine," he said as I read the entry forms for the Island's marathon. I squealed with delight and jumped in his arms.

Now we were at the airport waiting to board our flight. Exhaustion somewhat lessened my giddiness, but it would reemerge once Eric arrived with coffee. I spied him in the distance scanning the airport trying to find me in the throng of travelers. He spotted me and made his way to where I sat. He handed me a coffee and asked if I wanted to grab a book in one of the airport's bookstores.

"No," I said. "I brought one. Go ahead, though. I'll watch our stuff."

Eric unloaded his awful backpack and placed it in the seat next to me. He caught me eyeing his pack with critical discernment, ready to defend its existence if I felt compelled to criticize it—again. The hour defeated me, so I yawned and buried my displeasure. Eric smiled, victorious, and kissed the top of my head and walked away. Content with the moment, I sipped my coffee.

Then my phone chimed.

I retrieved it from my purse and unlocked the home screen. A message waited for me. It was from Shawn.

"You've been offline for eighteen months. A trip to Easter Island is the best way to celebrate! The average Easter Island vacation picture receives 5,000 likes. Click here to re-activate all social media accounts."

I read the message a dozen times searching for any hidden meaning in the content. Why was he reinstating my privileges? I had been absent from social media for eighteen months. I had defeated it, even though I still experienced twinges of heartache every time I captured a moment with my camera and yearned to share it. It is clichéd and somewhat embarrassing to admit, but when Eric and I started dating, the desire to post my love for him often struck me. However, my suspension forced me to push any residual nostalgia regarding social media to the recesses of my mind. There they lingered dormant and latent. And now, for reasons unknown, Shawn offered another chance, a fresh start to share my new life, my *authentic* life. I no longer needed Vicarious Vacations' services. My real world now superseded anything that a third party could contrive. If I accepted Shawn's invitation, it would not be to perpetuate a lie but to highlight my new reality. The invitation beckoned me. Could I use social media in moderation? Use it to upload genuine pictures and not manufactured ones? I could be a responsible user, like people who drink without forming an addiction. I wanted to fall back into the warm embrace of conformity that social media provided. It would be different this time.

I spotted Eric coming my way, a newly purchased book tucked under his arm. How would he respond if I reactivated my accounts? The bigger question was would he even find out? He still refused to join the social media circus, so it was possible he would not even know if I returned to the grid. Sure, if he asked, I would admit my return, but I did not need to apprise him of something so…innocent. For over a year we had grown closer and fallen in love. Would he begrudge me something as innocuous as having an Instagram or Twitter account, especially if I did not use it to cultivate a fake life? I read Shawn's message one last time and clicked the hyperlink. My Instagram page came to life. I was back in! I pocketed my phone before Eric reached me.

CHAPTER 40

Eric's mid-morning coffee was getting cold. He was ten minutes late, so I sent a text asking where he was. He wrote back: "Coming." I dumped his stale coffee down the sink and poured a fresh cup. I added a liberal amount of cream right as he entered the breakroom.

"What took you so long?" I asked. I handed him his coffee and, because we were alone, gave him a quick peck on the lips.

"I was talking with Ryann," he said.

"Yeah? What were you talking about?"

"Our trip."

I sat at our usual table and braced myself. "What did you tell her?"

"I told her it was the best week of my life."

My heart fluttered. "It was the best week of my life, too."

"Are you back on Instagram?" Eric asked.

I did not balk at his question. Instead, I pulled my phone from my pocket and placed it on the table between Eric and myself. I averted my gaze to avoid his stare, not wanting to risk breaking character. "Yes," I said. "I'm back on social media."

"When?"

"Shawn lifted the ban while we were at the airport."

"Did you think I wouldn't find out?"

"How did you find out?"

"How do you think, Paige?"

"Ryann saw our pictures?"

"Yeah. Each one has thousands of likes."

"Shawn estimated they would."

"Yeah? How many are real?" Eric asked, raising his voice for dramatic effect. Eric's performance was so believable, I had to focus to keep from laughing.

"I'm sorry, Eric."

"When were you going to tell me?"

"When the time was right."

Eric paced. When he reached the far side of the room, he smiled and pumped his fist. Stuck to the breakroom's fridge was a magnetic dry erase whiteboard. Eric took the attached marker and wrote: "When are we talking to him?"

I walked to the whiteboard and erased Eric's questions and wrote: "Tomorrow."

Eric wrote: "What time?"

I replied: "One o'clock. He thinks we're going over marketing strategies."

We returned to the table where my phone remained untouched. Eric leaned toward the phone and said: "This breaks my heart, Paige. We'll discuss this later. I have work to do." Eric winked and walked to the door. "By the way," he said. "You're sleeping on the couch tonight, and don't even think about using the hide-a-bed." Eric gave me one last departing flourish and walked out. *Hide-a-bed?* That was gold. I buried my face into the crook of my elbow and laughed; I only hope Shawn confused my amusement as sobs.

CHAPTER 41

We did not meet in Shawn's office. Eric called ahead and told him we had four additional guests, so he should prep his conference room. When Shawn asked who else we were bringing, Eric answered: "Our defense team." This was partly true. Two of our four additional guests were lawyers. Newage Technology now kept a lawyer on retainer, and Eric requested that another lawyer accompany our current one for "dramatic effect." The other two members of our entourage were Ryann and Heather. They wanted to come. Eric considered it and told them, "Okay, but dress like lawyers. I want him to think we have an entire team on this."

Eric and I sat in the center of the large conference table, while two members from our "defense" team sat on either side. Shawn entered, assessed our cavalry with confused skepticism, and sat down across from us. I gave Eric's leg an affectionate squeeze and sat up straight and placed my hands on the table.

"So," Shawn began, "something tells me we're not discussing marketing strategies."

"We need you to forfeit your stake in Celebrity Encounters," Eric said.

Shawn glanced at me; I looked away. "You're kidding, right?" he asked.

Eric motioned to the woman—our real lawyer—sitting next to him. She reached into her bag and brought out a folder. She opened the folder, removed a stack of papers, and handed them to Shawn.

"Five months ago, Paige and I switched cell phone providers, therefore terminating our contracts with our previous providers," Eric explained. "We got on the same cell phone plan with a new provider. That provider is Global Optics. I believe you are familiar with Global Optics, aren't you, Mr. Preston?"

Shawn studied Eric, wondering where he was leading him, and sensing wherever it was, it was not good. He tapped the conference table and nodded. "Global Optics is my cell phone provider," he said; we already knew this.

"The two women to the left of Paige are members of the Global Optics defense team." They were not; the two women were Ryann and Heather. I glanced at both. Ryann appeared confused, and Heather was under dire straits to keep from smiling. "The man and woman to my right are members of Newage Technology's defense team," Eric continued. This was not a lie—entirely.

"When Paige and I terminated our old cell phone contracts and signed new ones, we did so under two conditions—one: in the event of your resignation, Global Optics would gain your share of Celebrity Encounters. And two: Global Optics needed to honor the lifetime social media ban that you, Shawn Preston, tricked Paige Reynolds into signing when you hired her as a Vicarious Vacations fitness ambassador."

"Tricked her?" Shawn laughed. "That's absurd. All of this is. I would never agree to this."

Eric waited for Shawn's laughter to subside and said: "But you did agree." Shawn frowned, trying to assemble the scattered puzzle pieces Eric was placing in front of him. "Paige's contract, that you drafted, stated that if she revealed any of the inner workings of Vicarious Vacations, she was subject to expulsion. The first infraction resulted in a ten-day suspension; the second: thirty days, and a third violation earned a lifetime suspension. Now you can implement those suspensions at your own discretion, but once instituted, you cannot lift the lifetime ban. You lifted Paige's suspension nine days ago, Mr. Preston."

"I have that right."

"No," Eric interjected. "You *had* that right, until you agreed to your contract. The new contract outlined that, no matter the circumstances, you would never suspend the ban."

"I didn't agree to that."

"Yes, you did," Eric informed him. "After Paige and I signed our new cell phone user agreements, Global optics sent a software update. The new service terms were in the update. You accepted it on July 29 of this year. Fingerprint verification shows that *you* were the one to accept the new user agreement."

Shawn's confident demeanor vanished. "You can't…"

"We didn't. Global Optics, your cell provider, did," Eric said. "They can send users unfamiliar terms of service or updates whenever they need to revise their software or service agreements."

"But I didn't read it."

"Don't you know, Shawn, you should always read your updates." I sneered.

Shawn stared daggers at me. He now recognized what Eric and I had spent months planning. We knew how Vicarious Vacations systems operated. We knew because Eric assigned Newage Tech engineers to study them for the better part of a year. Shawn's algorithms updated him whenever I, or anyone else under suspension, tried logging into their social media accounts. Shawn could request any user's online activity, and our data showed that he often requested mine. If I tried logging into any social media account, Shawn would know. So that was what I did. Several times a day I tried to log in, knowing that Shawn watched every failed attempt. He interpreted my failed efforts as the burned-out junkie trying to reclaim a fix.

Shawn knew how much Eric despised social media. He knew because every week Eric and I staged scripted arguments where I feigned heartbreak for having lost my social media privileges. Eric met my supposed sadness with a catalog of invective language ridiculing my addiction. We fought—all for Shawn's benefit. We saw he was listening because, as part of our new partnership with Global Optics, we could tap into Shawn's conversations just as he could listen to ours. And it was all legal because it operated under the umbrella of "Capitalistic Integrity."

The Capitalistic Integrity Laws state that a business may monitor customer online activity, while also having access to intercept any verbal or nonverbal exchanges, when a said business believes their brand could become compromised due to "consumer negligence." The Capitalistic

Integrity Laws is how Shawn legally listened to mine and Eric's conversations (we were Vicarious Vacations' clients), and how Eric and I listened to Shawn's (he was our client because we owned a majority share of the Celebrity Encounters division of Vicarious Vacations).

In other words, Newage Tech engineers, at Eric's request, had developed their own algorithms (modeled after Vicarious Vacations') that flagged certain words associated with our product. If a user said anything inflammatory or otherwise—using any of the predetermined flagged words—about our business, we had the right to listen, along with the right to mete out suspensions if necessary.

Although Shawn said nothing inflammatory about Celebrity Encounters, he said countless things about me. Our intel taught us that Shawn still harbored resentment towards me for exposing Vicarious Vacations to my co-workers. He also detested that he did not own a majority stake in Celebrity Encounters. He wanted to absolve all connections with Newage Tech to that aim. In short, he had two goals— make my life miserable, and figure out a way to assume full ownership of Celebrity Encounters. Shawn theorized that if he lifted my ban, I lacked the resilience needed to stay off social media. The drug always tempts the junkie. If I started using again, mine and Eric's breakup was inevitable. We guessed his plan and played our parts to perfection, acting out a narrative Shawn was sure would lead to our breakup.

"You devised this to get back at me?" Shawn asked.

"Not at first," Eric said. "Initially, we just wanted out of our contracts with you. We wanted our privacy back."

"Why didn't you ask for it?" Shawn asked. "You could have negotiated that when you brought Celebrity Encounters to me."

"Because I didn't want my ban revoked," I said.

"Why?" Shawn asked.

"Because I lacked confidence in my self-control," I said. "I needed the suspension to stay in place, so I would not have the option of relapsing."

Shawn tapped his finger on the conference table, digesting everything we had revealed. "I won't resign."

"You have to," Eric said. "You violated your contract. Global Optics now owns your twenty percent stake. You allowed Paige back onto her social media platforms. That directly violates the contract you agreed to uphold."

"Why is being in bed with Global Optics better than remaining partners with me?" Shawn asked.

"Because Global Optics agreed to sell us Celebrity Encounters at market price," Eric answered.

"So, you'll own it free and clear?"

"No," Eric said. "Kenny and Paisley's agencies still own twenty percent. But we'll own sixty which gives us the authority to manage it how we see fit. And we intend to shut it down."

"The agencies won't agree to that," Shawn said. "They'd lose a fortune."

"It's not for them to decide. We are the majority stakeholders. If we must, we'll expose Celebrity Encounters. We'll tell the world it's a lie."

"You think two of the most powerful Hollywood agencies will allow that?"

"Yes," Eric said. "They will because they're so powerful. Together, Kenny and Paisley's agencies represent over two hundred clients. What do you think those clients will do if the public learns they agreed to fake picture postings with fans to earn an extra buck? Imagine the public outrage. Greedy celebrities milking their fans for even more money. The agency's high-profile clients would leave and sign with a new agency. It would be career suicide for everyone involved, a PR nightmare. It's in everyone's best interest to allow us to dissolve Celebrity Encounters quietly, amicably."

Shawn leaned back in his chair and did the math, carrying zeros to bottom-line revenues he could not fathom we were throwing away. "I don't understand," he said. "You're dismantling a multibillion-dollar operation."

"That's correct."

"Why?"

"Because it's a lie," Eric said.

"Who cares?" Shawn said.

"We do," Eric countered. "The money we've earned allowed us to fund other projects at Newage Tech. We're solvent now. We don't need Celebrity Encounters."

Shawn shook his head. "Nothing you're saying makes sense." Shawn rose, ready to conclude the meeting.

"There is one other thing," Eric said. I motioned to his chair, and Shawn returned to it, fearful of what was coming next.

"Since you violated your contract with us, it dissolves our contract with you."

"What?"

"We can now speak openly about your business without penalty. We can inform the world about Vicarious Vacations."

Shawn studied Eric and then shifted his gaze to me. He seethed. "You plan to expose Vicarious Vacations?"

Eric and I had already discussed this exact scenario. We agreed Vicarious Vacations should not exist, but we disagreed why. Eric believed a company that perpetuated lies and phony online personas should dissolve without question. I argued people had the freedom to make choices, no matter how ridiculous. One view we both supported, however, was that a corporation should not spy on its customers. Vicarious Vacations hijacked people's privacy, and that was not acceptable. Eric agreed that if this day ever arrived, Vicarious Vacations' fate rested in my hands.

"You can buy our silence," I said. Shawn sat back and crossed his arms, listening. "We won't reveal what you do under one condition: suspend all current contracts granting Vicarious Vacations the right to monitor people's devices. No more listening to their conversations and no more posting pictures of them without their consent. Your business is despicable, but it isn't for us to dictate whether consumers use it. They have that right, but you don't get to infringe on theirs. Stop spying, or we talk."

Shawn eyed me with unabated frustration. We had bested him, and it stung to become a victim to his own manipulations. "This could sink my business."

"Yeah, it could," I said. "But you don't get to rob people of their privacy because it's good for business."

Shawn stroked his chin, pretending to contemplate the terms of our demands. His performance was comical. He had no leverage; we were not seeking his approval. He pursed his lips into a stoic grimace and gave a slight nod.

"Newage Tech will oversee all new contracts and user agreements," Eric said. Shawn thought to protest but stopped himself. He recognized he was not in a position to negotiate.

"Are we done?" Shawn asked.

"There's one more thing," I said. All eyes settled on me. "Can you guys give us a minute?" I said to Eric and the others. Eric's expression was pure confusion. I gave him a slight nod, and whispered, "Trust me." He smiled and ushered everyone from the room, closing the door as he left. The room's sudden calm was thick with emotion. Shawn seethed and refused to look at me. The oversized clock that hung above the conference table ticked like a metronome death rattle. I counted fifteen clicks before breaking the silence. "I want you to know that we will grant you your privacy, too."

"What?"

"Eric didn't tell you, but we've been listening to you ever since we partnered with Global Optics."

I watched as every muscle in Shawn's neck and jaw clenched. "Why are you doing this, Paige? You came to me, remember?"

"Yes, I do, and that is why we're not exposing your business. I understand you and I were never really friends, Shawn, but for better or for worse, Vicarious Vacations is the best and worst thing that ever happened to me. I promise you that if you give people their privacy, we'll give you yours, and we will never expose your company."

Shawn pursed his lips, pushing the hatred and animosity he felt towards me to the fringes of his mind. He gave a slight nod. I stood and walked to the door. "Hey, Paige," Shawn said.

"Yeah?" I asked.

"I'm not naïve enough to ignore the fact that you could destroy me. If the roles were reversed, I'm not sure I'd extend your same level of understanding."

It was impossible to determine if this were a simple revelation or a subtle threat. "Is there a question in there?" I asked.

"Yeah," Shawn said. "Do you really believe in a person's right to privacy?"

"That's part of it."

"What's the other part?"

"Sometimes you do the right thing even when you won't benefit from it."

His face contorted in consternation. "What are you talking about?"

"When my boss assaulted me, and you offered to give me the recording. You didn't have to do that."

Shawn considered this. He stood and moved to the oversized windows of the conference room. He stared out into the parking lot and tried to organize his thoughts. "Had I not invaded your privacy, I wouldn't have had it," he said.

"I'm aware."

"So, you admit mass surveillance is necessary?"

I ruminated on his point. "I admit it's beneficial to some and detrimental to others," I said.

"You didn't seem to have a problem with it when it benefited you."

"And you seem to have a problem with it now that it's detrimental to you," I countered. Shawn scoffed and turned back to the window, satisfied that he had made his point.

"Take care, Shawn," I said and left the room. Once in the hall, I waited a beat, and then pressed my ear to the door. The clock's steady ticking echoed through the thick wood, and I sensed, but could not confirm, that between each rhythmic tick were the incoherent musing of a jilted man plotting his revenge.

Eric stood outside his car waiting for me. When I reached him, he lifted his arm and I slid into him, assuming my familiar place under his arm. He kissed the top of my head. "Everything okay?" he asked.

"Yeah," I said. "Let's go home."

Eric read Queen's Bath had limited parking, so it was best to arrive early. We did not talk during the forty-five-minute drive to the trailhead. Eric seemed preoccupied and distant; I observed him cautiously, stealing glances of him from the corner of my eye. The forecast promised zero percent chance of rain, a prediction that appeared true. A red warning sign mounted to a wooden post greeted us at the trailhead. The sign contained several bulleted items. Each item warned: Careless people die here—proceed with caution. Eric read the outlined warnings and, without saying a word, stepped onto the trail.

It was about a half-mile hike to the cliffs. The terrain was slippery with formidable tree roots circumnavigating the trail every which way. I wondered how anyone traversed the trail in less than ideal conditions. As we approached the cliffs, Eric spotted a makeshift placard tacked to a rock. It read: "UNEXPECTED LARGE WAVES WILL KNOCK YOU OFF THE ROCKS & SWEEP YOU OUT TO SEA!" Above this premonition lay another sign. "QUEEN'S BATH DROWNINGS." Next to it someone had carved a crude mockup of a skull and bones, and underneath were a series of tally marks—one for each life lost on the cliffs. Eric studied the sign for some time and ran his finger over the tally marks, contemplating which one represented Alexis.

He journeyed past the marker and stepped out onto the cliffs. A vast expanse of rock lining the never-ending ocean greeted us. We were awe-struck, speechless under the rising Kauai sun. The majestic cliffs, frightening and beautiful, beckoned us. Eric glanced back at me and offered a hurt smile. I wore my own solemn expression and nodded, silently telling him I supported whatever reasons had brought him here. I gave him a fifteen-foot cushion and followed his wake toward the tide pools. A handful of other tourists, teenagers, had beaten us to the pools. They were jumping from the cliffs into one of the larger pools. They laughed and swam and lived how teenagers should.

Eric watched the teens with envious awe as I made my way to his side. The impulse to take his hand seized me, but a greater urge not to impose on whatever thoughts penetrated his head kept me at bay. It would have been a futile gesture because his hand was sunk deep into his pocket, thumbing something inside.

"Can you give me a minute, Paige?" Eric asked. Even over the sound of the tide, I heard his voice break under the weight of his request.

"Sure," I said. I turned and walked fifty feet toward a different tide pool where I watched the waves crash into the rocks before pulling back into the limitless ocean. I pictured Alexis surveying the rocks, determining the best place to snap a selfie. I imagined a rogue wave crashing against the cliffs with a force great enough to pull an unsuspecting Alexis from the rocks and into the sea.

She had come here to spite me and paid with her life. The reality struck me that were it not for her jealousy and my fictions, she would likely be alive today. I may have well followed her to this ominous ground and shoved her into the unforgiving ocean myself, such was my role in her demise. The thought gave me pause, and I quaked with sorrow.

In the distance, I watched Eric approach the edge of the cliffs. He stared transfixed into the water. Whatever object he hid in his pocket, he removed. The distance proved too great for me to tell what he held. Eric mouthed a few words and tossed the object into the sea. He turned to me and our eyes locked. His stare was a mixture of pain and...optimism? I wanted to run to him and be swept into his arms and told everything would be all right. But *would* everything be all right? When he mentioned two months ago he wanted, *needed*, to come to Queen's Bath, I did not say much. I simply eyed him with discernment and said, "Okay." We were here now, and for the first time since he kissed me two years ago to cap our third date, I wondered if he regretted the path his life had taken him.

We continued staring at each other for a moment, then I lowered my head, unable to understand what lay beneath his stoic gaze. A moment later, a hand touched my shoulder. I did not need to turn to see it belonged to Eric. His touch was more familiar to me than my own. He pulled me toward him, took my face between his gentle hands, and kissed me tenderly on the forehead. Another wave crashed into the cliffs. Then, without saying a word, Eric Vandross took my hand in his own and led me away from the rocks.

ABOUT THE AUTHOR

Michael Wojciechowski is a native Utahan. He is of average height, weight, and intelligence. By all accounts, he is extra-ordinary. *Vicarious Vacations* is his fifth novel and probably his best.

NOTE FROM THE AUTHOR

Word-of-mouth is crucial for any author to succeed. If you enjoyed *Vicarious Vacations*, please leave a review online—anywhere you are able. Even if it's just a sentence or two. It would make all the difference and would be very much appreciated.

Thanks!
Michael

Thank you so much for reading one of Michael Wojciechowski's novels.
If you enjoyed the experience, please check out our recommended
title for your next great read!

Three Days by Michael Wojciechowski & Felicia Case

While flying home, Kadie rushes to finish the latest Kurt McCarthy novel. When she does, her nosy seatmate, Paul, asks if she liked it. She claims it's average at best and argues that McCarthy has lost his edge. Unbeknownst to her, her seatmate is Kurt McCarthy. Kurt McCarthy is Paul's penname—a secret Paul doesn't reveal.

Paul's headed to Chicago for his first public reading—a sold out performance in which Kadie has a ticket. However, minutes before Paul takes the stage, Kadie calls and asks him to meet her for dinner. Paul abandons the reading and his 1500 fans.

Over the next three days, they fall in love. Paul never reveals he's Kurt McCarthy, and he flies home promising Kadie he'll return in two weeks. Unfortunately, an unexpected development unfolds, preventing him from returning. Can they reunite, or will the prospect of what might have been haunt them forever?

View other Black Rose Writing titles at
www.blackrosewriting.com/books and use promo code
PRINT to receive a **20% discount** when purchasing.